Not Quite Home

A Novel

Temple Lentz

Sibylline Press

Published in the United States by Sibylline Press,
an imprint of All Things Book LLC, California.

Sibylline Press is dedicated to publishing the
brilliant work of women authors ages 50 and older.
www.sibyllinepress.com

Sibylline Digital First Edition
eBook ISBN: 9781960573629
Print ISBN: 9781960573896
Library of Congress Control Number: 2025931623

Cover Design: Alicia Feltman
Book Production: Aaron Laughlin

For Andy and Ed Lentz, who made reading and writing as natural to us as breathing and blinking.

CHAPTER 1

Claire rapped her knuckle against the microphone for attention.

"As many of you know," she announced, "I'm up here on this stage alone today because my husband, Chris, is dead and couldn't make it."

The typical luncheon sounds of forks and plates tinkling stopped. The ladies who lunch shifted uncomfortably in their expensive seats. Claire knew she had just broken an unwritten rule of high-society events—never mention the unmentionable—but she took a deep breath and continued.

"Chris hated these events. He always said award dinners and banquet lunches are just physical reminders of the hubris and arrogance of the people who attend them."

She looked up at the screen that flanked the stage and took in the larger-than-life photo of Chris and his kind grey eyes, crinkled in a smile. For a fleeting moment, it was just the two of them again.

Someone in the audience coughed, pulling Claire's attention away from Chris and back to the banquet hall. Scanning the room, she took in the audience of lily-white gray-hairs just like her, patting themselves on the back for being such open-minded, thoughtful, generous members of Portland's philanthropic elite. Glancing down at her notes, she realized nothing she'd planned to say made any sense anymore. She'd already blown the script ... might as well say what she was really thinking.

"And Chris was right. I didn't realize it until I got here today and saw this thing through his eyes. We're all here to congratulate ourselves because we think—we are *told*, over and over again—we are so *amazing* for donating money. We are pillars of the community for our generosity. But then, because we've given money, we don't actually *do* anything. Well, most of us don't. We write a check, clock out, and then complain when the problems we think we are paying to solve don't just magically go away."

Claire glanced down and saw Carol Connor at the table directly in front of the stage, folding her arms across her chest and frowning—well, it would be a frown if she didn't have so many fillers in her cheeks and lips.

"But, unlike all the rest of us," Claire continued, "Chris actually engaged. He gave money, yes, but he also found ways to perform good works with his own hands."

She looked down at her hands and thought of his strong, tanned fingers clasping hers. Tears began to pool in the corner of her eye and she inhaled sharply to pull herself together.

"When my husband died, he was halfway across the world, building houses for people who don't have anything. Literally *nothing*. And here we sit today, paying $150 for chicken salad and chocolate mousse with a marionberry drizzle, and we call ourselves heroes."

She crumpled her page of prepared remarks and tossed it to the ground. "This entire display is disgusting."

Bruce Bishop, the CEO of Portland Promise, stepped out from the offstage curtain and started crossing toward her. Claire managed to get in a few more sentences before cutting herself off so she could walk away on her own. Just before he got to her, she stepped away from the podium, turned on her heel, and strode off the stage and out of the room with her head high and shoulders back.

She crossed the hotel lobby, noticing for the first time its obscenely shiny marble floors and the cloying scent of the lilies in the enormous floral centerpiece. Chris had hated flashy displays of luxury like this, but they'd never bothered her before. Just as she reached the elevator and punched the button to take her to the parking garage, she realized her keys and phone were in her purse at Table One, at the very front of the room she had just stormed out of.

Well, shit.

She couldn't go back in, but she also couldn't go anywhere without her purse. This thing had to be ending soon, and she could sneak back in after everyone had gone out. She looked around for somewhere to hide and wait it out, saw the door to the ladies' room, and slipped inside. She locked herself inside a stall and leaned back against the door, running a hand through her shoulder-length white hair.

She'd been invited to speak to the Portland Promise luncheon as one of their major donors and supporters, and hadn't intended to have a "mic drop" moment on stage. But something got into her as she stood backstage waiting to go on, and none of the remarks she'd prepared made sense anymore. If she was going to honor Chris's memory and accept an award, none of the hollow words she'd written the night before were appropriate. Sure, they were "appropriate," but they were meaningless. Something overcame her when she went onstage, and ... it was Claire speaking, but it was a totally different Claire than the one any of the people in that room were expecting. Hell, it was a totally different Claire than even Claire was expecting. And running to hide in the bathroom? No idea which Claire came up with *this* brilliant plan. She was someone new, too. In hindsight, Claire realized she could have just had the hotel call a cab, and figured it out from there. She had a spare key in the ceramic frog and, like, fifty credit cards at home. But no. She ran to the damn bathroom. And now they were almost done and they'd see her if she tried to leave. This was like one of those horror movies where the victims ran upstairs instead of out of the house and all you could do was scream at them for making poor choices.

Right on cue, women started to stream into the bathroom. Poor choices, indeed. Claire inhaled and plotted her course. Now that the luncheon was wrapping up, she just needed to get comfortable standing next to the commode and wait for the opportunity to sneak out.

She turned around so her feet would face front and rested her forehead against the cool, heavy wooden door of the fancy hotel bathroom. With any luck, she'd go unnoticed in the stall and, with even more luck, her performance wouldn't be the subject of bathroom gossip.

"I thought Bruce recovered from her meltdown on stage quite well ..."

"He works with the homeless, sweetie; her tantrum can't be the worst thing he's seen."

No luck. Claire rolled her eyes and tried to place the voices.

"I don't know, I feel bad for her."

"Well, I'd feel bad for you, too, if you did something like that, dear."

Carol Connor, Claire thought. Of course. From philanthropy to tennis to grief, she made everything a competition.

"It's only been a couple of months since Chris died, you know," said a voice Claire couldn't place. "And she wasn't even with him when he went. That's hard. I don't know if I'd be able to handle it."

"She wore a dress with *pink flowers* on it. So much for grieving, am I right?"

Claire looked down at her sheath dress and barely kept herself from punching the door and shouting. Pink on a black background! Black shoes! Black belt! Understated and appropriate! At sixty-three years old, putting herself together well was one of the few things she felt she had mastered.

"I thought it was tasteful. Black belt, shoes, purse. She found balance. And she still looks great for someone our age."

Ah, that was Dorie Rogers. Thank you, Dorie.

"Nothing about that display was balanced," Carol said from a stall on Claire's left. "I was so offended at the way she talked about us. We are all here to give charitably and support the less fortunate, and she talked about us like we're wolves."

Claire turned her head toward Carol's voice, growled, and bared her teeth.

"Did you hear something?"

"Yes, dear, but it's impolite to talk about bathroom things."

Claire started to laugh and then caught herself. She wasn't going to be able to keep quiet much longer. While they were still in their stalls and before anyone else came in, she slipped out. As she left, she heard Carol's voice.

"Can you believe that woman just left without flushing or washing her hands?"

★ ★ ★

There was still a decent-sized crowd in the lobby, so Claire stayed at the edge and pasted a benign smile on her face as she avoided eye contact and made her way back to the hotel ballroom where the luncheon had taken place. As she approached Table One, she saw Bruce standing near the stage with his back to her. He appeared to be lecturing a young woman standing in front of him. As long as he kept his back to her, Claire thought as she crept forward, she could just get up to the table, grab her purse, and get out. She was done attending these luncheons, not that she'd ever be invited to one again. What she'd do instead, she had no idea. For now, she just needed to escape.

Bruce was whispering, but she was pretty sure she heard him hiss the word "raccoons." Claire shook her head like she was trying to clear her ears and got a closer look at the girl he was facing. The young woman was dressed for a construction site, not a luncheon. Her work boots had a heavy crust of dirt, her jeans were grubby, and her heavy flannel shirt was rolled up at the elbows. She looked sturdy—like she'd be hard to knock over and you probably wouldn't want to try.

As Claire edged past them, the young woman turned and gestured directly at her.

"She was right about all of this being pointless! Maybe if you spent less time hustling people like her," the woman shouted, "and more time with the people you're supposed to be helping, you'd understand!"

Bruce whipped around, and Claire froze with her hand extended toward her bag.

CHAPTER 2

Erica had slipped into the luncheon a few minutes after it started. She'd been working since before dawn and having to stop in for the fundraiser schmoozefest made a long day even longer. She put her curly black hair into a short ponytail, then took it out and played with the elastic band. She leaned over to one of the other outreach workers standing along the back wall.

"He do it yet?" Erica asked.

"Not yet. Just getting going."

Erica was not a banquet person or a luncheon person. She was not a smile-and-be-polite person or a press-the-flesh kind of person. And since she'd gotten sober seven years ago, she couldn't even be a hide-in-the-bar-until-the-party's-over kind of person. She loved her work but avoided the fundraising events whenever possible.

However, staff attendance at Portland Promise's annual fundraising luncheon was not optional. Staff had to sit at a couple of tables in the back so Bruce, the CEO, could point in their direction during his speech and say none of this would be possible without their hard work, then spend the next twenty minutes talking about himself and how great and important he is.

Unfortunately, Erica wasn't going to be able to escape after Bruce's hollow thank-you this time. Bruce was after her for "breaking the rules" again, and insisted she come find him after the luncheon so they could "get back on track." Bruce didn't actually speak in air quotes, but it felt like everything he said actually meant something else, and no matter what she did, it never meant anything good for Erica.

Unlike some of the other outreach workers who had easier client loads, Erica's client list contained mostly tough characters, people whose unmanageable problems had pushed them to the street: addiction, mental illness, personality disorders, trauma from abuse. Although the case load was difficult, she preferred it this way. These were people who didn't just need help, they needed *her* help.

Her caseload hadn't started that way, but had started to shift gradually as her co-workers came to her with questions about difficult clients, problems they couldn't solve, and situations they need her support on. Eventually, she just became the first stop.

It had been a tough sell to convince her parents that working so close to people suffering this much was a good idea, given her own history. They'd been there to catch her when she finally stopped drinking, and they were still more than a little cautious on her behalf.

"Most of the other outreach workers mean well," Erica had told her parents, "but they don't have any lived experience. I have a lot to offer here. It's important for me to do this." Although it meant she had the heaviest caseload of all of the outreach workers, and her working hours were out of hand, she felt like she really was making connections. Erica had found she could reach a lot further when she could honestly tell people she knew where they were coming from, and the truth was, it didn't just help them. Helping people this way was also a big part of her own sobriety.

What Erica couldn't get over was why Bruce made her life so miserable about it. Working these crazy hours with such a heavy workload, you'd think he'd be trying to help her. But every time she turned around, he was on her back about something else. She'd rather be anywhere than here at this luncheon.

When the rich lady with the white hair and flowered dress came to the podium to get some award, Erica zoned out and started looking at her phone. She knew exactly what was coming. First, the rich lady would talk about how great it was to be rich and donate to Portland Promise, and then the agency would trot out one of the more-presentable clients to tell a story of hardship followed by success because of the agency's work. The stories were always true and heartfelt, but they were also completely engineered to make it seem like those stories were the rule, not the exception. Tears would flow, and donors would open their wallets.

Erica had seen this lady before, doing the same thing. She would breeze in for ribbon cuttings, give hugs and kisses, and act like she had done something just by showing up. She was just like all the others who threw their money around. Erica knew all that money helped make sure she got paid. But she didn't have to like it, or listen to whatever empty, useless crap this lady onstage was going to spew. As far as she was concerned, if you're giving money away because you want people to clap for you, you're doing it for the wrong reasons.

But something in the way the lady was talking made her check back in. This was not a normal rich-lady speech. She was ... Holy shit—she was taking Bruce and the whole charade to task. She was actually calling people out for being shallow, and she was getting *real.*

"You have my attention, Rich Lady," Erica said quietly.

The well-dressed white folks at the nearest table put down their spoons and stopped eating the chocolate mousse the lady had just called them out for. People shifted in their seats, unsure how to respond. Bruce started walking toward her slowly, like he was approaching a wild animal.

"I can see Bruce is ready for me to be done here," the lady said. "So just one more thing: If you came here today planning to give money, you still should. Support the mission. This stuff up here is all meaningless—the big fancy party, the posturing, the chocolate mousse. But there are people out there who need help. And you can help them. So do it. Not because you'll get to see your name on a donor wall, but because it's the right thing to do. And if you, like me, feel that we also need to *do* something, then I'll see you out there."

"Nice!" Erica started a slow-clap but dropped it when Bruce whipped his head toward the back of the room and glared like he knew it was her. Erica doubted that Rich Lady would even know where to begin on "doing" something, but she liked the fire. This luncheon hadn't seen anything like that in ... well, in ever.

The lady walked off the stage like she had somewhere to be. It looked like Bruce was considering going after her, but then remembered he had a thousand people in the room he needed to ask for money. He started in on his speech, and as soon as he thanked the staff, Erica slipped outside for a cigarette.

One of the admins from the main office at Portland Promise was out there, too. Standing the requisite twenty-five feet from the entrance of the hotel, they smoked and took in the scene around them. Even right downtown among all the fancy hotels and well-heeled professionals, tents occupied by people with nowhere else to go filled the edges of the sidewalk.

The admin gestured toward the tents. "Has it always been this bad?"

Erica tried to remember the girl's name. Bruce had a hard time keeping office staff, so this young woman was relatively new. Jennifer. Erica was pretty sure her name was Jennifer.

"Depends what you mean by 'bad,'" Erica said. "If you mean, 'Ew, homeless people,' then I think you might not be working for the right place. If you mean, 'Have there always been this many people in need of help that no one seems to be offering,' then no. It hasn't always been this bad."

Jennifer looked chastened at the correction and nodded.

Erica inhaled and let the smoke out in a long, slow breath, reminding herself not to take out her frustrations on this girl who was just trying to make small talk. "It's gotten a lot worse in the last few years."

She explained to Jennifer that Portland wasn't unique in this regard—homelessness is increasing everywhere.

"Overpriced housing combined with low wages. Untreated mental illness and addiction. Domestic abuse, medical problems, and lack of structural supports."

"And," she added, "the people who are able to do something about these problems are failing. For every speech they make about helping those most in need, the City Council gives tax breaks and incentives to developers building luxury condos. And as addiction rates are skyrocketing, the county is closing sobering centers and reducing treatment beds. And for every minute they fight among themselves about who should pay for what or who gets to take credit, or whose ego needs to be stroked, fifty more people fall through the cracks. They've created a generation of people who will never be able to come inside."

"Thanks for the pep talk," Jennifer said.

"Sorry," Erica sighed. "I'm getting jaded, I guess."

"Is that why you did the tent thing?"

"You've worked here like thirty seconds. How do you know about the tent thing?"

"Everyone knows about the tent thing."

"The tent thing" was exactly what Bruce was going to yell at her for.

Erica *had* become jaded, and the job she used to love had been getting harder to do, especially if she followed the insane number of rules that kept being added. So she had started breaking those rules. She spent her own money on cigarettes and socks and clothes and food, which she traded with clients to build trust and make deals. She got to know the main low-rent landlords in town and started working directly with them to help her clients get around the three-year wait for subsidized housing.

On all these transgressions, Bruce looked the other way. He gave her a hard time, but she got results and took the clients none of the other case workers wanted. But when she found a donor who could hook her up with cheap tents and she started handing them out to clients, it was apparently a step too far. When someone tipped off the City Council that an agency that received public funds was handing out tents, all hell broke loose. They interpreted the effort as Portland Promise trying to make it easier for people to stay on the streets. Instead of protecting Erica, Bruce offered her up as a sole actor. She had to go in front of City Council, where she had to promise not to give out any more tents, as a condition of employment. She agreed, but not before fully dressing down the mayor in front of a packed audience.

The reason Bruce wanted to see her now was that what she'd technically agreed to was to not pass out any more tents as an employee of Portland Promise. She didn't make any commitments about what she'd do or not do on her off-time ... and, yes, off-duty Erica had indeed continued to unload tents whenever she saw the need.

People started drifting out of the hotel. The luncheon must have ended. Erica nodded to Jennifer, ground out her cigarette, and tossed the butt into the ashtray nearby. She slowly headed inside, hoping Bruce would be caught up talking to his donors. He was, but as soon as he saw her he beelined her way, caught her elbow, and pulled her into the banquet room. She shook her head at the ridiculous contrast of him smiling and waving to people as he gripped her arm tightly and almost dragged her across the room.

"I just learned new tents are popping up all over the city," he whispered sharply when they reached the front of the room. "Like *someone* is handing them out to the people on the street."

"Wow," Erica deadpanned, "I guess there are people out there who want to try to actually do some good."

"God damn it, Erica," he hissed. "This has to stop. You know as well as I do that we need to get them off the street, not make them more comfortable. Handing out tents is just ... feeding the raccoons. It's not truly helping anyone."

Erica was so shocked, she laughed. "Raccoons? Seriously?"

Bruce flapped his hand in front of his face. "You know what I mean."

The rich lady was walking up behind Bruce, but he hadn't seen her yet. "Actually, Bruce, I don't," Erica said, raising her voice above a whisper now. "My clients ... your raccoons ... are pretty grateful for a dry tent. I mean, they still have to use a parking curb as a pillow, but at least they have some kind of shelter. Come on, Bruce! The system has totally failed these people. Now we are also going to let them die of exposure?"

"Your job is to connect them to service, not to get personally involved."

Erica turned and pointed directly at the rich lady, who froze. "She was right about all of this being pointless! Maybe if you spent less time hustling people like her," Erica shouted, "and more time with the people you're supposed to be helping, you'd understand!"

Bruce pivoted and saw Claire. He quickly straightened up and reached out to push Erica's hand down by her side.

"Claire!" Bruce beamed and reached for her shoulders to give her an awkward hug. "You really gave us the what-for today. I hope we can have the opportunity to win back your trust!"

Claire stepped back from his hug quickly and Erica saw a look of confusion pass across her face before it was replaced with a bland politeness.

"Sounds like spirited conversation over here," Claire smiled, looking past Bruce to Erica, who snorted.

"Claire Anderson," Bruce said, "this is Erica Ford, one of our outreach workers. Erica, Claire is one of our top donors, and ... spoke from the stage earlier today."

"I was here," Erica said, and maintained eye contact with Claire. "Oscar-worthy performance, if you ask me."

"No one asked," Bruce said quickly.

Claire smiled at Erica. "Thank you for your hard work for the organization."

Erica stood silently until Bruce nudged her. "Uh, you're welcome?"

The three stood together saying nothing until Claire broke the silence. "Outreach worker? So, you go out and talk to the homeless?"

"The unhoused," Erica corrected her. "The folks we serve. Every single day"—she glanced at Bruce—"and most nights and weekends, too."

"Erica keeps us on our toes," said Bruce. Looking past Claire, he raised his eyebrows and looked relieved. "Claire, will you please excuse me? It looks like they need me in the lobby."

"Of course."

"And Erica," Bruce said, "we'll finish this conversation later."

"Can't wait," Erica muttered.

As Bruce walked off, Claire picked up her purse to get her keys and check her phone. "Sounds like he's not too thrilled with either of us today."

"I don't know about you," Erica said, "but for me this is just a normal Tuesday."

"Hm," Claire said, taking Erica in. "No, this one's unusual for me. This is the strangest Tuesday I've had in a very long time."

CHAPTER 3

After the luncheon, Claire returned home to change clothes and head to yoga class, reflecting on her new commitment to "do" something to make a difference. She and Chris—well, now just she—lived in Portland's Northwest quadrant, on the edge of the West Hills. Just outside of downtown and past an industrial district that had been turned into luxury condos, the Tualatin Mountains gave the city a huge vertical leap. In Portland's turn-of-the-twentieth-century glory days of lumber barons and railroad titans, the city's wealthy built their sprawling homes up on the sides of these low-lying mountains. And even now, just past the turn of the twenty-first century, being able to afford one of these rambling old houses was a sign of stature that many people in Portland could only imagine. What better way to signify your power than to force the rest of the city to always be looking up at you?

Claire and Chris had bought their little piece of social domination almost forty years ago. Even as she bristled against the snootiness of the neighborhood, Claire had known having a home in this area was an important part of being a leader in the city's philanthropic class. She also had to admit, she *loved* these houses. Yes, they communicated an elitism she didn't want to admit she was a part of, but they were also just gorgeous. If you could afford to buy one of them, why wouldn't you?

Their 1925 Craftsman-style house was one of the first homes built on the hill and was on the historic register, giving them extra status points. Their home had huge picture windows with leaded glass, charming built-ins, spacious rooms with graceful tile mosaics inset into the hearths of the many fireplaces, a service call-button system that still worked, a back staircase that went up to the third floor that was intended for "the help," and original claw-foot bathtubs in all the bathrooms. They'd retained all the original details they could while also upgrading to a fully modern luxury kitchen and master bath, bringing the best of all possible worlds into one home. Most impressive of all, throughout the house and exposed and highlighted on the house's many porches, were thick wooden beams that were single cuts from old-growth trees. Fancier, newer, more modern places were being built in other neighborhoods these days, but none of them could compare with the old builds that had details like this one. Claire knew that the timber baron who built the place didn't come by his wealth because of fair labor practices or sustainable harvesting—but she balanced whatever guilt she felt about perpetuating his legacy with the fact he was long-gone and the details and original woodwork in the home were simply *stunning.*

This duality, Claire realized, could also be described as hypocrisy. Wasn't that exactly what she'd been ranting about at the luncheon? Yes, somewhere in the back of her mind she knew that her luxury and comfort were dependent on someone else's hardship—but she made up for it by making huge donations, right?

She wasn't so sure any longer.

Walking in the back door from the garage, Claire dropped her keys into the valet tray next to the kitchen counter and glanced into Chris's study on her way upstairs. Even before he died, this house was way too big for the two of them. And now that it was just her, five thousand square feet seemed ridiculous. But lonely as it was, he was there with her. He was there in the study, in the bedroom, in her car, wherever she went. He was in her head, and he sometimes talked to her when she needed him. She loved that she could still hear his voice and see his face. Sure, talking to her dead husband as though he was sitting right next to her might not have been the picture-perfect definition of mental health, but it's not like he was telling her to commit crimes or anything.

She changed quickly out of her luncheon dress and into her yoga clothes and headed back out. She had just enough time to get to her yoga class on foot, so she left the car at home. The fashionable NW 23rd Avenue shopping district was just a ten-minute walk from her house, down the large hill. It had trendy restaurants and coffee shops and clever little gift stores, as well as her new yoga studio, located on the second floor of a building tucked behind a fancy ice cream store that charged twelve dollars for a milkshake and always had a line around the block.

She'd only been going to this studio for a few weeks. Before Chris's death, she'd gone to a different place downtown. But she had made the mistake of going to a class too soon after he died, thinking it would help her process things. And it did, but stretching to open her heart and chest made the perfect place for a ten-ton weight of grief to land right on her solar plexus. She wept through the class and was so mortified that she had no intention of ever going back.

Shielding her eyes from the early spring sun, she stood on the sidewalk and took in the dissonant view of high-end shops and restaurants with tents and tarps propped up along the road. "This has to change for so many reasons," she said. "It's inhumane, but it's also such an eyesore!"

If you don't like looking at it, imagine how they feel having to live in it, she heard Chris say to her.

"I always thought I was doing my part by donating."

What did I always say? The money matters, but so does being engaged. So does doing the work.

She shook her head. After years of being a leading philanthropist, people were still huddled in tents on the streets. Something had to change, and it was looking more and more like that something was going to have to be her.

A loud voice jolted her out of her reverie.

"Hey! *Stop*!"

Claire stopped abruptly and noticed a yellow blur in the periphery of her vision at the same time as she heard the loud, long bleat of a truck horn. The yellow blur was now stopped right in front of her, and her heart was pounding in her chest.

A woman's voice yelled at her from a few feet away. "Christ, lady, that truck almost made you a hood ornament!"

She had almost stepped right in front of a rental moving van. There was a guy in the driver seat yelling and gesturing wildly.

"Oh my God," she said to the truck driver and held up her arms, waving her hands in front of her. "I'm so sorry!"

A woman with long blonde hair in a braid stalked toward her and waved off the driver, who continued to yell through his closed passenger-side window.

"Yeah, we know you're upset! Go on, already!" the woman yelled and pounded on the truck's hood. "Keep it moving!"

Claire took in the woman's baggy, threadbare jeans and a T-shirt that revealed heavily tattooed arms. She was standing in front of a tent-and-tarp setup on the sidewalk between two street trees. She was much younger than Claire had originally thought. This girl, who couldn't be more than twenty-two, looked terrifying but also a little familiar.

"Thank you," Claire said quietly. "I ... I wasn't paying attention ..."

"No shit," the girl said, expressionless. "It must be nice to walk around feeling untouchable."

"Thanks for stopping me—for stopping him—for stopping me from getting run over by him."

The girl sat down on an overturned orange bucket and waved her hand toward where the truck had been. "He probably wouldn't have hit you, but you definitely would have got even more shook up than you are now." She looked Claire up and down. "And you might have dropped that fancy purse."

"You look very familiar," Claire said.

The girl folded her arms and kicked her legs out in front of her, crossing them at the ankles. "You all look the same to me."

Claire smiled. "I appreciate your honesty."

"Oh!" The girl's face lit up. "I know how I know you!"

"How?"

"You're the moneybags who lost her shit at the thing downtown!"

Claire squinted, confused. "*You* were at the Portland Promise event?"

The girl laughed and plucked at her T-shirt. "What, you don't think someone like me gets invited to fancy parties?"

"I … I didn't mean …"

"Ha. Forget it. I'm messing with you." The girl shrugged. "I'm the charity case they brought up after you. I'm Wendi."

"Oh!" Claire exclaimed. "I'm sorry I didn't recognize you. I'm Claire." She scanned the girl for familiarity, noting her long hair and pale face, but still something looked off. "Did you … change clothes?"

"Yeah," Wendi said. "They told me this look," she nodded down toward her tattooed arms and grubby jeans, "wasn't the most 'poor little homeless girl makes good.' So they made me wear some scratchy dress."

"Huh." Claire crossed her arms. This still wasn't making sense. "So a few hours ago, you were there, in a dress, and now you're here, not in a dress."

Wendi rolled her eyes, clearly wondering how a lady this slow was allowed to be out on her own. "Yeeeeeeeeeesssssss."

"But I thought you said Portland Promise helped you."

"They did. They do."

"But you're here."

"Yup." The girl looked around like she had a secret and leaned in closer to Claire. "I don't know if you know this," she whispered, "but *you're* here now, too."

Frustrated, Claire shook her head. "Psht. I know. I mean—" she gestured toward the tent and the tarp. "You're *here*."

Wendi just shrugged. "Yup."

"Is this where you live? I walk past here all the time."

"Are you asking, have you walked past me every day on this corner like I don't exist, but now you know I do exist, you don't know what to do about it?"

"Well ... I guess, something like that."

"I kind of want to say yes just to mess with you," Wendi said. "But you already look like you're about to cry. So don't worry. No, you haven't walked past me like I'm not human for months and months."

"Oh. Good."

Wendi stared at her for a beat. "You walked past my friend Paula like she's not human for months and months."

Claire shook her head sharply. "What?"

"That's her tent. I'm visiting my friend Paula. I have two kids, so I don't usually have the time to hang out on the corner."

"That's right, you have kids." Claire remembered hearing something about the guest speaker having kids and looked around. "Where are they? And where's your friend?"

"Well, not that it's any of your business, my kids are sleeping off a sugar coma from that party. They're in the back seat of my car, which is right there," she pointed to a banged-up forest green Honda Accord just across the street.

"Are they okay?"

"Of course they are," Wendi said, getting a little bit of an edge in her voice. "I take care of my kids. The windows are rolled down partway and I always got my eye on them."

"Where's your friend?"

"Paula had some stuff to do. So, I'm watching her space."

"Where do you stay?"

Wendi nodded her head toward the car. "My humble abode is right there. I'd offer you a tour, but the maid hasn't cleaned it yet today."

"I'm sorry I'm not getting it," Claire said, "but you were just at this luncheon where they used you as a success story to bring in more money, and now you're telling me you're living in your *car*?"

"Yeah?" Wendi shrugged.

"No offense, but that's not much of a success story."

"No offense, but I never said I was a success story."

"But that's why they had you speak."

"Maybe," Wendi said. "I don't know. They just wanted me to talk about my story, and it also meant the kids and I got showers and clothes and a meal on real plates. And they also got like four years' worth of sugar from that chocolate pudding stuff. God, they were unbearable until they finally passed out for their nap."

Claire folded her arms in tighter. "But Portland Promise is supposed to help you. With housing, with support, with something *besides* chocolate pudding and a dress you don't even want to wear."

Wendi shrugged. "Don't know what to tell you. I'm on their housing list. They help me out when they can. But maybe you noticed ..." she looked up and down the street, which was sprinkled with tents. "It's a long list. I'm not the only one with this problem."

"But it's not supposed to be like this."

"No shit, *really*?" Wendi opened her eyes wide in fake shock.

"What about your kids? How can they sleep in the back seat of a car?"

"Same way I sleep in the front seat. Easier for them, actually, their legs are shorter."

"But—what about education and nutrition and ... you can't be bringing your kids up in a car."

"I can and I do." Wendi sat up a little straighter and then stood up to look Claire in the eye. "I take good care of my kids. They may not have," she passed her hand in front of Claire, "all the fancy things you think they need. But I take good care of them, and I don't need you telling me how to be their mom."

"I just ..."

"Look, it's been nice saving your life and all," Wendi said with a harder edge in her voice. "But—could you move on now? Paula will be back soon and she's not as friendly as I am."

"Sure ... sure ..." Claire said, and started to walk away. Then she stopped and walked back, digging into her purse for her wallet. She pulled out two twenties and held them out to Wendi.

"Here."

Wendi looked down at the bills, then back up at Claire. "What's that for?"

"Just ..." She fanned the bills toward Wendi. "Just take it. It's all I have on me. To help you and your kids."

Frowning, Wendi grabbed the money. "I'll take your money, but I don't need your pity."

"Of course you don't."

"I don't."

"I'm serious"

"I know."

"Okay."

"Okay."

They stared at each other, not moving.

"Would you *go* now?" Wendi asked, irritated.

"Right." Claire nodded and turned. "It was ... nice to meet you, Wendi," she said.

"Yeah," Wendi said and waved her off. "Super. Have a nice life."

CHAPTER 4

Back at home after yoga, Claire tried to follow her routine and read a book in the living room, but she couldn't focus on any of the words. She got up and paced from room to room, searching for something she couldn't identify.

I know what you're thinking, Chris's voice said in her ear.

"Of course, you do," Claire said, "You're in my head."

You were always such a literalist, he teased.

"So, what am I thinking?"

You're thinking about how our house has four empty bedrooms.

"Maybe I am."

So what—are you going to open a boarding house? That could be fun.

"What is this, 1932?"

A shelter, then? A home for the wayward? The Fanciest Flophouse in Forest Park? You know I'm on board.

Claire rolled her eyes. "Some parts of you I miss less than others, old man."

Package deal, my love.

Their banter brought up a swell of emotion. She shook it off and used her finger to dab away the beginning of a tear. She went upstairs and moved from room to room, standing in each doorway and imagining the bedrooms with people in them: sleeping, reading, talking, playing games, listening to music. Just being there and living lives, bringing more life and vibrancy to the house than had been there in—well, surely not since she and Chris had moved in, just the two of them. Yes, it was madness to think about inviting homeless strangers to come stay with her. But what a waste of all this space! Her society friends would tell her she should be worried about them being dangerous. But this was a rail-thin young woman and two small children. How were they to know *she* wouldn't be dangerous to *them*? Of course, she's the furthest thing from dangerous, but still. Who knows anything about anyone these days?

"It wouldn't exactly be a shelter, I just ..." She struggled to articulate exactly what she was feeling. "It doesn't seem right that I have so much, and they have so little. I know I don't know anything about them, and I'm just a woman with a house. I wouldn't even know where to start after that."

You want to help. That's good.

"But I thought I was—we were—already helping! I thought that was the whole point of all this giving!"

Well, Chris said, *when there are big, messy problems like this one, giving like we do is one way to help make our money go farther. Portland Promise can do a lot more than we would be able to do alone.*

"But are they?" Claire asked. "They say they are, but she has two children sleeping in the back seat of an economy sedan and here I am, pacing around an empty house that has a front door made from a single piece of old-growth timber that is probably worth more than her entire car!"

Oh, it definitely is, Chris said as Claire made her way downstairs to stand in the foyer. *You have handbags worth more than that car.*

She raked her hands through her hair. "I just feel so ..." She dropped her arms to her sides. "I don't even know!"

Yes, you do. You feel so ... what?

"Helpless, Chris. I feel helpless. Even with all I have, there's nothing I can do for them."

You and I both know that's not true.

She meandered into the kitchen. She wasn't hungry but opened and closed the fridge then walked over to the pantry and stood in front of it. Just as she was about to give up and leave the kitchen, she had a thought: She couldn't house them, but maybe she could help feed them.

She reached for a jar of peanut butter that hadn't been touched since Chris passed, found a loaf of bread, and made a stack of peanut butter sandwiches. Then she grabbed a jar of jelly and made another stack of peanut butter and jelly sandwiches. Putting each sandwich into its own plastic baggie, she placed them all into a public radio tote bag and headed out of the house. She walked back down to the corner by her yoga studio, where she'd met Wendi.

* * *

The Accord was gone and a dark-haired, dark-skinned woman close to Claire's age was sitting in front of the tent at the corner. Claire approached her tentatively.

"Is ... Wendi ... still here?"

The woman sat on the orange plastic bucket, cutting an apple into slices and eating them off the knife's small blade. "Nope," she said, not looking up.

"Are you ... Paula?"

The woman with the knife slowly raised her eyes and said flatly, "Who's asking?"

"I'm Claire. I met ... I saw her at ... I talked to Wendi here a little while ago."

"She's not here."

"I brought some sandwiches." Claire held up the bag.

Paula reached out her hand. "I can help you out with those."

"Well, I ... They were for the kids." Claire pulled the bag back.

Paula shrugged and lowered her arm. "No kids here now."

Claire took another step back. "Do you know where they went?"

"Back to the Hilton so they could shower and order room service."

Claire blinked and dropped her arm. "Wait, what? The Hilton?"

Paula laughed. "How the hell would I know where she is?"

"Well, you're ... friends—aren't you?"

"Do you know where all *your* friends are right now?"

"No." Claire dropped her shoulders. "Good point."

Paula looked at the bag in Claire's hand. "For real you're not giving me those sandwiches?"

Claire looked down, surprised and distracted. For a moment, she'd forgotten she was holding a bag of peanut butter sandwiches she'd invested with the magical power to lift two small children and their mother out of a life of poverty. "I ... well, I guess you could have one or two." She took out one of each kind of sandwich and handed them to Paula. "I need to save the rest for the kids. If I were going to go try to find her, where would I look?"

"Seriously, lady, I don't know where she's staying tonight. She usually stays where there's other people around."

Claire sighed. "Please. Anything. Anything would help."

"Anything would help me, too," she said. "How about ten bucks and the rest of those sandwiches?"

Claire hesitated but realized this might be the only way to find Wendi. She handed over the bag of sandwiches and reached into her purse to find cash.

"I only have a twenty," Claire said.

"That'll work."

Paula took the bag and the money and settled back onto her bucket. "There's a couple camps up in Delta Park where people with cars go. I know she stays there on the edges sometimes. You could try there."

"Delta Park! That's so easy!" Claire gasped and caught herself before she reached out to hug Paula. "Thank you! Thank you so much!"

"It's almost dark, though. You shouldn't go tonight."

"Oh, I'll be fine," Claire said excitedly. "It's right off the freeway. This is fantastic."

"Seriously," Paula said. "Not tonight. Go tomorrow."

The sharp edge in her voice stopped Claire cold.

I think you should listen to her, Chris said in her ear.

Claire nodded. "Okay. Okay. Tomorrow. I'll go to Delta Park tomorrow and go home tonight."

"Good girl." Paula turned back to her apple.

Claire started walking back home and considered going against Paula's advice and heading straight to Delta Park that night. But she looked around. It was starting to get dark. She decided not to press her luck.

Good choice, Chris said. *Let's get home, Babe. They made it this long without your peanut butter sandwiches, they can probably make it another night.*

"I feel like you're making fun of me."

A little.

Claire walked up the hill in silence and leaned against the kitchen counter when she got inside the house. She shook her head at her own ridiculousness. What good is being helpful if you can't even find the people you want to help?

"It's the thought that counts, right? But what kind of a thought is a peanut butter sandwich? 'I want you to have protein so you can carry on, and also, I hope you don't have a nut allergy?'"

She stretched her arms out along the counter and laid her cheek on the cool marble.

"I miss you."

I know, Chris said.

"I feel like I'm falling apart."

You're not.

"All I had was you. Without you, none of this matters."

I'm right here.

"No, I mean *here*!" Claire raised her voice. She slapped the counter and propped herself up on her elbows. Her eyes welled with tears. "You never should have left. I never should have let you go."

I didn't die because I left, babe, I died because I had a heart attack. It could have happened anywhere.

"But it *didn't* happen anywhere." Tears started to run down her face and she pressed her cheek against the cool marble countertop.

* * *

The call that Chris had died came while Claire was at the grocery store, standing in front of the almond milk. She'd just talked to him the night before. He'd suggested that when she came to meet him in Sri Lanka, instead of heading off to the beach in Thailand as they'd planned, she stay with him in Buttala so they could get even more work done.

"This is your passion, Chris, not mine," she'd said.

"Come on, babe, we both love to give back."

"We do, but we've talked about this before. As much as I love you and as much as I want to make a meaningful difference,

I prefer the ways that aren't doing manual labor in the tropics, in a pool of my own sweat."

"You don't know what you're missing!"

"I know exactly what I'm missing."

He laughed, and even on the phone across thousands of miles, she could see the corners of his clear, grey eyes crinkle as he laughed that beautiful laugh and ran his strong, tanned hand through his short, white hair.

"I miss you, babe," he'd said.

* * *

Cheek pressed against the kitchen counter, Claire squeezed her eyes tight to hang on to his image. Of all the people in the world, of course Chris would end up being the person who literally died doing what he loved.

"The only thing in my life that had any meaning was you," she whispered.

Chris laughed gently.

"Don't laugh at me!"

I'm sorry. I love you. I don't think—I never thought—anything about you was meaningless.

She wiped her face with the back of her hand. "But it is. It all is."

I don't think so. But if you do, you're the one who's going to have to figure that out.

"Oh, come on!" Claire yelled. "I don't need you to be wise, I need you to be *here*! And if you can't be *here*," she said, "then just be quiet."

Okay, babe. I'm here when you want me. I love you.

She sank to the floor and turned to lean against the cabinet. Tears continued to roll, and she hugged her knees to her chest as she sobbed. “This is the part where you’re supposed to be here, holding me.”

When Chris didn’t answer, she cried harder.

CHAPTER 5

Erica Ford was not a morning person. Until this job, she'd only ever greeted sunrise at the back end of a bender. But here she was, at 6:17 on a Wednesday morning, watching the sun rise over an industrial lot under the Fremont Bridge. She sat on the open tailgate of her beat-up white pickup with its even more beat-up truck cap, smoking the third cigarette of the day and nursing a now-lukewarm paper cup of coffee. It wasn't winter-cold out anymore, but mornings in the spring were still chilly, damp and relentlessly gray. She tugged the hood of her sweatshirt down over her eyebrows and settled in. At least it wasn't raining.

Remembering she'd missed (ignored) a text from her mom last night, Erica fished her phone out of her pocket and ran her thumb over its cracked screen to bring it to life. For a few moments she distracted herself checking socials and email, but then remembered that she was supposed to be checking the text from her mom. It's not that Mom-texts were necessarily *bad* ... they could just sometimes be a lot. She took a deep breath and tapped the green icon for messages.

All her mom's text said was, *Seriously?* And then there was a link to an *Oregonian* article about the City Council meeting about the tents.

Erica leaned her head back against the rim of the truck cap and sighed. Of course, her mom had seen the article.

I'm famous, Ma! she typed back, followed by the little sunglasses face emoji.

Are you OK?

Erica stubbed out her cigarette and settled in for a longer text conversation. A responsive daughter was the least her mom deserved after all her parents had done for her.

I am. It's all good, I swear. Bruce is not a happy camper. So to speak. But what's new?

There was a pause, then three little dots showing her mom was typing, then they went away. Then they came back, then went away, and then Erica's phone rang.

Erica sighed. After a few lines, her mom always gave up on texting and just called. This time, she skipped "Hello," and started in with a raft of questions.

"Are you really okay? Is he pissed enough to fire you? How are you feeling? When was your last meeting?"

"It's fine, Mom," Erica said slowly, hoping her calm pace would slow her mom down, too. "I went to a meeting last night and I'm good. That's where I was when you first texted, and I just forgot to get back afterwards. Bruce is mad, but everything I do makes him mad. He knows he needs me. It'll be fine."

Erica wasn't one hundred percent sure about that, but she didn't want to worry her mom. If Mom thought there was even the slightest chance Erica could lose her job and potentially be on the streets like her clients, she would drive down to Portland from Olympia immediately to assess the scene herself and, if necessary, bring Erica back to her childhood home for as long as necessary.

"From the comments on the article," her mom said, "some people think you're a saint and some people think you're the devil incarnate."

"It's just giving out basic supplies to help people who have nothing. It's not being a saint or a sinner, it's just being a decent human."

"I'm only a call, a text, or a short drive away, Miss E.," her mom said. "And if I see another article about you fighting homelessness single-handedly, I'm coming down there."

"I know, Mom. I love you, and it'll all be okay."

"Love."

"Love."

Erica's parents still lived in Olympia, Washington, where she grew up. Oly was about two hours north of Portland and about ten times smaller. As Washington State's capital city and home to a public college, it housed a strange mix of government workers, university people, and random hippies and drifters. Once a year, legislators swarmed the place for a few months, but they generally stayed up on the Hill, where they didn't impact the townies much at all.

Growing up, Erica knew she'd probably end up working to help people in some way. A teacher, maybe, like her dad, or something in government like her mom. She never firmed up those ideas, though, because the summer she turned thirteen, she discovered Boone's Farm wine. It quickly went downhill from there.

To her parents' credit, they knew from experience that a person can only really stop when they're ready to stop. Her dad was in open recovery and mom had been by his side the whole time. They knew you can't force the process. There were a few hard fumbles early on, and they stepped back, trying to support her without enabling. But Erica kept on drinking, and one day she and a friend got loaded and went out for a drive. Erica was the passenger, and she walked away with some scrapes. Her friend who was driving didn't make it. When Erica decided the next morning that it was time to quit, her parents were right there for her, helping her navigate the harsh curves of grief and sobriety at the same time.

She finished her GED since high school had been a bust, went to Evergreen College where her dad taught, and graduated at twenty-seven. Shortly after graduating, she moved to Portland to get a little distance. She'd started with a job at a domestic violence shelter and went over to Portland Promise when a job there opened up. A lot of her clients were affected by addiction—whether it was themselves or a family member. Not only was she helping people who needed it, she was also helping herself. The twelfth step is helping others navigate their own paths through the steps. Doing that work—that step—was often the only thing that kept her going on some of the toughest days, because it reminded her of where she'd been, how far she'd come, and where she didn't want to be.

A pair of headlights fixed her in their glare as a car drove in her direction. Erica held her arm up to shield her eyes and squinted. She was supposed to be meeting Sarah, one of her off again/on again clients who was going to borrow a van and come meet her to get some tents. This vehicle rode too low to be a van, though, and when the driver parked and left his lights on, Erica noticed the spotlight on the side. This was a damn police cruiser. Great. That's all she needed now. Erica braced herself for an inquisition as the driver opened his door and stepped out. She reminded herself that while it may not be normal, sitting in one's parked, licensed, and properly insured vehicle under the Fremont Bridge is not illegal. Neither, technically, is giving away tents to the unhoused.

The cop walked toward her slowly, chest puffed up and hand near his hip. He walked directly in front of his headlights, so his face was in shadow.

"Good morning," he said as he advanced. Then he stopped abruptly, dropped his shoulders, and folded his arms. "Ford? What are you doing out here?"

Erica's forehead wrinkled in confusion. "Jacob Wright?" she called back.

"Who else did you think they'd send to respond to a complaint about someone who looked homeless parking under the bridge?" he answered.

Jake was the city's "Officer Friendly." At least, that's what Erica called him even though he hated it. He was the sole cop in the department who had genuine compassion for people who were struggling, so they rolled him out as the face of their homeless response team. He was dispatched to most of the calls related to people on the street. Over the last couple of years, they'd gotten to know each other because a lot of his calls turned out to also be Erica's clients or potential clients. She wasn't inclined, as a rule, to trust cops. But he'd proven to be alright.

"What the hell, man?" Erica responded as she pushed herself off the tailgate to stand in front of her truck. "Turn off your damn headlights, will you?"

He went back to the car and switched off the high beams and the spotlight. Erica blinked rapidly to adjust her eyes.

When he returned to the truck, he put his forearm against the top of the cap over the truck bed and leaned down to look inside.

"You know they told me to watch out for you," he said. "To make sure you weren't giving out those tents."

"You see anyone here I'm giving tents to?"

"So, you're telling me this is not a truck full of tents?"

"The truck is not full. That's like a solid fifty percent. Half full. Or half empty, if you insist on being a pessimist."

He rolled his eyes. "Taking a few friends camping?"

Erica pinched the cherry out of her cigarette, ground it out with her heel, and dropped the cigarette butt into her coffee cup. "I'm quite outdoorsy."

"I'm going to have to call this in."

"For what?"

"I'll figure it out."

Jake returned to his cruiser and Erica boosted herself back up onto the tailgate, pulling her legs up under her. She pulled out her phone and started typing a text message to Sarah.

You're late. Don't come now. 5-0.

As she hit send, Jake walked back to her truck and stood in front of her, hands in his pockets.

"Turns out I'm having some trouble with my radio," he said, and rocked back on his heels.

"Really," Erica deadpanned.

"I'm going to have to go back to HQ and get it fixed."

"So ..." Erica said, "you're not calling it in?"

"Like I said, my radio isn't working right."

They looked at each other. Erica smiled. "Thanks, Officer Friendly."

"Don't call me that. And don't thank me. It's a radio malfunction."

"Got it." She stuffed her phone in her pocket, picked up her coffee cup, hopped out of the truck, and closed the tailgate.

Just after she'd started the truck and was about to pull away, she rolled down her window to thank him. At that same moment, his radio crackled with a call. Erica shook her head and laughed while Jake moved to silence the radio.

"Sounds like your radio got fixed," Erica said.

"Maybe so."

"I'll get out of here so you can deal with it."

Jake patted the truck twice and she pulled away, back out onto the road.

★ ★ ★

Once she was clear of the parking lot, Erica lit another cigarette. Sarah had been crashing lately up at Delta Park, so that's probably where she was now. There was a group of tweakers who had carved out a space for themselves at the edge of one of the camps up there. Erica was pissed Sarah was staying with them because it probably meant she was using again. But as long as Sarah trusted Erica, Sarah would keep taking her calls. And a call meant a chance to talk, a chance to extend a hand, a chance to try again.

Erica headed north on I-5 and dialed Sarah's number. She put it on speaker and turned up the volume before tossing the phone into the seat next to her.

"Sorry, sorry, sorry," Sarah answered.

"Where the hell are you?" Erica shouted at the phone in the seat next to her.

"Here."

"You're gonna have to give me a little more than 'here.'"

"Delta. I overslept."

"Come on, Sarah. I'm about to get fired for these stupid tents. Even the cops are looking out for me. The least you could do is show up so I can hand them off to you."

"I thought you said the cops showed up there."

"They did, but if you'd been on time we'd have been out of there before then."

"But I was late."

"Sarah, I swear to God."

"What?"

Erica sighed. "Nothing."

"Sorry."

"Yeah. You're at the camp?"

"Yeah."

"I'll be there in a few. Don't go anywhere."

"I can't. I wasn't able to get the van after all."

"Wait, what—? Sarah, please hang up now."

"K, see you soon."

Erica banged her head against the headrest, muttering as she neared the Delta Park exit, "Why. Do I. Even. Bother?"

⋆ ⋆ ⋆

The camps look the same as always, Erica thought as she exited the freeway and looked out from the offramp. Total shitshow.

The sprawling wreckage looked like someone took the worst, most run-down trailer park, threw it into an industrial dumpster, and then tossed a bomb into the whole thing. Shrapnel in the form of garbage was strewn everywhere. Since these weren't residences or businesses, the city didn't provide garbage pickup. So anything tossed aside stayed exactly where it landed. And in rainy Portland, water and mud turned all of it into a gray muck that was a stinky swamp when it was wet and a hard, impenetrable crust when the sun came out and dried it.

Erica parked on the side of the road on the east end of Delta Park and texted Sarah her location. As she waited, she looked out on the line of broken-down campers and the tents clustered just beyond them. It was such a mess. So many people needed so much help.

"I'm like the Sisyphus of tents and camping equipment. Solve one problem, and another one pops up," she said to herself.

"Actually," she muttered with a wry smile, "I guess that's more Whack-A-Mole than Greek mythology."

Finally, Erica's phone buzzed with a new text from Sarah.

There's a lady here giving out sandwiches and money! It's like Christmas!

Erica looked up toward the encampment and saw Sarah at the edge, waving at her. Erica sighed and shook her head.

Come get these tents, she texted back.

No srsly! This is funny & the sandwiches r DELUX!

Erica groaned. Damn it. She was hoping to just stay at the edge and not go in. But now Sarah was distracted and there was some random person giving out sandwiches. She should probably check on that person, too. These "Good Samaritans" who showed up from time to time were a real problem. Most of them had no idea what they were getting into and were putting themselves and others in danger.

She stepped out of her truck and walked toward the camp. As she approached, Sarah pointed her toward a white-haired lady with an expensive coat, a tote bag, and muddy sneakers, leaning into a tent with her wallet open.

"These people." Erica rolled her eyes.

"I know, right?" Sarah said, bouncing up and down. "I got twenty bucks and a super fancy sandwich from Whole Foods. This lady is sandwich Jesus."

As the lady straightened up and turned to the next tent, Erica saw her face. It was the same woman from the luncheon yesterday. The major donor who'd freaked out.

"Fuck me," Erica said under her breath.

"Yeah. I know," Sarah said. "I should have held out for more money. But I'm hungry, and this sandwich is *fire*."

Erica turned to look at Sarah and shook her head. "What? I'm not talking about that. Eat your sandwich, and then we'll get your tents. I'm going to go talk to her."

"See if you can get me another twenty!" Sarah called after her as she sat down on the ground. She bit into her sandwich. "Oh my God, roasted peppers? This is so deluxe!"

Erica came up behind the lady as she was talking to people inside a tent. What was her name? As she walked up, she heard a man's voice inside the tent say, "I mean, five bucks is nice and all, but I see you've got a couple twenties there and that'd be even better."

"Well, I ... That's more than I ..." Claire stammered.

Erica cleared her throat loudly, "Excuse me."

Claire looked behind her and backed out of the tent opening when she saw Erica, who looked inside the tent and recognized the guy asking for more money.

"Oh hey, Jim," she said. "Five bucks is just fine, isn't it?"

"Oh, come *on*," Jim said. "Seriously?"

"Seriously," Erica said.

"Screw off, Erica."

"Always good to see you, too, Jim."

Claire looked confused and handed Jim the five-dollar bill she was holding, then stepped back and turned her attention to Erica.

"Hello," Claire said, clearly thinking Erica lived at Delta Park. "Are you hungry? Would you like a sandwich?"

Erica rolled her eyes. "No, Mrs. Philanthropist of the Year. I don't need you to feed me."

"How do you ..." Claire started, and then squinted. "Ohhhhhhh," Her eyes went wide as she recognized Erica. "You're the one who was arguing with Bruce yesterday."

"Yep, that was me. Can I offer you a suggestion?"

"Certainly."

"Follow me out of here," Erica said. "Don't stop to give out any more money. Just walk out with me."

Claire pursed her lips and folded her arms. She looked down at her nearly empty bag of sandwiches and at her wallet, which Erica presumed was also nearing empty. Claire looked like she was weighing her options, then shrugged slightly.

"I guess I was almost done anyway," Claire said, and followed Erica.

Sarah came up next to them and started walking, too. "Thanks for the sandwich," Sarah said brightly.

"You're very welcome," Claire said. "And I appreciate your sunny disposition."

Erica rolled her eyes and quickened her pace. "Sarah, what are you doing?"

"Coming to get my tents," Sarah said. "And thanking this nice lady for her generosity."

"Have you thought about where I might find that young woman with the car?" Claire asked Sarah. "I have a few more sandwiches. Would you like another?"

"Oh my God, yes," Sarah answered. "And, you know, I need gas, too. To get to a job interview next week. It's a really good job. If you had any money for gas, that'd be amazing."

"Well, let me see," Claire said. "I may still have somethi—"

They'd reached Erica's truck, and Erica slammed her hand on the hood. "*Sarah.* Stop."

Sarah leaned toward Claire conspiratorially. "Someone sounds hungry. She should have had a sandwich, huh?"

"Take your tents and get out of here," Erica hissed.

"Fine," Sarah said, and walked around to the back. She popped open the tailgate and grabbed three of the tents.

"Here," Claire said. "Since your hands are full, why don't you just take this bag and put it over your shoulder. You can share what's left as you see fit."

"Oh, thank you!" Sarah said, bowing into something that was almost a curtsey.

Claire leaned in and whispered, "And here's a twenty. Good luck this week!"

Erica leaned her head back and looked skyward. "I saw that. I heard that. You don't think I heard and saw that? You," she pointed to Sarah, "stop being a predator. And you," she pointed to Claire, "stop making it so easy. Take your stuff and get out of here, Sarah."

"Going." Sarah slung the bag over her shoulder and used both hands to drag the tents across the field. "Thanks, E! Thanks, sandwich lady!"

Erica closed the tailgate and leaned against it as Sarah walked away.

"What a nice young woman," Claire said. "She lives *here*?"

"You know there's no job interview, right?" Erica said. "There's no tank of gas. There's not even a car."

Claire blinked like that thought had never crossed her mind. "Well ..." Claire said, "if a few sandwiches and some cash can help her out, then I'm glad to help."

Erica cocked her head. She was still amazed when she learned some people really are this blind. "She's going to smoke that twenty before you and I are even out of here."

"I ... I just wanted to help."

"Seriously? You're the top donor at Portland Promise. I don't even know how much money that means you've donated this year."

"A lot."

"What is the agency's largest single donor doing walking through a homeless camp giving out twenty-dollar bills and twelve-dollar sandwiches?"

Claire looked chastened. "I'm looking for someone. I thought maybe having something to trade would help me find her."

"Who are *you* looking for out *here*?"

Claire's entire body brightened as she realized Erica might be able to help her. "Wendi," she said. "The young woman who spoke at the luncheon yesterday."

"Let me guess. You want to take her out to a five-course meal tonight?"

Claire hesitated. "Kind of? Not exactly. I saw her yesterday afternoon, after the luncheon. We chatted briefly, and ... I don't know, I wanted to know more about her. I wanted to help her and her children. We'd just been to this luncheon where hundreds of thousands of dollars were raised, and then later in the day I saw her sitting outside a tent on 23rd Avenue."

"You thought after the luncheon she'd magically get a house and start paying a mortgage?"

"No, I just ... What are we paying all this money for if we aren't helping the people who need it? Especially the one who they pulled up on stage to speak to us about the value of our giving?"

"Welcome to the conflict of my life and work," Erica said flatly.

Claire pointed at the open tailgate on Erica's truck and asked, "May I?"

Erica shrugged. "Help yourself."

Claire arranged her coat behind her and perched gently on the edge.

"Look," Erica said, "you seem like a good person and a nice lady, and I thought your little speech yesterday made that luncheon hands-down the most entertaining thing I've seen all month. But handing out sandwiches and cash isn't going to get any of those people any closer to living inside. It may make *you* feel better, but it doesn't actually help."

"They have so little, and I have so much. I just wanted to help."

Erica sat down on the other end of the tailgate and tucked one leg under her, leaning against the frame of the truck cap.

"There's an analogy my boss uses," she said. "I hate it, but there's a little truth to it."

Claire nodded for her to go on.

"It's like ... feeding the strays. You see a stray cat in the neighborhood, and you feel bad for it, so you put out some food.

It comes back the next day, and you feed it again. Then the next day. And the next day. But then you go on vacation or get busy and forget, and the stray is left out in the cold. What you should have done if you wanted to help that stray was take it in and commit to caring for it, or take it to the Humane Society where they could help it get its needs met."

Claire frowned and folded her arms across her chest. "Are you comparing homeless people to stray animals?"

Erica half-nodded, half shrugged. Bruce had actually compared their clients to raccoons, which was way more antagonistic and, frankly, racist than she wanted to deal with. She would stick with cats.

"It's an imperfect analogy," she said.

"It's kind of rude, don't you think?"

"So is assuming that swooping in and spending a few hundred or even a few hundred thousand dollars to make yourself feel better makes any kind of a difference."

"Wow." Claire winced a little. "Don't pull any punches."

"You can't just bring them a sandwich and assume everything else will change."

"You've made your point about the sandwiches, okay?"

"Okay. But I'm going to keep bringing it up because, seriously? Twelve dollars for an egg salad on wheat? Come on."

"It was whole grain, and the eggs were from pasture-raised chickens."

"Now you're just telling jokes."

"I need to defend myself."

"Those sandwiches are indefensible."

"Have you ever had one?"

"No! People who live normal lives and have normal jobs and go to normal grocery stores do not spend an hour's wage on a sandwich. That's just not a thing."

They eyed each other for a beat before Erica continued.

"Helping people who are living on the street, especially those who are the toughest of the tough, isn't about helping them with one-time quick fixes. It's about staying with them and helping them along. About providing services and support and making that new life seem more attractive and worth fighting for than the old life, and being there for them when the fight is hard."

"It already seems pretty hard, to me," Claire said.

"It is," Erica said. "And it may take a while. And when they fail or relapse or lose hope, you pick them up and sit with them until they're ready to try again."

"That sounds ... draining," Claire said.

Erica nodded. "It sure as shit is. But when someone succeeds, it's the best feeling in the world."

They sat together in silence for a while, looking out at the camp. Then Claire sighed heavily.

"So ..." Claire started. "Here's another question for you. You're smacking me on the wrist and lecturing me about not giving one-time solutions that make it easier to stay here ..."

"Yes ..."

"But at the same time, you're handing out tents."

"Yeah?"

"How does a nice, clean, new tent help someone come inside? Aren't you helping them with a short-term fix, too?"

Erica pursed her lips and sucked in on her teeth. "It's not the same."

"How? Because right now," Claire said, "it seems to me what you're saying is it's okay for *you* to ... feed the strays, as you put it ... but it's not okay for me to. That seems arbitrary."

Erica stood up and walked a few paces away. She lit a cigarette and shook her head. How could she tell this rich lady the truth she didn't want to hear? That the system was broken, that the safety net had so many holes in it people dropped through in piles every single day? People always say they want to help until they realize how big and broken and messy the system is.

Erica turned to Claire and jabbed the air with her cigarette. "People always say they want to help until they realize how big and broken and messy the system is. But the thing is, that mess is what's true. These people are out here because our system has failed them. It's gotten big and unwieldy and unhelpful. People wait for years to get into public housing because we aren't building enough of it. But then the city doesn't add shelter while we wait on the housing because they say our goal is housing, not shelter. And then they say we can't give aid and tents to people on the street because that would just encourage them to stay on the street. But since there's nowhere else for them to go, they stay on the street and they freeze because they don't have a decent tent."

Claire took a deep breath and moved in a little closer. "Don't take this the wrong way, but I'm wondering something."

Erica took a step back. "Whenever someone says, 'Don't take this the wrong way,' they are about to insult you."

"Not this time," Claire said, moving forward and closing the gap between them. "You clearly care a lot about this. And you have plenty to say about how to do it wrong. Where's the vision of how to do it right?"

Erica threw her hands into the air. "That's all I know! I know what's wrong, but I don't know how to fix it." She stepped back and punched the truck with the side of her fist. A beat later the pain hit and she walked away to pace in a circle, shaking out her hand.

Claire let her walk it off and then a minute or so later, cleared her throat. "You just said we can't fix the whole thing."

She paused and waited for Erica to look her in the eyes.

"But can we fix part of it?" Claire asked. "If you could fix one thing, knowing it wouldn't solve everything, but it would make things a little bit better, what would you do?"

Erica stopped pacing and cocked her head. She smiled a little. "Like, if I had a magic wand and wouldn't get fired for even suggesting it?"

"Yes."

Erica stared at Claire for a few seconds and then stood a little taller. "Okay," she said. "I've actually thought about this. But if we're going to keep talking about it, I'm going to need some more coffee."

CHAPTER 6

Claire and Erica relocated to a diner in one of the aging strip malls bordering Delta Park. They sat opposite each other on orange vinyl booth seats, with a window view of the parking lot and the camps just past it. The place was nearly empty: just them, an older couple who looked like they'd been sitting in that same booth every day for the last thirty years, and a ragged-looking middle-aged man who was nursing a cup of coffee and muttering quietly to himself.

Eventually, the server ambled over with a coffee pot and two mugs.

"Coffee?"

"Yes. Two, please," Claire said brightly.

"And a whole lot of cream," Erica said.

The server gestured with her chin to the bowl of individual creamers by the wall, then poured them each a mug of coffee.

"I'll probably need more than those," Erica said.

Wordlessly, the server reached into the pocket of her apron and scattered a handful of creamers on the table.

"And ..." Claire said, "what else do people get here? Pie? How about a piece of pie?"

"I don't think you want the pie," Erica said quietly.

"What's wrong with pie?" Claire asked. "And a piece of cherry pie," Claire told the server, who shrugged and went off to place the order.

When the pie arrived, Erica looked smug and Claire tried not to grimace. A bright red pool of goo seeped out from a triangle of crust that could have been cut from a cardboard box. Claire thanked the server and gently pushed the pie toward the edge of the table.

"Told you," Erica said and shrugged. She dumped sugar and creamer into her coffee.

"Need a little more sugar?" Claire asked lightly.

"No, I'm good—" Erica started to respond, then looked up and met Claire's eyes.

Claire grinned. "I was just thinking you might need a little more. There might still be one molecule of unadulterated coffee in there."

"Shut up," Erica said, but without any bite behind it. "You drink enough bad coffee, this is what you learn to do."

"I like this girl," Claire whispered to herself.

"What was that?" Erica asked.

"Nothing," Claire said. "This may sound strange, but it's refreshing to talk with someone who has no problem telling me to shut up."

"All due respect," Erica smiled, "I have a feeling this won't be the last time."

Erica smoothed out the Kiddie Klub paper placemat she'd been marking up with a complex-looking network of hubs and spokes and turned it so that Claire could read it. Gesturing with a blue crayon, she pointed out multiple small-scale types of housing and services she felt were lacking in the current system.

"Some of these small programs already exist and just need to be strengthened so they can grow," she said, "and some need to be started up. For the people who are reluctant to come inside, managed sites offer a reasonable alternative. But they need to be small and well-resourced, and governed by the people who live there."

Claire took a sip of coffee, suppressed a shudder, and pushed the mug away. "I guess that makes sense."

"The self-governing part is huge," Erica said. "It's a level of ownership and responsibility that helps make it all work. And having peer support is important, too—it's been demonstrated to help people stabilize more quickly and with fewer setbacks."

"But isn't someone with a more stable life in a better position to help than someone who's also struggling?"

"No, think about it," Erica said. "When someone who has a totally different life from you comes in and tries to tell you what to do to fix your life, how does that go over with you?"

Claire thought about all the people who had endless advice for her after Chris died. And none of it was helpful because none of *them* had just lost their husband.

"Not well," she said.

"Exactly. But when someone can honestly say, 'I've been where you are and here's how I got through it,' that's different, right? It's not telling someone what to do, it's saying here's what worked for me; your mileage may vary."

Claire nodded. "It seems like this is something you know personally."

"I do."

Claire waited to see if Erica would offer more.

"I'm seven years sober, Claire," Erica said. "I'm lucky enough never to have been homeless, and to have a family that went to great lengths to help me. But I still lost a lot. I know what it's like to have a problem that's bigger and tougher and meaner than you could imagine. But I have also learned how to deal with it, and to how to use that experience to help others."

Erica held up her hand to get the server's attention, and gestured toward their coffee mugs.

"Thanks," she said as the server refilled her mug and dropped another handful of creamers onto the table.

"More for you?" the server asked Claire.

Claire looked down at her mug of truly awful coffee. She'd only had about a quarter of it, but she nodded and pushed it out to the center of the table.

The server nodded. "Good choice. It's bad when it's hot, but deadly when it's cold." She winked and walked away to check on the older couple.

"Are we done naming alcoholics now?" Erica asked. "Can I get back to telling you how I'd save the world?"

Claire smiled. "Absolutely."

"We've gotten to this weird place," Erica said, "where the state and the feds and the donors like you are totally fine with spending tens and hundreds of millions of dollars on warehouses to stick people in. But then when we need to pay for the services that will *keep* people in housing, everyone cheaps out and says there's not enough money. I want to flip it. Let's invest more in people and service. That's where real change happens, and it's where we've consistently cut funding."

"How expensive would doing this be?" Claire asked. "What you've laid out here."

"I'm sketching this out on a children's placemat, using a Cornflower Blue crayon," Erica said. "We aren't really at the budget spreadsheet place."

"Give me a ballpark."

"So, I've got a lot of small operations here on my list of ideas. Everything all together? About twenty million to start and then half that again each year to keep them all running."

"How much was that building I contributed to last year with Portland Promise?"

"Twenty-five million. For forty-eight single-unit apartments. And that's just the structure, before adding in any services."

"So ... Using your model, we could help a lot more people for half as much."

"Yeah, but don't let that difference make you think your money was wasted. It wasn't. That apartment building you helped pay for filled up immediately. We needed it. But we also need more and different."

Claire leaned forward and tapped the placemat sketch. "You're saying we need all this in *addition* to what we are already doing?"

"Essentially. And more on top of that."

"Oof."

"Yeah, it's a lot," Erica said. "But the money is there. Whether it's in this system, in the hands of donors like you, or in other funding areas that may be bloated."

"Like what?"

"Well, for example, more than two-thirds of city and county budgets go to law enforcement, jail, and the courts. And about half the people in the jails and the courts are people without housing. Jail is our most expensive and least effective form of shelter. Maybe we wouldn't need to spend so much on cops and lawyers and wardens for those people if we spent a little more on helping them solve the problems that put them there." Erica continued thrumming her fingers on the table.

Claire looked at Erica's hands and looked up at her face. "I don't condone smoking, but you clearly need to step outside."

Erica held her hand still. "I'm fine."

"Ha," Claire said. "Go have a cigarette. I need a little time to process all of this."

Erica looked relieved and scooted out of the booth.

Claire looked down at the paper in front of her with Erica's blue-crayon scribbles. The fact that she chose to use a crayon didn't do her justice. This girl was smart.

Seems like she's the one who should be in charge, Chris said in Claire's ear. *Not that guy Bruce.*

"I agree." Claire nodded. She looked up from the paper and out the window to where Erica was smoking and staring out at the camps. She picked up a fork and poked at the piece of pie sitting at the edge of the table.

She's clearly frustrated where she is.

"She is, but no one's going to put that angry little woman in the pullover hoodie in charge," Claire said.

You could, Chris said.

"I'm a donor, Chris," Claire said. "I don't run the organization."

I don't mean put her in charge of Portland Promise, Chris said. *I mean start something new and give her a shot. You both want to make a difference. So do it.*

Claire considered this and stuck the fork into the triangle tip of the piece of pie. "I don't know ..." she said. "That's a big commitment. Here on paper she makes it look simple, but it's not that easy."

You've got to start somewhere.

"True enough."

Claire lifted a bite of the pie to her mouth and chewed, then coughed and reached quickly for her coffee. "Oh God. Serving that pie should be a crime," she said.

* * *

As much as Erica knew smoking was bad for her health and bad for her wallet, the short breaks to step outside also gave her a much-needed chance to slow down and think.

Staring at the economic, public health, and social service disaster that was Delta Park, she let herself entertain the possibility that this weird rich lady might be the key to doing something meaningful. She finished the cigarette and pushed through the door to come back inside, and from the front door to the diner it looked like Claire was talking to herself. Although Erica was used to seeing people talk to themselves, it wasn't necessarily what she was hoping to see here. But then Claire tasted the pie and pushed it away like it had attacked her ... so, at least she wasn't completely nuts.

"Seriously," Erica scolded as she eased back into the booth, "what did I tell you about the pie?"

"I should have listened."

"Who were you talking to?"

"Hm?" Claire said, looking up quickly. "No one. Just me."

"I thought you were on your phone when I first walked up. But you weren't, and it looked like you were talking to someone."

"Nope," Claire said, and smiled. "Just an old lady talking to herself." She took a paper napkin from the dispenser on the table and laid it over the plate, covering the pie. "I can't even look at it."

Erica laughed a little. "So where were we?" she asked.

Claire clasped her hands, rested her elbows on the table, and leaned her chin on her hands. "It sounds like you have a workable plan here. How do we get started?"

Startled, Erica laughed sharply. "To do everything on this page? Um, make me queen of the world and then find me thirty-million bucks just to get started?"

Claire smiled and leaned back, laying her hands flat on the table. "Well, I can't do either of those things. But ... say I could do *something*. Say we could find ... a million. If you had that, what would you do?"

Erica pushed herself all the way to the back end of the booth and extended her legs long on the bench seat. She looked over at Claire. "If I had a million dollars to start my own program?"

"Yes. You can pick one thing from your list. What would you do to make a real difference right now?"

Erica sighed deeply and closed her eyes, leaning her head against the wall. "God, I don't know." Sure, she'd been thinking about these plans for years. But they had always seemed like dreams, not realities. It was harder than she'd expected to go from railing against the system to actually trying to repair it.

She sat there for a few seconds, feeling Claire staring at her. Then she popped her eyes open and pointed at one of the lines on her brainstorming placemat.

"A managed site for women. Independent but cooperative transitional housing in a managed, self-governed community. Tiny houses with a common area. Women only, maybe also kids. Strong peer support and a full slate of services."

Claire beamed and sat up straighter. "Then that's our plan."

Erica shook her head. She must have misheard something. "What are you talking about?"

"Well, you just identified our project. Where do we start?"

"Um ... I thought this was a hypothetical."

"It doesn't have to be."

Erica picked up a spoon and pointed it toward Claire. This woman was something else.

"Look, I looked you up," Erica said. "After the luncheon. I looked you up to see what your story was and the most you've ever given the organization in a year is $400,000. And don't get me wrong, that's a hell of a lot of money. But this is a whole lot more. Don't make promises you know you can't keep."

Claire didn't blink. "I give to a lot of organizations, not just Portland Promise. A million dollars *is* a lot of money, but it's not unmanageable. Let me worry about that."

They eyed each other across the table.

"A big part of me thinks you're full of shit," Erica said.

"What about the other part?"

Erica paused. She didn't want to get her hopes up, but if this woman *wasn't* nuts or straight-up lying, this thing could be amazing. "If you're not messing with my head? Cautiously optimistic."

"Well, that's better than nothing," Claire said and shrugged. "And I'm not messing with your head."

Erica rolled her eyes. "If we actually did this," she said, "it would need to be in a place that's easily accessible by transit, has access to utilities, and has enough space. At least an acre, preferably more."

"Great," Claire said. "I'll start looking for a location. You start planning it."

Erica pursed her lips. This was definitely not how she'd expected this day to unfold. And she had no idea if this woman was for real or not. But on the very off chance this time might be different, she didn't want to shut out the opportunity altogether. She decided to go along with it for now. If it turned into something, she'd be there. And if this lady dropped out like she probably would, well ... then Erica could get back to fighting her everyday battles.

"Alright," Erica said. "I need to get going now, but you start looking for a site and I'll start thinking about the framework."

"Excellent." Claire clapped her hands and pushed out of the booth to stand up. When Erica stood, Claire pulled her in for a hug. "This is going to be great."

Erica initially resisted Claire's hug, but Claire held on until Erica finally gave in and hugged her back.

CHAPTER 7

In the week since they'd sat at that diner, Erica had heard very little from Claire.

She had, however, heard from Bruce.

After a few days of irritating voice mails reminding her she was on probation, he had called Erica into his office for a meeting at "9:00 a.m. *sharp.*" And as usual, she was on time and he was nowhere to be found. From past experience she knew she had ten minutes or so until he graced her with his presence, so she settled in.

His office was arranged with an audience in mind. He'd filled the wall behind his desk chair with accolades: his degrees, letters from the governor about how great he was, framed newspaper articles with large pictures of him. And on the desk, all the photos faced out, not in. Normal people faced their family photos inward, to remind them of what they love. Bruce set up his desk to remind others of why *they* should love *him.*

Erica had been up most of the night trying to help a client find a detox bed. Her phone was buzzing with texts, but she wouldn't have time to get through them all before Bruce walked in. So she decided to go for a ten-minute power nap instead. She sank into the chair, put her feet up on the edge of Bruce's desk, pulled her hoodie down over her eyes, and shoved her hands into her pockets. This, she had found over years of experimentation, was the best position to catch some sleep in his intentionally uncomfortable chairs.

She jumped when a pair of hands loudly clapped three times, right next to her ear.

"Fuck, Bruce!" she spat as she straightened up in the chair and put her feet flat on the floor.

"Good morning to you, too."

"*Unnecessary.*"

"Glad you were able to get some sleep on agency time," he said, making a big show of brushing off the edge of the desk where her feet had been.

"I was up all night for the agency," she said flatly. "Want me to just bill you for that time?"

"Cute." He sat magnanimously in his desk chair, which was cranked up to put him at least three inches higher than she was. She wondered if his toes dangled off the floor.

"Not cute, Bruce," she said. "Dead serious."

Bruce exhaled loudly. "Well, speaking of dead serious, let's talk about why you're here." He reached into a desk drawer to grab a thick file folder. "This is *your* file, Ms. Ford. It contains every write-up, every complaint from the authorities, and every example of your policy violations since you started work here."

The corner of her mouth lifted into a wry smile. "I'm impressed. You're thorough."

"Your file is more than twice as thick as anyone else's."

"I'm an overachiever."

"It seems so," Bruce said. He dropped the file onto his desk and some of the papers slid out. He shook his head as he pushed them back in. "Your latest antics are the last straw."

"Antics? I don't know what you could possibly mean, Bruce."

"Oh, I think you do."

Erica inhaled slowly. She was having fun, but she also knew she was close to the edge.

"You were specifically directed to stop giving away tents," Bruce said.

"Indeed," Erica confirmed.

"But you didn't stop, Erica. You kept doing it."

"No, I didn't."

"Yes. You did."

"I swear I stopped, Bruce."

"Don't bullshit a bullshitter, Erica."

Shit. Did Bruce actually know she was still giving away tents even though she wasn't supposed to, or was he trying to get her to say it herself?

"I have evidence and an eyewitness account."

Say as little as possible, she reminded herself, and wracked her brain to think of who would have given her up.

"Hard to have evidence of something that didn't happen, Bruce," Erica responded.

The last time she'd given away tents was a week ago when she'd seen Jake under the bridge and then met Claire at Delta Park. Jake hadn't indicated he was turning her in, and he'd have told her if he did. And Claire wouldn't have, because they were on the same team now and she was out searching for land, occasionally texting Erica with questions. And Erica had been so busy with clients, she hadn't had time to do any more tent drops since then. Who else would it have been?

"Am I ... boring you, Ms. Ford?"

"No, Bruce," Erica said, determined to keep up her bravado. "I find everything you say endlessly fascinating."

"Well then you'll love this part," Bruce smirked. "I have photos and a testimonial from one of your own clients."

Don't react, don't react, don't react, Erica thought. Shit. Sarah. It had to be Sarah. She'd dime someone out for a bag of chips. Erica tried to keep her face neutral. Don't admit anything. You still don't know what they have.

"That's unfortunate," she said.

"Indeed," Bruce said, and walked around to sit against the front edge of his desk. This was his "I'm approachable" stance. Bruce always adopted the approachable stance before he lashed out.

"Look, Erica, I can't ignore this."

"You've been threatening to fire me for three months. Why haven't you done it, Bruce?"

"You're on thin ice here, Ford."

She stood and pushed her chair back a little more aggressively than she'd intended. It caught on the rug and tipped over. "You haven't fired me, Bruce, because even if you don't like me or how I do things, you know I get results."

She leaned past him and stabbed the folder on his desk with her index finger. "You call that a stack of mistakes and violations, but you can tie every single one of them to a success or a forward step for clients who would otherwise fall through the cracks. You haven't fired me, because what I do works and no one else gets the results I do." She stood upright and folded her arms in front of her.

Bruce puffed up his chest and opened his mouth to reply but stopped when he heard a timid knock at his door.

"*What*?" Bruce bellowed.

His administrative assistant cracked the door and leaned in. "I'm sorry, Bruce."

"I *said* not to interrupt us."

"I know," she whispered. She looked down at the tipped-over chair and back up at Bruce. "I'm sorry. It's just ..."

"Spit it out."

"It's the call from the foundation you were waiting on. The really important one about the grant funding?"

"Damn it." Bruce looked at Erica and then looked at the phone on his desk. "I need to take this."

Erica rolled her eyes and picked up the chair she'd knocked over. "Well, I need a smoke. You take your call and kiss some ass for money, and I'll be back in a bit."

"Don't go far, Ford," he said as she walked out. "We aren't done."

* * *

In the agency parking lot, Erica leaned against her truck and lit a cigarette. This wasn't good. Bruce was heading toward firing her or making her life so miserable she'd quit. She'd never pushed him this far before.

"Well, God," she said as she looked to the sky, "maybe *this* problem has become unmanageable now, too."

She carried her seven-year coin in her pocket. It was both a personal talisman and a piece of evidence if she needed to show clients she was in recovery. She reached into her pocket and rubbed the coin's surface with her hand. She'd been sober long enough she wasn't feeling the need to go straight to the bar—but she did feel the need for some help and guidance. She made the mental note to hit an AA meeting right after she was done with Bruce, so she could clear her head and re-focus.

Her phone buzzed in her pocket, and she remembered she'd been ignoring it. If she still had a job later, it seemed like it was going to be a busy day. In her notifications she saw a few client calls and texts, as usual, and a huge number of texts and calls from Claire. There was also one long text from Sarah. In the preview window, that one started with, *I'm sorry.* So it was definitely Sarah who'd busted her. Damn it, Sarah. Instead of reading that one, she opened the texts from Claire.

Call me.

I have great news, call me.

Where are you?

There were also voicemails, so she tapped the first one to listen.

"Erica! I did it! Call me back!" The air filled with Claire's voice, breathless and excited. "We have land!"

"No shit?" Erica said to her phone.

This woman was too much. Erica had assumed she'd get bored and give up. In this crazy housing market, any land she found was probably too small and in the wrong place, but she had to give Claire points for follow-through. Erica hit the button to call her back.

"Finally," Claire said when she answered before the end of the first ring. "Where have you been?"

"Pretty sure I'm getting fired."

"Well, good."

"Um, excuse me?"

"I mean … I'm sorry, that's terrible. But it's good you'll have time now. We have a women's housing site to build."

Claire was just as amped up as she was when she left the message.

"So you're serious. You found a piece of land?" Erica asked.

"*Yes*," Claire shouted, then laughed excitedly. "And it checks all your boxes. Not too far out, close to transit, almost a whole acre, on city utilities and sewer."

"Wow."

"I just signed all of the papers and take possession tomorrow. Now what do we do?"

Erica coughed. "Wait, you actually *bought* it?"

"Of course, we have no time to lose!"

"But what if it's …" Erica slapped her forehead with her hand. "I haven't even seen it yet."

"I'll take you now. Of course, I bought it. We need to keep moving."

"I … I don't even …"

"Oh," Claire added, slowing down a little, "when I said I was happy you were getting fired, I should have also said I meant 'good' because I'm your new boss. I mean, I *want* to be your new boss. Or partner, maybe. Yes, let's say partner, not boss. I planned to pay you to run this. You're the brains behind the whole thing. You need to leave that job and come to this one. So … you're hired. Wait, no. You're partnered. I don't know. It's something. You have a job. What do we do next?"

Erica blinked and looked at her phone. For someone who wasn't drinking, she was sure racking up a pile of surreal days lately.

"Well," she said, "I need to go to a meeting before I do anything else. And then once I've got my head right, I have some calls to return. And then … if this hasn't turned out to all be a hallucination that causes me and my whole family grave concern in a couple hours, I guess we'll need to start building some tiny houses."

"Let's *do* it," Claire cried. "I'll text you the address. You can come meet me there when you're ready."

Erica ended the call and stared at her phone, then looked up at the sky.

"Seriously?" she asked the sky. "I was expecting, like, a dog to walk by and give me a meaningful look. This sign was a little on the nose, don't you think?"

The text from Claire came through with the address, and Erica looked it up. She zoomed in and checked it out.

"Well damn," she said. "I know that area. That could totally work."

She stuck the phone back in her pocket and lit another cigarette. She paced outside the building, other hand in her pocket turning the seven-year coin over and over. This was a big change. A huge jump. Something that would probably give her mother a panic attack. But it was also exciting, and she knew she couldn't keep on with Bruce this way. If he didn't fire her today, he would when she eventually punched him in the face. She put out her cigarette in the ashtray outside the building.

She walked back into Bruce's office and the admin tried to stop her.

"He's still on that call," the admin said.

"No problem," Erica said, and kept going right into his office.

Bruce saw her and gestured angrily toward his headset. "I'm on the *phone*," he mouthed, then spoke into the mouthpiece. "You don't say, Mrs. Redfield. I never thought about setting *Hamlet* on a desert island. That must have been a fascinating production."

Erica nodded affably and kept walking toward him. She leaned in close.

"I'm sorry, Mrs. Redfield?" Erica yelled toward the mouthpiece. "So sorry to interrupt. Bruce is going to have to call you back." Then she put her finger on the receiver and ended the call.

Bruce ripped off his headset and stood up, pushing back his chair and glowering at Erica.

"You just made this very easy," he seethed.

Erica folded her arms across her chest and grinned. "For both of us. Nice knowing you, Bruce. I quit."

CHAPTER 8

Erica walked the perimeter of the lot and took in everything she was seeing, shaking her head in disbelief. It was good. It really was the perfect site. Flat, on city utilities, large enough for the housing units plus a common building and a small parking area. Two blocks from a good bus line, and—best of all—ringed by mature evergreens on three sides, adding privacy.

"How did you find this?" Erica asked Claire. "In Portland's insane real estate market, this lot shouldn't exist."

"That's what the real estate agent said, too." Claire bounced on her toes and clapped her hands. "She said lots like this don't come along very often, and it's a good thing we were right here to grab it. It was a perfect storm!"

"I know you're excited," Erica said, "but please stop bouncing. And 'perfect storm' usually means something bad."

Claire rocked back on her heels and up on her toes. "Well, then, the opposite of that. A perfect ... sunny day? I don't know ... Whatever. It was the perfect something."

Erica smiled, "I'm impressed."

It really was some kind of positive perfect storm: a mix of the right timing and the right seller. It also didn't hurt, Claire said, that she was able to show up with the equivalent of a suitcase full of cash.

"You didn't really give him a suitcase full of cash, did you?" Erica asked. "I've seen how you hand out twenties like they're candy."

Claire swatted at her. "No, silly!"

She paused. "And there's no way that much cash would have fit in one suitcase anyway."

Erica rolled her eyes. "I literally would have no idea."

Claire continued, "I just have a lot of liquidity right now. We've been moving assets around with Chris's death, and I had a chunk set aside for a few major gifts in his name."

Erica looked nervous. "You were planning to use this money for something else? I don't want to mess anything up ..."

"Not at all." Claire waved dismissively. "I hadn't figured out what to do with it yet. None of the proposals I'd received or ideas I'd had were working. This is very exciting and worthwhile."

"Okay," Erica said. "As long as you're sure."

Claire nodded. "I'm positive. One thousand and ten percent."

Erica told herself to stop doubting and take this strange woman at face value. If it didn't work out, it's not like *she* was the one who was going to be out piles of cash. And it wasn't going to work if she didn't stop doubting and just go for it—like this lady clearly was.

"... So how did you find this site, anyway?" Erica asked.

"Luck and good timing," Claire answered.

⋆ ⋆ ⋆

In the days since she had sat at the diner with Erica, Claire had started and stopped her search for a property a hundred times. Truthfully, okay, it was more like five—but it felt like a hundred. She wasn't used to having to work for what she wanted. She was used to naming the thing she wanted, and then just having all the pieces fall into place.

After coming up short on properties close-in to downtown, the real estate agent had convinced Claire to look much further east than she'd originally intended. Lots near downtown were just too small and too expensive.

The city doesn't stop where the Michelin guidebook ends, Chris teased her when she'd commented on how far away some of these lots were.

"Psht, I know that, Chris," she said.

Are you sure about that? He laughed.

"... Yes?" Claire's voice went up at the end.

Yes, technically, she knew the city went very far east, well past the downtown core, the trendy hipster neighborhoods, and even the outer ring of the interstate with its strip malls, used car lots, and restaurants offering food from other countries (but she wasn't sure which ones, because their signs weren't in English). But she'd never had much reason to go out there, so it was easy for her to forget that this, too, was a part of the city.

"I feel like a pioneer," she'd whispered as the real estate agent navigated her car off the freeway and onto Holgate Boulevard.

You probably don't want to lead with that, Chris said. *This isn't actually the wilderness.*

The place off Holgate hadn't worked out. Days passed and, even looking out near the edge of the city limits, they still weren't finding anything suitable. Just when they were about to give it all up and Claire was trying to figure out how to break it to Erica, the agent got an alert on a brand-new property that had just hit the market, For Sale by Owner. They raced to see it.

It was perfect. In the southeast part of the city, pretty far out from the city center but well-located for public transit and access to all basic services. It was a double lot in a quiet, working-class neighborhood that was platted long before it became a part of the city. The houses here were small, but had large lots that were nearly an acre each, and this one was a double. The seller used to live in the house next door, and this property had been in the family for a couple generations, as their sole asset.

"I don't have any kids," he'd told Claire. "No one to pass it to." He'd sold his house next door a year earlier, and used it to get a condo that was easier to take care of. "I miss the old neighborhood," he said, "but I don't miss having to mow the lawn! Now I'm thinking I can sell this lot and get myself another condo down in Arizona for the winters."

Even though he was ready to sell, most of the buyers interested in the lot were developers who wanted to put in high-rise, high-end apartments. The neighborhood that had once seemed almost rural was quickly becoming more and more dense as those large lots filled in with apartments, condos, and houses that the people they were displacing wouldn't be able to afford.

"They are *sharks*," he said. "They want to turn this neighborhood into the next hot place, but it's a quiet neighborhood, full of regular people just trying to get by. Some of those guys offered me a lot of money for this lot, but I didn't want to do that to my old neighbors."

When Claire told him the plan, his eyes softened.

"You'd use my family's property to help women who don't have anywhere else to go?"

She told him yes and assured him it would be clean and quiet and respectful of the neighbors. He liked that.

He seemed to like it even more when she told him she also didn't need to get a loan and could close immediately.

* * *

Erica walked the lot and turned to squint at the sun, her mind already jumping ahead to the best placement for the common area.

"Is your contractor friend coming soon?" Claire asked.

"She'll be here," Erica said. "I called her right after you and I talked. She was coming from another job."

From the moment this idea seemed like it might be real, Erica knew exactly who she wanted to help them plan it out and get it built. Her friend Samara was a union carpenter who was also one of Erica's earliest client success stories. Trying to escape a bad home situation on the southern Oregon coast, Sam had run away to Portland at seventeen. But with no job, no connections, and no high school diploma, she had ended up on the street with a guy who was almost as bad as the stepfather she was trying to get away from. Erica had helped Sam find a transitional youth shelter and get her GED, then found her an apprentice program for women carpenters because she liked working with her hands.

"In the retelling," Erica told Claire, "It sounds like a seamless success story."

"A *great* one," Claire gushed. "What an inspiration."

"It was actually pretty bumpy. Sam went back to the boyfriend once and he beat the hell out of her. She also almost bombed out of the apprentice program more than once. For a while, she was the worst client I had, and I wanted to kill her on the daily. But she hung in there. She's doing amazing stuff now and working for a lot of different homebuilders and construction contractors."

"That's fantastic," Claire said.

"It is," Erica nodded. "But it didn't always seem like it was going to be. Not everyone's stories turn out like Sam's."

Waiting for Sam, Claire and Erica walked the double lot and talked about what the site could possibly look like. They wanted to give everyone privacy and their own safe space, while also creating community.

"This is your vision," Claire said. "Tell me what you're seeing."

"We're going to have separate, single-resident tiny homes," Erica said, and pointed toward the back end of the lot. "One or two will be a little larger and have room for a couple of kids to live there with their mom. And then up here," she said, and stood in the center of the lot with her arms out to the side, "a central shared space with a full kitchen, laundry, bathrooms and showers, and a main lounge space. Having the common spaces together like this not only keeps costs down, it ensures community interaction and participation. There'll be a few parking spaces over there," she gestured closer to the road, "and also space for a couple of tents if the community agrees to have guests or wants to help someone out with an emergency place to sleep."

When Erica had talked with Sam about it on the phone, Sam said she was sure they could do the tiny homes from scratch, which would not only allow for easy customization, but also ensure the first residents were involved in the creation of the site. Building the common building from the ground up, however, would be a heavy-duty construction project so she'd recommended a pre-fab unit that could be delivered and dropped into place.

* * *

They'd reached the middle of the lot, Claire stepping carefully to avoid the muddy spots, while Erica was explaining something about "cool pre-fab" units. Claire shook her head—she was glad Erica had a vision, even if she couldn't quite see it so clearly yet. What she did see was a middle-aged white man waving at them from the roadside.

"Ahem. Uh, hello … neighbors?" he called out, still waving.

Erica nudged Claire. "You go talk to him," she whispered.

"Come with me."

"No, you go."

Claire narrowed her eyes at Erica, but stood up straight and threw her shoulders back, put on a broad smile, and walked to meet the man at the road.

"Good morning," she sang.

"Are you, uh, the ones who bought this?"

"We sure are," Claire said. "Do you live nearby?"

"Across the street. I'm Doug." He jerked his thumb over his shoulder and Claire looked him over. He had a little paunch, readers propped up on his forehead, short-sleeved button-down tucked into belted khakis, thinning gray hair. He seemed like someone who had held the same reliable, respectable, status quo job for the last twenty-five years. He was probably an accountant for a mid-size company.

Claire extended her hand to shake. "I'm Claire, and that's Erica."

Doug shook her hand limply. "I'm head of the neighborhood association. Welcome." He stuck his thumbs through his belt loops. "We're not one like one of those HOAs that tell you what you can and can't do down to the type of grass you can grow," he said.

"Good to know," Claire nodded. Her snooty neighborhood did have an HOA, and it contained a long list of ancient and strange rules, ranging from the vaguely racist to the outright absurd. She hadn't thought about HOAs when looking for lots, so she was pleased not to have to deal with one.

"So, uh," he continued, "when Stan told us he was selling, he said he wasn't going to let it become fancy condos or some huge luxury mansion." He glanced at her Mercedes. "You're ... not doing that, are you?"

Claire laughed and clapped her hands. "Oh no, not at all! We are doing something very different."

As she explained their vision, Claire watched Doug's face darken. This didn't seem to be going over as well as it had with Stan.

"And Stan was okay with this?" Doug asked when she finished.

"Yes! That's why he sold to us."

"You're telling me you want to bring a bunch of street people to live right across the street from me? Right next to these good, hardworking folks and their little kids?"

Claire clasped her hands behind her back. "Well, I'd frame it a little differently—"

"No matter how you 'frame' it, that's what it is, right? The camps downtown and all along the freeways and in our parks aren't bad enough, now you want to bring them here?"

"This isn't one of those camps," Claire said. "This is to help them get *out* of those camps and become self-sufficient."

"We don't need that here. This is a good, quiet place with good, quiet people. I feel bad for those women, but they don't need to come here. There's other places for them to go."

Erica, who had been watching and listening from behind Claire, was suddenly beside her.

"No, there aren't," Erica spat. "They *don't* have anywhere to go. That's why they're on the street. We're trying to help and make a difference, and it's people like you who keep that from happening."

Claire put her arm around Erica's shoulder and drew her back from Doug. "Erica, I don't think that tone—"

Erica shook her off and turned back to Doug. "And if you think 'they' aren't already here, you are clearly blind. There are people living in tents two blocks from here, and even more back at the freeway offramp. Would you rather have disorganized camping like that, or have something managed and controlled that helps people?"

Doug jabbed an index finger toward them. "I worked hard for what I have. So did every single person on this block. You tell your women to go get a job and stop freeloading, and then they can come buy a house here like everybody else."

Erica stepped closer to Doug and reached out to smack his pointing hand away. "These women have had everything ripped out from underneath them. They aren't going to bother you in the slightest. You wanting to stand in their way says a lot more about you than it does about them."

Claire moved between them, pulling Erica back. "Look, this isn't helping anyone. Doug, I assure you this will be a well-run operation."

Doug nodded and folded his arms across his chest. "I see."

Claire sighed with relief. "Oh, I'm so glad. You'll see, this will be a great—"

Doug held up his hand. "It may be the best operation in the world, but it's not going to happen here." He spun around and headed back across the street. "I wouldn't get too comfortable," he called over his shoulder.

⋆ ⋆ ⋆

The words were still ringing in the air when a truck pulled up behind Claire's car. A surge of relief hit Erica when she saw Sam step out of the truck. It was almost enough to still her rage until Doug's front door slammed across the street.

"Looks like that went well," Sam said to Erica as she walked up. "I could see how pissed he was from halfway down the block. She turned to Claire. "Hi, I'm Sam."

Claire looked like she was about to cry, but she straightened up and put out a hand. "Hi, Sam. I'm Claire."

Sam looked at Erica as she shook Claire's hand. "I see your people skills keep improving."

"Fuck off, Sam," Erica said.

Sam grinned, then walked onto the lot and looked around. "This is great," she said, placing her hands on her hips, elbows wide. In her brown canvas work pants with a brown T-shirt tucked in, she looked every bit the experienced carpenter ready to get to work. She looped her thumbs through her belt loops and turned to Claire and Erica.

"We can do a lot here," Sam said. She kept her shoulder-length black hair in a low ponytail, and a few strands escaped and framed her face as she looked around and nodded.

Erica and Claire walked to meet her in the middle of the lot.

"Unfortunately," Sam said, "I have a little more bad news."

Erica grimaced. "Neighbor Doug wasn't enough?"

"Yeah, no. There's more."

"Whaaaaaaat," Claire sighed.

"I checked out the zoning before I came over, and we have a little bit of a problem."

"No!" Claire shouted. "I checked the zoning. With the double lot we can do ten units."

"Yeah, except that zoning applies to single-family residences."

"So?" Claire asked. "We're only going to have one person in each house. Maybe some kids. So that's single family, right?"

"Unfortunately, no," Sam said. "Single family homes have this strict definition and there are minimum house sizes and distances for how far back they have to sit from the road, and all these other things. Tiny homes are in a totally different category, and the city's zoning hasn't caught up with the architects and builders. You're going to need to apply for a variance and have the City Council allow what they call an 'unusual use.'"

Erica sighed. "I knew this was too good to last."

"No, it's no problem," Claire said. "We can go to the City Council. I know the mayor and a couple of the councilors. This is fine. We can do this."

"Well ..." Sam said.

"What?" Claire asked.

"Part of the variance process is a public hearing and a survey of the neighbors to make sure they are okay with the change."

"Okay ...?"

Sam looked across the lot toward Doug's house, and Claire and Erica followed her gaze.

"Oh." Claire sank to the ground.

"Yeah," Sam said. "Neighbor Doug may be able to stop you."

Erica reached for a cigarette. "Well, shit." She sat down next to Claire.

"Pretty much." Sam shrugged and sat down, too. "Sorry."

CHAPTER 9

After they all sat around moping for a while, Claire summoned her fundraising socialite spirit. She clapped her hands brightly and shooed the other two back to their vehicles.

"Enough of this brooding," she chirped. "We have work to do."

"What are you talking about, Claire?" Erica whined. "If we have to go through a neighborhood review, there's no way that guy's gonna let us through."

"Erica Ford," Claire spat. "Are you serious? We haven't known each other that long but I did not think you were someone who would let the posturing of some schlub with a bad combover and Amazon Basics khakis put you in the corner. Is that who you're telling me you are?"

"I think it was a whole Amazon Basics outfit, actually," Sam chimed in.

"Even worse," Claire said and shook her head.

"And no shade to shopping on a budget, but seriously I find way better stuff at Value Village," Sam said.

Erica shrugged. "Okay, fashion plate. But back to the actual issue here. It's not like you've ever done anything like this before, either, you know."

"No," Claire agreed. "But my husband Chris put together big projects for work and for his charity activities all the time, and I was there all the way along. I know how projects work. And you know, I'm no slouch myself. You may think the ladies who lunch don't do anything ... and, well, most of them don't. But *some* of us tried to make ourselves useful from time to time."

"So, what's your big plan to defeat The Man?" Erica asked.

Claire snorted. "If someone had figured that out, none of us would be standing around this lot talking today. I may not know how to defeat The Man. But what I do know is the first thing we have to do is break this project down into manageable chunks. Let's go to my place. It's a lot more comfortable than standing around the hood of your truck."

★ ★ ★

She texted them both her address and had them follow her.

Once all had arrived, she told them to make themselves at home in the kitchen while she grabbed paper and pens from the office. Sam and Erica hung close to the back door, a little concerned about what they were and were not allowed to touch. The kitchen looked like it could have come straight out of a magazine. The fridge was restaurant-size, stainless steel with literally no streaks. The stove was also stainless, with huge gas burners and bright red knobs. Butcher-block counters that topped seemingly endless white cabinets and drawers were paired with a marble-topped island housing a ridiculously deep farmhouse sink and an eating bar with high stools. Across the room, an eating nook showcased the backyard from a huge bay window, and the white penny tile floor was just as spotless as the appliances.

"I've never been in a kitchen this nice," Erica whispered to Sam.

"I've never been in a *doorway* this nice," Sam snorted and whispered back.

"Is that marble?"

"Are we allowed to touch?"

"Are we allowed to breathe?"

Claire returned and saw them paralyzed in the doorway. "Come in, come in. What are you waiting for?" She pulled out two tall chairs at the eating bar and patted the gleaming countertop before reaching for coffee supplies. "Coffee?" she asked. "I could use some coffee. I also have tea and water."

"I'd go for some coffee," Erica said. "But I'm worried you're going to serve it in like a crystal goblet or something."

"What are you talking about?" Claire asked. "No one serves coffee in crystal. Get in here. Sit down."

Sam and Erica eased forward and sat gingerly on the chairs at the counter.

"I feel," Sam said, "like you're going to have to do a deep-clean after having us in here."

Claire set the coffeepot down on the counter, sighed, and turned to face them.

"Look," she said. "I get it: I'm rich, I have a fancy house, and I'm completely disconnected from reality."

Sam and Erica exchanged a look that essentially said, "Yeah."

"But I'm trying," Claire said. "This is where I live. This is who I am. I'm not trying to rub it in. I'm not saying I think it makes me better than you."

Sam and Erica didn't say anything.

"So, please." Claire continued. "Please stop perching on those chairs like you're afraid they'll break, and sit your entire butts on the seats." She banged on the counter a few times. "Don't act like it's all so fragile. For what I paid for this kitchen remodel, it should outlast all of us. No one besides me is ever in this place anymore, and this house was meant to have people in it. So please help me out by acting like people. If you want to go to your house next time, if my fancy kitchen makes you so uncomfortable, then fine. You never have to come back here. But we're here now, and we have work to do."

Erica cleared her throat. "Fine. Just promise that if one of us does break something, you aren't going to freak out?"

"Deal," Claire said. "Now shut up and drink your coffee."

Sam leaned over to peek underneath the counter to see how it was constructed, and smiled. "Your finish work frightens me with its awesomeness, and I have to admit that coffee smells amazing."

Claire poured them each a mug of coffee, and set sugar and half-and-half in front of Erica.

"Hopefully, you won't need quite so much of these this time," Claire smiled.

Erica tasted the coffee and nodded. "Definitely not as much."

After doctoring her brew, she held the mug to her nose and inhaled with satisfaction. "Fancy counters are intimidating, but you may have something here with this fancy coffee."

Claire shook her head and smiled. "I like it, too. Maybe we aren't as different as it seems."

They all sipped quietly together and then Erica started laughing a little to herself.

"What?" Claire asked.

"It's just—" Erica said. "I think we're still pretty different."

Claire reached behind her for a napkin and tossed it at Erica.

Erica caught it and held it up for Sam. "See what I mean? *Cloth* napkins."

* * *

A couple hours later, after three phone calls to the city's planning department, two to the permitting department, and a long text exchange with a homebuilder Sam trusted, they had a full sense of what they needed to do and a list of tasks assigned to each of them. Claire was assigned to contact City Council and the mayor, to make a personal appeal for their project and make sure they got onto the council meeting schedule as soon as possible. For any of the rest of it to work, they needed this variance.

They agreed that even though the City Council thing could sink the whole project if the council voted 'no,' they also couldn't afford to wait around. They needed to keep going as though they'd succeed. People on the street needed help and failure was not an option.

While Claire worked City Council, Erica and Sam were tasked with keeping the project moving as much as possible. Sam was going to go in-person to the planning and permitting departments to personally walk through the building checklists. She was also going to get the ready-made commons building designed so they could order it immediately after approval.

Erica was to start recruiting residents and designing the service program. If residents needed help with addiction, mental illness, job skills, money management, whatever—she would get them connected. Eventually, they wanted the community to be self-governed with an application process for new members, who would be vetted and selected by the current members. But to get started, Erica would be hand-picking the residents to be sure there was the right mix of women who both needed the help and would be engaged enough to help design the self-governance program.

* * *

At the planning office later that week, Sam showed city staff her plans for the ten tiny houses and one common building. In Portland, the "tiny house" movement had been gaining some momentum, largely practiced by wealthy people who wanted to build themselves something cute and trendy, but weren't prepared to truly live small. Many "tiny houses" that could be seen around the city were not so tiny, coming in at almost 1,000 square feet.

"If it's bigger than my studio apartment," Sam muttered to Erica, "no one has any business calling it a 'tiny house.'"

Sam planned for truly tiny homes, designed for people who didn't have much, who might not be comfortable with a lot of open space when they'd been living cramped in a tent. Her own experience informed this perspective. Sam had spent months sleeping first in her car and then in a tent after the car was towed. Erica finally found her a room in a motel that had been converted into a shelter, and it was a rocky transition. She was supposed to be able to relax and feel safe, but instead she was always on edge.

"In the car and in the tent," she had told Erica, "I got used to being able to see every corner all the time. I knew every inch of that space. Every sound, every smell, how the air felt. Suddenly having this whole big room ... even though it was what I wanted, it was really hard to get used to."

Based on her own lived experience, Sam had decided that around 150 square feet, with high ceilings and the option for a loft bed, would give the women more space to spread out, while still retaining that safe closeness she had so wanted after being on the street. The common building would be the place with all the main bathrooms, laundry, and kitchen. This pod of tiny homes would be more friendly and homier than a shelter, but not necessarily someplace you'd want to be forever. Eventually, you'd want to move on, and that was the point. It was going to be both a landing pad and a launching pad. A safe place to land, and a safe place to take flight when the time came. It was almost home, but not quite.

* * *

Claire started her calls with the mayor, whom she'd met a few times at fundraisers. She knew he'd take her call, as would the rest of City Council. As much as she hated to admit it, the ability to write a check meant your calls got answered. She scheduled one-on-one meetings with all of them. When they heard the vision and looked at the plans, most of the Council members were politely receptive, showing some concern behind their smiles.

"So, you've already purchased the land?" the mayor asked when Claire met with him. Instead of bringing her into his office, he'd met her in a conference room. They sat at one corner of a very large table in a room overlooking the park across the street from City Hall. That park, like almost every other park in the city, was dotted with tents and full of people with nowhere else to go, sleeping on benches and clustering in corners.

"Yes," Claire answered. She gestured toward the park. "As we all know, this is a pressing issue, so we were not inclined to wait."

The mayor pursed his lips.

"And," Claire continued, "we are in process of applying for the variance we'll need to allow the tiny homes. That's why I'm here talking with you."

"Which social service agency are you working with on this?"

"None of them," Claire answered.

"Who is providing service, then?"

"We are," Claire said.

"But how are you integrating with the system already in place?"

"My partners are a woman who has worked in outreach and knows the system, and a woman who is formerly homeless and has been trained as a professional carpenter. We will contract out for supportive services to help the women with mental health and addiction treatment if necessary, and provide peer support for recovery and for job and life skills training and job placement."

"Who's the outreach person you're working with?" he asked.

Claire told him about Erica, describing her as an outreach worker who had previously been with Portland Promise. She told him about Erica's deep experience, her past successes, her commitment to the work and the people, and her innovative ways of thinking and approaching problems.

The mayor frowned. "This isn't the girl who just got fired from there, is it?" he asked.

"She didn't get fired; she quit."

"As I understand it from the director, Bruce," the mayor said, "that was simply a matter of timing."

"She has a strong spirit and needs the freedom to be creative at work," Claire said. "She gets results, and that's apparently something Bruce didn't like."

The mayor pushed himself away from the table and started pacing in front of the window.

"In addition to distributing contraband tents when she was expressly forbidden to," he said, "when we brought her to City Council to account for her actions, she was rude and insubordinate, insinuating that her mistakes were *our* fault and problem."

Although she wanted to say, "Aren't they?" Claire knew to keep her mouth shut. She quietly waited for him to finish.

"You want to come to the Council," he continued, "and ask us to give you special dispensation to do a project coordinated by someone who berated us a month ago?"

"That's exactly what I'm asking, Mr. Mayor," Claire said calmly.

"Well, that's—" he sputtered, before Claire cut him off.

"Let me finish," she said. "You and I both know there is far more need in this city than there is service." She gestured toward the chair he was pacing behind. "Please sit down."

Slowly, grudgingly, he sat back down.

Claire smiled and spoke in a low voice. "Are you seriously telling me you're going to deny help to a community in crisis because a girl half your age was … mean to you?"

The mayor's eyes turned icy cold. Claire eased back in her seat and hoped he couldn't see her heart racing.

"Personalities aside," the mayor said stiffly, "this is a big project. And I'm not sure a couple of relative amateurs are up to it."

Claire didn't flinch, even though it took almost all her self-control not to.

"I'm sure you understand," the mayor continued, "that homelessness is a complex problem and thus will require a complex, systemic solution. One-off projects often harm that process, not help it."

Claire worked to keep her eyes from rolling at the mayor's lecture.

"With all due respect, Mr. Mayor," she said slowly, "you'd be in a much better place to lecture me about how to successfully solve the problem of homelessness if the city had shown even the smallest measure of success in doing so over the last decade."

"Well, like I said, it's very complex …"

Claire sat up straighter and leaned in. "It's actually very simple," she said, and firmly tapped her index finger on the table with each sentence to make her point. "Fund the system (*tap*). Fund the services (*tap*). Make it a priority instead of a talking point (*tap*). Stop screwing over the people who can help (*tap*)." Then she pointed out the window toward the park. "And focus on serving the people who need it."

The mayor leaned back, bristling. "And your degree in social work is from ... where?" he asked.

"Don't condescend to me, Mayor," Claire said evenly. "I'm presenting you with a huge opportunity here. I am fully funding this project and taking all the responsibility. I am taking ten people at a time off the street and giving them the support they need to get stable. I'm not asking you for money. I'm not asking you for staff. I'm not asking you for land or a tax break or a fee waiver."

The mayor nodded.

"When this is a success," Claire continued, "you'll be able to say you supported it. We may even let you cut a ribbon and be in the photo. Your lift on this is easy. It's just a variance. Based on how you've been getting beaten up over the last few months about all the people sleeping on your streets, I suggest you take an easy win where you can find it."

The mayor sucked his teeth and glared at Claire. "Noted," he clipped.

CHAPTER 10

Erica sat in the driver's seat of her pickup, parked outside a closed Kmart that had been turned into a mega-church. In one wing of the cavernous building, the church had set aside the former Home & Garden section to be a shelter, staffed by volunteers from the congregation. The operation was a little heavy on Jesus and a little light on real services, but their hearts were in the right place and they weren't harming or coercing anyone. The folks who slept there got a warm place to rest their head, a decent dinner, and a little breakfast before they were sent on their way each morning. Three times a week, the mobile shower truck was there and people could get washed up. Erica knew at least one of the women she was looking for would be leaving here this morning, so she was staked out to wait.

Since she and Claire first sat down in the diner, Erica had been thinking about who to recruit as residents. It was nuts to think they could pull this off, but on the off chance they could, she had the opportunity here to help ten women. She remembered a moment with her dad, back when she was ten or eleven. They were walking downtown in Olympia, waiting to pick her mom up from work so they could all go to dinner together. They passed a panhandler, and her dad gave the guy a buck. After they walked by him, she asked her dad why he did that.

"You know how I've talked to you about being an alcoholic, and how I work the Twelve Steps?" her dad responded.

"Yeah."

"Well, the Twelfth Step is about giving back. I go further into my journey of sobriety when I try to help others. Whether it's alcoholics just beginning the program who need support, or members of my community at large. I had a dollar to spare today, and it seemed like he could use it more than me."

"My teacher said giving money to bums just encourages them."

"No one is a bum, Little Bear." He stopped walking and bent down to look her in the eye. "You can never tell what someone's been through just by looking at them. A little grace and compassion are the absolute least you can offer. And if you have a spare dollar, go ahead and throw that in, too." He moved a piece of hair away from her eyes. "And remind me I need to make a visit to your teacher to talk about some things."

She nodded. At age ten, she knew her dad was smart and right about a lot of things, so she took what he said at face value. Years later, by the time she reached the Twelfth Step on her own path, she knew it with her whole being. The step didn't really talk about or mean you should hand out money on the street, but if that's one of the ways her dad interpreted it, then that's what worked for him. But that step, and living up to the spirit of her dad's big heart, were definitely major parts of why this work mattered so much to her. She loved outreach because she was helping people, and also because she was helping herself at the same time.

Just then, Marta walked out of the shelter with a small bag over her arm. She walked slowly, taking care with her bad back. Erica stepped out of the truck and waved at her. She beckoned Marta toward her, but knowing Marta's back injury slowed her down, she hustled over to her side. Erica loved talking to Marta. She was in her late fifties, and even with all her troubles, Marta had a mom vibe, this combination of kindness and a total lack of patience for bullshit. When they hugged, Erica noticed Marta had taken her turn on the shower truck last night. She smelled like industrial shampoo and the gold-colored Dial soap the guy who ran the truck bought in bulk. Her black hair was pulled up into a bun as usual, and she was wearing layers that indicated she planned to spend most of the day away from the shelter.

Marta was born in Honduras but barely remembered it. Her family fled when she was a child and ended up in Portland after a few stops in other cities. She became a naturalized citizen, graduated high school, and had finished some college, going to Portland State University on a scholarship. But her aging parents needed help, so she dropped out. All she could find were two full-time, low-paying jobs to support them and some of the other elders in her extended family. Early in her twenties, she got pregnant and the father took off. Marta loved her daughter, but a child's arrival also meant Marta needed to work harder to support everyone in the house.

"I have something I think you might like," Erica told Marta as she walked beside her toward the bus stop.

"You pushing drugs now?" Marta said with a smile.

"Not even gonna touch that," Erica said.

"Good girl," Marta said. She was on her way to the public health clinic to get her week's dosage of Suboxone.

Marta had never been someone who did drugs. "I never even drank because it gave me a headache!" she'd said when she met Erica. But a bad fall at work, insufficient health insurance, and a lack of treatment options led her down a dark path of painkillers that eventually led to shooting heroin. She stole from her family and friends to support the habit, and soon she had no one left and nowhere to go. When she met Erica, she'd been staying at the Kmart shelter. They allowed her to trade volunteer work helping clean up in the mornings, in exchange for a prime bottom bunk. Erica found her a medication-assisted treatment program and Marta had been diligently going to her weekly appointments, even though it took the entire day to get there and back on the bus.

Erica explained the tiny homes project to Marta and asked if it was something she'd want to be a part of.

"Your own place, with your own real bed," Erica said, and paused as she prepared to launch into a longer description.

Marta put her hand on Erica's arm and stopped her.

"I'm in," she said. "You had me at 'real bed.'"

Erica smiled and reached out to hug her.

"This will be amazing," Marta said. "You think I can get totally clean there?"

"We can definitely try," Erica said.

"I want to get off all of it," Marta said, nodding toward the bus that was going to take her to get the Suboxone. "But I'm nervous. They say if you stop doing it, the withdrawals are so bad you just go right back. I can't do that. I won't."

"Having a safe and stable place to stay will help a lot," Erica said. "Let's get this project up and running, and then we can set you up to detox the right way. And when you do, you'll have our place to come back to and all of us to help you."

Marta nodded. "I like it."

She gave Erica a quick hug as the bus pulled up.

"Call me soon about it, right?" Marta asked.

"Soon as I possibly can," Erica said.

⋆ ⋆ ⋆

Moving in closer to downtown, Erica went looking for Cheryl and Heather. These two, both in their late twenties, tended to hang around in the same places. They weren't related, but they might as well be sisters. They were both tall and bone-thin, with mouse-brown hair and a tough meth habit.

They didn't meet until adulthood, but had almost identical stories. Dirt-poor families, abuse and neglect, malnourishment, and leaving the trailer park in their teens because some guy said "I love you" before he disappeared forever and left them stranded. Heather liked to say her mom nursed her with a meth pipe, and Cheryl always nodded right after Heather said it. Methamphetamine leaves a mark; between them, they had maybe one full set of teeth. Cheryl wasn't concerned about it at all, but Heather had learned to smile and talk with a nearly closed mouth, never fully showing her teeth.

She found them in a camp near the foot of the Broadway Bridge. They both looked even thinner than the last time Erica saw them, so she took them to get Happy Meals at the McDonald's a few blocks away. Normally, she'd want to get them something with a little more nutrition, but Cheryl would not shut up about the billboard she saw with the Polly Pocket toy in the girls' meal, so Erica just sucked it up and took them over there.

They sounded interested in the project, but Cheryl stiffened when they talked about basic rules around drugs, like no using and no holding. Cheryl slumped down so her shoulders were level with the table in their booth and held her Polly Pocket in both hands, making the toy hop up and down on the table.

Erica asked Cheryl directly if the drug policy was going to be a problem.

"No ..." Cheryl said reluctantly and without meeting Erica's gaze.

"Seriously?" Erica asked. "Because that's not what I'm picking up here."

Heather reached over and took the Polly Pocket doll away from Cheryl, holding it hostage.

"What's going on, Cher?" Heather asked. "We're both clean now, so what's your damage?"

Cheryl rolled her eyes. "I just want options."

"Not a good set of options, Cheryl," Erica said.

"Fine," Cheryl said with a whine. She stuck out her hand and made a grabbing motion with her fingers. "Gimme."

Heather cocked her head and held the doll out of Cheryl's reach.

"Fi-nuh," Cheryl said again, making it two syllables. "No using, no holding."

Heather eyed her for another second, then dropped the doll into Cheryl's hand.

"When can we move in?" Heather asked Erica, brightly.

* * *

One woman who'd been on the prospective resident list since the first day was Wendi. Claire had insisted they include her, and Erica agreed. While she didn't know Wendi well, she knew where to usually find her, and when they talked, the young woman seemed very interested in the prospect of a better place to stay. Both Erica and Wendi realized Claire's fixation on her was probably about wanting to "save" the two kids, but it was clear that Wendi needed the help. She was a survivor of domestic violence, and Erica had seen too many women who fled a bad scene go right back because they ran out of options. If this project gave Wendi a stable address while she sorted out custody and tried to get a steady job, then it would be a huge positive.

* * *

For the next two days, Erica worked her way through her list of prospective residents for the site, while also closing out her client accounts at Portland Promise. Finally, she reached nine confirmed residents for the ten spots. She felt the mix was good, and even though there'd be a lot of trial and error, the women on the list could handle those challenges and help each other make it work.

"There's no way I'd be allowed to do this at Portland Promise," she told herself as she walked back to her truck from meeting another prospect at her campsite. Not only was this project too experimental, but the intentional selection process was also *not* standard process in the "system." Portland Promise placed people on a first-come, first-served basis. Which, Erica knew, made sense so everyone was treated equally. But equality could often pose a challenge to equity. Getting people off the street isn't a one-size-fits-all solution, and she'd seen so many placements go wrong because the agency didn't take individual needs into account. It was a fine line. Programs shouldn't show preference or exclude some people because of personal biases. But they also need to meet people where they are and recognize that person's reality.

As she reached her truck, her phone buzzed with a new text. She was expecting it to be Claire with news from City Hall, so she eagerly opened the message.

Hay, you got any vouchers? Frank said I had to go.

It wasn't Claire, it was Sarah.

She hadn't heard from or seen Sarah since the day she learned Sarah had ratted her out about the tents. Erica knew she wasn't supposed to be mad or hold grudges with clients. Patience and second chances were a part of the job. But so was accountability.

Yeah, no, Erica texted back. *Almost got fired bc u thought it was cute to sell me out. No vouchers today sis.*

Sarah: *Whaaaaaaaaa?*

Erica: *Actions have consequences. Thanks for nothing, now we both lose.*

Sarah: *Oh man I'm so sorry*

Erica: *Too little too late*

There was a long pause before the next text from Sarah.

You know someone else cn hook me up? I had to leave evrything back there at Franks

Erica shook her head. This girl. Bouncing from one dirtbag's tent to another. She could totally get it together if she would just get away from those creeps. She was always taking whatever they were taking, breaking whatever laws they were breaking ... Erica took a deep breath and slowly lowered her forehead to the steering wheel. Sarah was such a pain in the ass ... but she was a great candidate for the pilot.

"Ugh," she whispered to herself, then raised her head and started typing on her phone.

I can probably hook you up for a few nights

She gritted her teeth and hesitated, but then also typed, *There's also this other thing you might want to be a part of ...*

* * *

With Sarah, Erica now had a full list of residents. She called and texted each of them to confirm their placement. As she did so, she realized that even though the lot wasn't built out yet, they had all this space and these women needed places to stay *now*, not later.

She called Claire to run it by her.

"This way," Erica said over the phone, "they can also give input as we build, and participate in the process so they have a real sense of ownership."

She was making up justifications on the spot because she thought Claire would say no. But Claire was all over it.

"Of course!" Claire said. "That's brilliant! Of course, they should come stay now! We have the space and it's silly to say, 'Please wait.' Let's make sure we have everything we need. We can order some pizza for tonight, and I'll go shopping for some basic food and stuff. And you'll set up whatever we need for bathrooms and such?"

Erica had expected resistance because that's all she'd ever gotten at her old job. But she didn't even have to argue here. Claire gave her a credit card number to order a couple of portable toilets and go to the surplus store to get some basic camping equipment to go with the tents she still had in her truck.

Within a couple of hours, Erica and Sam were helping the new residents move to the lot. They worked into the early evening, helping the women set up their tents and move things around. They'd snagged a cot for Marta so she wouldn't have to sleep directly on the ground, and set up tarps to shield the site a bit from the neighbors. While they worked, Claire set the pizza boxes up on a folding table and made sure everyone had enough to eat.

With everything set up and bellies full, the sun was setting. They turned on a few battery-powered lanterns and started to wrap things up, bagging the pizza boxes for a run to the dump and settling into their tents. Erica and Sam had decided to stay overnight with the women while everyone adjusted to the change. Claire, even though she had never been camping in her life and couldn't imagine a world where a foam pad, sleeping bag, and tent were somehow preferable to her pillow-top mattress and Egyptian cotton sheets, also wanted to stay. She asked Erica if she had an extra tent and sleeping setup.

Sam and Erica exchanged a glance, then shrugged and pulled out equipment for Claire. Claire gathered it all up, smiling as she dragged it to an open spot near the others.

"You need a hand with that?" Sam asked.

Claire shook her head. "I'm sure I can figure it out."

Sam grinned and leaned against Erica's truck at the street. Next to her, Erica lit a cigarette. They watched Claire struggle with her tent for a while and then finally accept some help from two of the residents, Linda and Salina.

Sam nodded toward the scene. "It was nice of them to help her." She laughed a little. "That is not a woman I'd ever expect to see sleeping on the ground."

Erica exhaled a stream of smoke. "Right? I didn't think she'd actually want to stay overnight. She's going to freeze in that silk twinset, though."

Erica opened the passenger door of her truck and reached behind the seat for an extra sweatshirt she carried around in case she ran into someone who needed it.

"We'll see how she does by morning, but I'll say I'm impressed, at least for now."

"Agreed."

Erica stubbed out her cigarette and they headed back toward the group to make sure everyone had what they needed for the night.

CHAPTER 11

Shortly after the sun started to rise, Erica crawled out of her tent. Her apartment across town might be small, but she knew she was fortunate to live indoors with a nice, soft bed. Missing it, she was even more grateful this morning. Her body screamed at her as she slowly stood up and headed for her truck. At least it wasn't cold or raining. Things had moved so quickly the day before, that when she'd grabbed a box of camping equipment from her basement storage unit, she hadn't verified it contained everything she'd need. She sighed with relief when she found the camp stove, a full-enough can of propane, and—most important—the coffee pot. She grabbed the coffee they bought on yesterday's grocery run and set up a coffee station on her tailgate. Once things were ready and she was waiting for it to boil, she looked out over the site.

They'd kind of just thrown things together the night before. Tents were scattered haphazardly around the site, but they all fit with plenty of room to spare. Since the portable toilets wouldn't arrive until today sometime, they had set up a makeshift bathroom with lidded buckets and a bag of sawdust hidden behind tarps at the back of the lot, as far away from any neighbor as possible. It wasn't ideal, but it did the trick.

Sam and Claire were stirring in their tents. Sam emerged with a groan.

"I don't miss this at all," Sam muttered.

"Coffee soon," Erica replied.

"I knew I loved you."

Rustling and grunts came from Claire's tent. Sam and Erica turned to look.

"Where the—" They saw Claire's hands fumbling against the tent from the inside. "I can't find the—"

Erica snorted. "Zipper's at the bottom, Claire."

"Ah. Found it."

Claire unzipped the flap and sat in the opening, looking a little dazed. Erica smiled as she took in the socialite's messy hair and twisted-around sweatshirt. Claire looked down at herself and ran her fingers through her hair like a comb. This clearly wasn't how she was used to waking up.

"Sleep well?" Sam asked.

"I have no idea," Claire said. "But if I had ever doubted that people need a decent place to sleep indoors, that doubt is gone."

Erica smiled. "Wait till you have to go to the bathroom."

Claire glanced at the bucket setup area and then looked back at Erica. "I plan to hold it."

"Good luck with that," Sam said.

"Coffee's ready," Erica said.

"I would love to get some of that when my knees and back decide to join the party and I can stand up," Claire said as she sank backward onto her sleeping bag. "Which should be somewhere between three and forty-five minutes."

Sam and Erica shrugged and let her be.

Erica whispered, "As far as complaining goes, that's almost nothing."

"I know, right?" Sam replied. "Tougher than she looks."

They took their cups of coffee and walked further in on the lot, away from the tents and toward the trees, to talk about where to site the tiny houses.

★ ★ ★

"This ring of trees is great for shielding us from the neighbors on the sides and back," Sam said. "Once we have everything built, we are also going to want to do some plantings at the front. We could even make them rolling planter boxes, so the space could be more flexible. The common building can be up closer to the street, and with a fence and some trees, we can make the whole thing blend in real nice."

Erica nodded. "I love your idea about having the building open onto a patio and gathering area in the back. That'll be about in the center of the space, right?" she asked, pointing toward where most of the tents were clustered.

"Yep," Sam said. "That's the natural gathering spot, and we can have little paths from each of the houses."

Each of the tiny houses would be spaced out so residents didn't feel cramped together and could get their privacy, but close enough there would be a strong feeling of community. Sam and Erica wanted the project to rely heavily on a pleasant, attractive common space to encourage the residents to spend time together. Learning how to live as a community would help build resilience as well as responsibility.

"And over there," Sam said, "some raised garden beds for flowers, fruits and vegetables. Both as dirt therapy and as a way to get some fresh food."

As she pointed to the southern part of the site with the best sun, shouting erupted near the street.

"I don't care if you're the president of the U.S.A.," Sarah yelled. "I'm supposed to be here and you're not!"

At the curb next to the road, Sarah was standing nose-to-nose with the neighbor from across the street, whose face was bright red and whose fists were clenched by his side. Erica and Sam rushed toward them. As they neared, Claire scrambled out of her tent. Most of the other women were awake now, watching from their tents. Claire got to the fight first and placed herself between them, facing the neighbor. Sam and Erica grabbed Sarah, walking her a few steps away. They turned her to face away from the guy and stood by her side, talking to her softly and trying to calm her down. Claire stayed facing the neighbor, who was still beet red and trembling.

"What's the problem here ..." Claire asked, desperately trying to remember his name. Dan? Dave? Doug? Right, Doug. Doug the Slug. "... Doug?"

She approached him with her palms open and reached out to place her hand on his shoulder. He shrugged her off.

"The problem?" He spat. "I'm looking right at it. What the hell is going on here? This is a residential neighborhood, not a homeless camp."

Claire kept her voice low and slow and trained her eyes on Doug.

"Doug, I own this property. We are having a nice campout in my yard. We aren't breaking any laws or rules here."

"We'll see about that," Doug said. "The cops'll be here any minute."

Sarah, who had finally calmed down, heard him mention the cops and lost it all over again. She jumped away from Sam and Erica and started screaming.

"He called the *cops*? What the fuck, man?"

Sam held her back and leaned in to her, whispering quietly and turning her to face away from Doug.

Claire touched Doug's elbow and gestured down the block toward one of the other houses. "Why don't we come this way to talk?" she said. She looked back and saw Wendi and her kids looking out from their tent. She winked at the kids and walked Doug a few paces away, with his back toward them.

As she did, Sam held onto Sarah while Erica moved quickly through the group, checking with all the women to let them know things were okay. She also whispered to ask if any of them had any outstanding arrests or warrants. They all said no, and she hoped they weren't lying. If they didn't have any outstanding business with the cops and kept their heads down, they should be alright.

Claire and Doug were talking in heated tones at the street when a police cruiser rolled up slowly. Erica only realized how tense she was when her shoulders dropped three inches and she sighed with relief as Jake stepped out of the car.

Doug was waving him over impatiently, and Erica moved faster to intercept him.

"Jake," Erica called.

Jake stopped mid-stride and looked over at her with surprise. "Ford? What are you doing here?"

That allowed her to catch up, and she walked alongside him, intentionally slowing her pace so he'd slow down, too. "These are some of our people. This asshole from across the street is mad over nothing."

"Well, let's see ..."

Erica rolled her eyes. "I hate that you're a professional, sometimes."

Jake held back a laugh as they approached Claire and Doug. Before he even finished introducing himself, Doug began ranting.

"I woke up this morning and looked out my window," Doug blustered, "and *this* is what I saw! A homeless camp right in front of me! Officer, you have to do something. This is unacceptable."

Jake scanned the lot and nodded at the women in their tents. "I am sure this was very surprising to you, sir," Jake said.

"You bet it was," Doug said.

"It's probably not every day you wake up and look out your window and see a bunch of tents and women sleeping in them on the property across from yours."

"You bet it's not."

"But," Jake said, "I'm not sure anything illegal is happening here."

"Ha!" Sarah shouted, leaping forward before Sam jerked her back.

"How is this *possibly* okay!?" Doug asked.

Jake looked at Claire and Erica. "Who owns this property?" he asked.

"I do," Claire said, and raised her hand. "Sale just closed. I own it outright."

"And do all of the people here have your permission to be on your property?"

Erica interjected, "All except *him*," pointing at Doug.

Jake looked at Erica and almost imperceptibly rolled his eyes at her, then looked back to Claire. "Is that correct, ma'am?"

"That's correct."

"Well, as long as there's not a noise disturbance or a code violation, there's not much for me to do here," Jake said.

"Thanks, Officer," Claire said, and smiled broadly. "We are just enjoying a backyard get-together." She looked around. "Well, I guess there's not really a front or back yard at this point, so it's just a yard. But it's still a pleasant get-together."

Jake glanced at Erica and smirked. "All due respect, ma'am," he said to Claire, and then nodded his head toward Erica, "if she's involved, then it's probably suspect." Then he smiled so she knew he was kidding. "But who you choose to hang out with isn't a police problem. As long as you get permits for any structures and don't disrupt the neighbors, then there's no reason for me to be here."

"Thanks for the vote of confidence, *Officer*," Erica said.

"Voice of experience, Ford," he answered quickly, and chuckled before nodding his head at the others. "Ladies. Sir. I'll be going now."

Jake walked back to his cruiser and Doug sputtered, hands on his hips. "I don't believe this. No wonder this city is falling apart."

"Doug," Claire said, and smiled sweetly, "would you like a cup of coffee?"

"I'd *like* you get this trash off the lawn," Doug said.

Claire flinched slightly then stood up taller and folded her arms. "I'll presume, when you use the word 'trash,'" she said, and turned to face him, extending one arm past him to point toward a trash bag sitting at the curb, "you mean that single bag of pizza boxes tied up neatly and ready to be removed."

Doug glared at her. "You may be able to get away with this for now," he said. "But I'm going to fight like hell and I'm going to get every single neighbor working with me to keep you out. This isn't going to last."

"These are good people, Doug, and this is a good project." She re-folded her arms and looked him up and down. "You look a little flushed. Getting worked up like this can't be good for your health."

"I've taken pictures and I'm watching you. One wrong move and it's over," Doug said.

"I'm sure all these women who have nowhere else to go and no one else fighting for them to succeed appreciate the vote of confidence, Doug," Claire said. "Now I think it's time for you to get off my property."

"This isn't over!" Doug called as he slunk back across the street.

"It is for today!" Claire called back a little too cheerily and waved as he walked away. "Have a good one!" She stood her ground and kept her gaze on him until he was fully inside his house.

Claire exhaled and heard a low whistle as she turned around to a smattering of applause from the women who'd come out of their tents to watch.

"Daaaaaaaaaaaamn," Cheryl said from her tent.

"Right?" Marta said.

"Rich white lady does *not* mess around," Jamilah said.

Claire smiled at them and then looked back toward the bathroom station at the back of the site.

"Porta-potties are coming today, right?" Claire asked. "It's a good thing he didn't know about the poop buckets. I can't imagine a world where those are to code."

"They're coming today, boss," Erica said.

"Great!" Claire clapped her hands. "Then let's have some coffee. Come on over, everyone."

CHAPTER 12

After they had all been sufficiently fed and caffeinated, it was time to get to work.

"I've marked out spaces for each of you to move your tents," Sam said to the group. "Each spot is roughly where your house will go. We'll start building your house platforms next, so we can get you up off the ground."

"What if we don't like where you put us?" Sarah asked.

"Honestly, it makes no difference to me," Sam shrugged. "Don't mess with the spacing in between each place but if you want to trade with someone else? Knock yourself out."

The women compared spots and a few traded. Jamilah wanted to be further away from the road and possible noise, so Barb offered to trade her spot.

"I can't hear out of this ear anyway," Barb said, and tugged on her left ear, laughing a little. "It sucks, but sure helps me sleep in noisy places. And here ain't noisy at all compared to most places, anyway."

"I wish I had that," Jamilah said. "I feel like I have super-Spider-Man hearing, especially in the middle of the night. I know it's not that noisy here, but sometimes even the smallest thing sounds like a monster truck to me."

Once the trades were made, they all helped each other move their tents and belongings to their new spaces. When the porta-potties arrived, Erica directed them to the right location and adjusted the tarps around the larger restroom area that now also had a hand washing station.

"The tarps really tie it all together, don't you think?" Salina joked as she helped Erica hang them up.

"I don't think we'll be on HGTV anytime soon," Erica said. "But hey, at least the dark green tarps kinda blend in with the trees."

Next, they moved on to set up the kitchen area near the power and water hookup. To get started, they had a couple of picnic coolers and two long folding tables, with the camp stove set up on the end of one of the tables. This wasn't going to be a great arrangement for long, but it would do for now. Erica made a note that she needed to get a camp-safe food locker for the non-perishables, to keep the critters out. Sam also planned to build a better lean-to structure that wouldn't need a permit but would create more privacy and storage space.

* * *

After they'd made strong progress, all the women and the two kids gathered in the center area, scattered in lawn chairs or sitting on the ground. Most of them liked the idea of raised garden beds, and only Wendi protested when the kids said they'd like a sandbox.

"You're not the ones who'll be cleaning sand out of their clothes all the time!" she'd cried. The other women agreed she had a point. They told the kids they were overruled, but they could have their own special section of one of the garden beds.

Sam had a few more small tasks for them all to do, and the women broke up into smaller groups and started to get to know each other as they worked. Claire made her way over to Wendi and the kids and sat down with them.

"I'm glad you're here and a part of this," Claire said.

Wendi kept her head down, focused on the kids. "I heard you went out looking for us."

Claire nodded. "I did."

"No offense," Wendi said, glancing up, "but why? You just met us."

"I know ..." Claire trailed off. She didn't exactly know why, and tried to figure out what to say. Wendi was right. She did barely know them, and it was weird that she went out looking for them. Claire didn't think it was *that* weird, but everybody else seemed to, so clearly there was something she was missing. She was just so lonely since Chris had died, she'd never had kids of her own, and these kids ... she knew there were hundreds of other kids in situations just like theirs, or worse, all over the city—but for some reason, knowing these two kids were on the street when she could help them, when she was a major donor to the organization that was supposed to help them, and they weren't getting the help they needed ... she just couldn't live with herself if she didn't try. But how do you say that to the child's mother, who's the one who's supposed to be caring for them?

The boy, Theo, was playing with a little plastic truck. Claire reached out to tap the toy. "I like your truck," she said and then looked over at Wendi.

"I don't know," she continued. "I just ... they had you up on that stage as someone who benefitted from the money I donate, but then I saw you sitting on the side of the road. It bothered me. What does help mean if you still don't have a home and your kids' bed is the backseat of your car? I just ... I wanted to help you."

"I'm not special or different," Wendi said.

"Of course you are," Claire said. "You're so articulate and your kids are so smart. It's not right that you're in this position."

Wendi laughed. "Are you serious right now?"

Claire looked confused.

"Look around you, Claire. "No one here *belongs* here."

"That's not what I—"

"Yes it is." Wendi interrupted "You may not think it's what you meant, but it's what you meant. Someone like me never mattered to you before," she said. "Why do I matter now?"

"I don't ..." Claire struggled. "You have these kids ..."

"Yeah, lots of people have kids."

"But they deserve better. Most people with kids aren't homeless and dragging their kids around with them," Claire sputtered.

"*Excuse* me?"

Claire put up her hands. "I'm sorry, that came out wrong."

"I hope it did." Wendi stiffened and started picking up the kids' toys. "Come on guys. Get your stuff together. Maybe this wasn't a good idea."

Claire put her hand on Wendi's arm. "No, please. Stop. You need to be here." Her eyes traveled down to Wendi's tattooed arm.

Wendi followed Claire's eyes then shrugged off her hand and stood up, slinging her bag over her shoulder and grabbing one child with each hand. "I don't need your pity or your judgment."

"I know," Claire said, backing off. "I'm sorry. That's not what this is." She shook her head. "I'm going to say this all wrong."

"You got a good start on that."

"I know," Claire nodded. "You're right. I apologize. Can we start over?"

Wendi released the kids and shooed them off to toward some of the other women, and slowly sat back down, eyeing Claire suspiciously.

"I'm staying because it's too late to find space in one of the shelters tonight, not because you're some great negotiator, okay?"

"Okay." Claire nodded. "I imagine it's got to be hard to not have a place to stay, and also have two small kids to take care of," Claire said.

"It's not great, but we get by."

"One of the reasons I wanted to find you those times I came looking for you was because I *can't* imagine. I thought that by donating to Portland Promise I was helping people like you get off the street, but it turns out that even with all the money they bring in and put into service, even the 'success stories' still live in their cars and their kids live in cars, too. I just ... I want to understand better. How did you get here, to this place?"

"I drove my car, which I live in."

"I mean ..."

"I know what you mean." Wendi sighed. "I'm just really tired of explaining myself to people," she said. "You probably don't ever have to explain yourself to anyone, but I—hell, I bet all the rest of these ladies," she said, waving her hand across the site, "we need to explain ourselves to people all the time."

"I'm sorry about that," Claire said. "I want to understand more. If I've learned anything in the past couple weeks, it's that I have a lot to learn."

Wendi smiled a little. "Yeah, you do. Look, the kids like it here and I like that there's a bunch of space here for them to run around and stuff. But you need to know I'm telling you about me 'cause I decided I want to, not because I, like, owe it to you or something."

Claire agreed. "You don't owe me anything."

Wendi exhaled. She crossed her arms and looked away. Finally, she brought her gaze back to Claire.

"I grew up in St. Louis," Wendi said, "and my high school boyfriend got a job out here. My dad was a drunk and my mom hit me since she couldn't hit him 'cause he was already hitting her. So I got out of there as soon as I could. We went to Marysville, up north of Seattle."

Wendi's boyfriend, Chad, had a high school buddy who found Chad a job working construction. It was low-skill, but there was a lot of work and it paid well enough for them to rent a decent apartment. Wendi landed a job at a call center and quickly got pregnant. They decided to keep it, and the boyfriend insisted she stay home to raise it. She was more than happy to quit her boring job and was excited by the prospect of having the American Dream life her parents didn't have. They even went and got a marriage license, and suddenly she was a wife.

"But it turns out," Wendi said, "babies cry and take up a lot of time, and Chad didn't like it. He wanted me to pay attention to him, not them. I couldn't keep up, the house was a mess, and the baby was crying all the time."

When baby Ella was a little older it got a little better, Wendi said.

"We even started talking about having a real wedding so we could invite our friends. We started to save up for it, but then I got pregnant again."

"And there went the savings?" Claire asked.

"There went the savings, and everything else."

Chad started yelling again. At her, at the kids, at anything and everything. One night he put his fist through the wall.

"Which wouldn't have been so bad," Wendi said, "except his fist was right next to my head. And it was while I was holding the baby."

"Oh, Wendi," Claire sighed.

"I hoped it'd get better when Theo got older, like it did with Ella. But it didn't. I was still so tired, and Chad was mad all the time, now. Sometimes he'd go and stay out all night and not come home till the next day. Those nights were good and quiet, but he never left us any money. And when I asked for some, he'd lose his shit, so sometimes I didn't even have any groceries. All three of us were real hungry most of the time. I started saving whatever I could, some change here and there, and even taking money from his wallet, not enough that he'd notice."

Then Wendi got pregnant again. She'd been trying to make him use condoms, but he said he didn't like them and she should just be careful. He also said he didn't want her to use birth control because he didn't want her to get fat. When she found out, she didn't tell him about the pregnancy. Planning to end it, she started taking more money from his wallet and quietly started selling some of the old baby equipment while he was at work.

The money wasn't coming fast enough, though. She started to show, and now Chad was yelling all the time, shaking the kids, and shoving her around. Her window to get rid of the pregnancy was closing. She told him she needed more money for the kids' clothes and to get a little more at the grocery store since they were eating more now. He tossed a few bills at her and said maybe she was the one eating more and she should stop being such a pig. She bristled at him calling her fat when she was just skin and bones apart from her rounding belly. But she sucked it up and asked him for money again a couple weeks later over dinner. He lit up with anger this time and shoved the table at her. With food, dishes, glasses half full, the table came charging into her belly. She screamed and the children started crying. Which made him angrier, and he did it again, pushing the table into her over and over, saying if she wouldn't try to lose weight, maybe he could force it off her.

He stormed out of the house and drove away. She made sure the kids were okay and gasped when Ella screamed and pointed at the blood running down her leg.

"I'd been saving up for the abortion but now all of a sudden I didn't need it," Wendi said to Claire. "I decided right there to use that money to get the hell out."

She cleaned herself up and quickly packed as much as she could for herself and the kids. She checked all his possible hiding places for more cash and grabbed the title to her car and the kids' birth certificates. She had thought about escaping so many times, all the moves were already in her head. She was able to act quickly and efficiently. She knew he probably wouldn't be back till morning at the earliest, so she had a few hours to get away. Maybe longer if he was out on another multi-day bender.

* * *

Claire shook her head and stood up. This was so much to take in, and she walked around in small circles while she tried to process it.

"Wendi, I just ..." she said. "He hit you so hard you miscarried?"

Wendi shrugged and looked away. "I guess."

"You must have been in so much pain. You were, what, four or five months along?"

"Something like that," Wendi said.

"What did you ..." Claire paused. "You were bleeding a lot, yeah?"

"Yeah."

"How did you ..."

"I don't know," Wendi said. "You just do what you have to do." She didn't want to spend the money on maxi pads so she'd used rolled up paper towels to soak up the blood while she moved around.

"That had to be so hard," Claire said.

"Not as hard as it could have been," Wendi said.

Claire took that in and sat back down next to Wendi. "I can only imagine what you felt through all that. I'm so sorry you had to experience it."

Wendi shrugged and scooted back a couple inches.

Claire recognized Wendi wanted a little more space and shifted back, too. "Thank you for sharing this with me."

Wendi looked up and met Claire's gaze. "Thanks for listening."

"Did he ever hurt the kids?" Claire asked.

"No!" Wendi snapped. "If he ever laid even a finger on one of them, we'd have been out of there that second."

Claire nodded. Wendi's entire demeanor had changed; her body lit up and she was ready to spring into action. It was clear she meant what she said, and Claire saw some of the energy that must have powered her through that horrible night.

"So," Claire asked after a little pause, "did you come here, to Portland, after that?"

"Not right away," Wendi answered. "All my, like, adrenaline and whatever ran out a couple hours into it, so I pulled over and we slept for a little while at a rest stop outside Olympia. When I woke up, it all kind of hit me how dumb it was to just run. I mean, we're married. The car is in his name. He's on their birth certificates. I didn't even have a bank account. I still don't, 'cause I don't know if he could use that to find me."

They'd gone to the bathroom at the rest stop and as she was holding the kids up at the sink to wash their hands, she saw a sticker advertising a domestic violence hotline.

"I never thought I was like a battered housewife or whatever, but he did hit me, and I knew I had nowhere else to go."

She called the number and they directed her to a shelter in Olympia. They stayed at the shelter for a few days.

"Oh my God, I was so tired," Wendi said, "and I swear to you those women were angels from heaven. They set me up with a doctor to make sure all my inside parts were okay, they had daycare people to watch the kids while I was gone, and one day they just let me sleep the whole damn day. It was amazing.

The only thing I didn't like was they told me I should figure out a way to return the car or leave it somewhere so it could get found and returned. I mean, I know—technically I stole it. But I needed that car so we could keep moving."

One day in the living room of the shelter, she was talking with another woman staying there, and mentioned the car situation.

"Yeah, they tell you to do everything by the book here," the other lady said. "They have to. But ... there's a guy I can connect you with who can do a trade for you."

"I knew it was probably definitely not legal," Wendi told Claire. "But if there was some other choice, I didn't know what it was."

If Wendi could forge her husband's signature on the title, this guy would "buy" the car from her. But instead of paying her, he'd give her a different, slightly shittier, car with a clean title. And then he'd sell her car or strip it for parts and pocket the difference.

Wendi did it, and received a green Honda Accord that wasn't great, but ran good enough and could fit all three of them and their stuff. She loaded it up, took a few extra supplies from the shelter, and bolted with the kids the next morning. They drove south, and she finally stopped in Portland. It was still a little too close to Marysville for comfort, but she was running out of money and needed to regroup. The domestic violence shelters in Portland didn't have any room. They told her they'd add her to a list and said she could try the regular homeless shelters.

"But I didn't think I was homeless then," Wendi told Claire.

"What do you mean?"

"I mean, I knew I didn't have a home, but I wasn't, like, a *homeless person*, you know?"

Claire nodded. "I guess ..."

"But we didn't have anywhere else to go," Wendi said. They tried the "regular" shelter for a night. It was a huge, open room with cots and mats, and it was loud and unruly. The kids were overwhelmed, and Wendi couldn't sleep. The next morning, she collected some information from the shelter operators about safe places to sleep in her car and where to find food pantries. And from there, they struck out on their own.

For the last year or so, that's what they'd been doing: moving around to different parking lots, usually churches but sometimes other clusters where they know the cops won't harass them. They get food boxes from the pantries, and she makes cash by selling plasma and sometimes doing medical studies at the university downtown.

"You and your kids have been living in that car for a year?" Claire asked.

"Yeah," Wendi said. "Our little house on wheels."

"How did you get hooked up with Portland Promise? How did you meet Bruce and get picked to go onstage?"

"I mean, I don't know why they picked me, but they've got a partnership with the food bank. I started volunteering there a couple times a week because they have a shower in the bathroom we can use, I get a good pick of the food boxes, and there's a daycare for the staff they also let me leave the kids at sometimes. I guess they figured I was like some model citizen or something."

Claire nodded. "It looks like you're keeping the kids clean and safe ..."

"I try to."

"What are they ... What are you going to do about their schooling?"

"That's not for a couple years yet, so I don't know. We'll figure it out."

"Early childhood education is very important," Claire said. "It can make a huge difference in a child's future." She looked at Ella. "She's old enough to be in a preschool program."

Wendi stiffened again. "We're doing fine."

Claire sensed Wendi closing down and backed off. "Oh, I'm sure you are. I was just thinking—"

"We're good," Wendi said and stood up again. "Thanks for the chat." Wendi walked over to where the kids were playing near some of the other women, and Claire watched her walk away. She pulled up a handful of grass and threw it off to her side.

⋆ ⋆ ⋆

Erica had been watching their conversation and walked over to Claire after Wendi left.

"You two seemed to be having a good conversation," Erica said. "Until you weren't."

"Yeah," Claire said.

"What happened?"

"I don't know. I was asking about her kids and school. I guess she thought I was getting too pushy."

"She's been through a lot," Erica said. "They all have."

"I know, I just heard about a lot of it. But tough situation or not, she should be thinking about those kids' future."

Erica sat down on the grass. "Claire," she said. "Seriously."

"I—"

"Take it easy," Erica said. "Just take it easy and take it slow. They're doing the best they can. Just like you are. Her best and your best don't necessarily look the same."

Claire pulled out more grass and tossed it. "I guess. I'd just hate to see those kids miss out on their opportunities."

"Oh my God, Claire, calm down. We'd all hate for them to 'miss opportunities.' But right now, their opportunity is to get into a house with actual walls. They're *her* kids, not yours. Let's help them get stable before you start picking which college the kids are going to and whether or not they have enough extra-curriculars to pass muster."

Claire rolled her eyes. "I'm not—"

Erica interrupted her. "You kind of are. So back off."

Claire rolled her neck. "Fine." She started to stand up. "Can you give me a hand? My knees are older than yours."

Erica stood up and reached down to help Claire. "Let's go see what Sam needs from us."

CHAPTER 13

A couple weeks later, the site was really coming along. With help from the residents, Sam had built platforms for the tiny houses, and the residents had moved their tents to the platforms. They'd set up the lean-to kitchen structure, run power from the drop at the edge of the lot, and Erica had brought over two little dorm fridges and a freezer to replace the coolers. On the externally facing side of the lean-to, a couple of the more creative but less handy residents had painted a mural of spring flowers.

Since leaving Portland Promise, Erica had been closing out her client list, handing cases off to other outreach workers and trying to tie up as many loose ends as possible. She'd been nervous about telling her clients she was leaving; she didn't want to be yet another disappointment and dead end in their lives that were already so hard. To her surprise, most of her clients were happy for her and excited about the new project.

"That's *exactly* what you should be doing, E!" one of them had told her when she showed up at his tent downtown to let him know someone new would be coming by. "Go show them how it's done!"

Erica was reminded how much she cared for these people she'd come to know so well, and how remarkable it was that they could be positive and find joy for other people, even when their own situations were so bad.

* * *

Sam had worked with the pre-fab building company to design and prepare the order for the commons building. All they needed now was the variance from City Council so they could place the order and get started on building the individual units. The City Council meeting was coming up in just a week, and Erica and Claire were preparing testimony and recruiting supporters to make a strong showing in person.

Erica and Sam sat on one of the platforms where Sam had been doing some work to make it more level. Erica looked over at a group of the women working together on four large, raised garden beds.

"It's nice seeing them calmer and working well together," Erica said. "Those garden beds were a great idea."

Sam nodded. "It's amazing how putting your hands in the dirt can just ... calm you down."

They watched in silence as Marta helped Sarah lift a bag of soil over the edge and pour half of it into the area they were working on. Claire was in there working, too, next to Wendi and the kids. Karyn and Jamilah were showing all four of them how to create little mounds of dirt and then drop a few seeds in.

Even though Karyn had grown up in rural Oregon and had very little in common with Jamilah, the two of them had bonded over the garden when they learned they'd both had grandmothers who taught them how to grow vegetables.

"I never heard anyone besides my grandma talk about the Three Sisters," Karyn had said.

"What's the Three Sisters?" Heather asked.

"Corn, beans, and squash!" Karyn and Jamilah said in unison, and then laughed.

"My grandma said it's the 'old way,'" Jamilah said. "And she also said it's the only way that works."

"*Huge* pumpkins," Karyn nodded. "We had to stop growing them because my mom's boyfriend liked to throw them at us when he was loaded."

"That's kind of dark," Jamilah said.

Karyn shrugged and flicked her long, brown braid. "Don't make it less true."

"I hear that," Jamilah said.

* * *

Erica flipped an unlit cigarette around and between her fingers. She was half-heartedly trying to quit again, which meant she'd been fantasizing about smoking this specific cigarette for the last hour.

"Seeing them all together like this," she said, "reminds me how much trauma they are all dealing with. They are all carrying around so much it's amazing it doesn't just spill over all the time."

Sam gestured to Claire. "Even Rich Lady?"

"Yeah, even her," Erica said kindly. "She's dealing with some heavy stuff. She needs to put her hands in that dirt, too. We all got here from somewhere."

"Yeah," Sam said, thinking about her own journey to get to this place. "Remember when we met? Who'd have thought that scared, beat-up girl would be sitting here with you now, with my own apartment and my own business, helping these other women ..." She glanced down at Erica's hand. "And watching you mangle that poor cigarette."

Erica looked down at the bent, wrinkled cigarette in her hand and smiled. "*I* thought it. I mean, about you, not the cigarette. I believed in you the whole way."

"I know," Sam said. "And a lot of the time, you were the only one who did."

"Imagine if we'd had a community like this for you back then?" Erica asked.

Sam sighed. "I don't know if I'd have been ready for it. But yeah, when I was finally ready, it would have been amazing."

While they were talking, Karyn brushed off her hands, stood up, and came over to them. Her braid swung behind her as she walked.

"We see you two over here slacking off," she said.

Erica deadpanned, "This isn't slacking. This is supervising."

Karyn smiled her crooked, closed-mouth smile. Like some of the others, she was working hard to recover from a meth addiction that had taken an extreme toll on her face and teeth. Between that and an ex-boyfriend who liked to use her face as a punching bag, her jawline was in rough shape. But as limited as her smile was, her huge, sparkling green eyes crinkled at the edges like she had a huge grin.

"Can we use your computer later?" Karyn asked.

"Sure," Erica said. "What you got?"

Karyn absently rubbed her hand against her thigh. She still carried a lot of nervous energy and some part of her was always moving.

"I found out it's real easy to get the bus to that new Amazon facility from here so I was gonna apply for a job," she said. And then she added, all in one breath, "I mean, I know I probably don't have a shot and we don't even know if we're going to be able to stay here but, hey, if I don't apply then I definitely don't get it."

"Let's do it!" Erica said. My laptop's in my truck. No reason we can't do it right now." She hopped off the edge of the platform and nodded to Sam, then turned to Karyn as they walked toward her truck. "Are there any other places you're looking at?" she asked.

Sam smiled as they walked away and stood up off the platform. That was Erica. Always ready to help you when you need it, and to gently push you just a little further than you think you can go. And Karyn taking the initiative on this application was huge. With a record for possession and use, and no strong work history, Karyn was having a hard time finding work. But she kept trying, thanks to Erica.

* * *

Erica and Karyn arrived at her truck parked on the street just as neighbor Doug zipped off in his Prius with another stack of the signs he was placing all over the southeast side of town. Erica waved with an overly friendly smile as he drove off, and flipped her middle finger just as he was out of sight.

"That guy," she muttered as she reached behind the front seat to get her computer.

They hadn't been the only ones keeping busy the last few weeks. Doug was calling the police on them almost every night, "Just to keep them on their toes." Finally, the police had told him that unless there was a mortal threat or a fire, he needed to stop calling 911. So then he'd printed a bunch of signs which said, "Your Neighborhood is Next!" and had a link to a website he'd designed himself, with a long, mostly incoherent screed about bad influences and threats to children. He was placing the signs throughout the area and was posting similar messages on different neighborhood groups' social media sites.

Although he was thorough, his message wasn't landing as well as he'd hoped. Erica and the residents had been taking turns going door-to-door, covering a few houses each afternoon, to introduce themselves and let neighbors know about the project. The responses were mostly positive, and neighbors were now stopping by from time to time to say hello and check in. These friendlier neighbors encouraged the women not to worry too much about Doug.

"He's a pain in the ass," one neighbor woman said, "but no one else wants the job of neighborhood president, so we just put up with him."

"That's funny," Erica answered. "Unfortunately, we don't really have the ability to ignore him. He's actively coming after us."

The neighbor looked around at the site, then over at Doug's property, on which he'd put up a row of the signs all across the front lawn. "I guess so," she said.

* * *

One late afternoon while Wendi's kids were napping inside her tent, Claire and Erica called everyone together in the common area to talk about the city council meeting.

"We're going to need all of you there who think you're up for it," Erica said. "I know it's not a place you're used to going, or even want to go—but to pull this off, we need to show the City Council that if they vote no, they are voting against real people. They are voting against *you*."

"Well, that sounds like a shit time," Sarah said. "No offense."

Barb laughed. "But how do you really feel?"

"Ha," Sarah said. "No, I mean it. Sounds like you're basically asking us to sit there and take it while a bunch of strangers talk shit about us."

Erica looked around and made eye contact with each person in the circle. "Pretty much. I'm not going to pretend it's something else. And it sucks. But showing up is the only way we can fight it."

"I don't know," Marta said softly, "It doesn't sound any worse than anything else I've heard people say about me when they don't know me at all."

Some of the women nodded. "Walking by and talking about us like we're not there or can't hear them," Cheryl said.

"Spitting," Barb said.

Karyn added, "Driving by and shaking their heads."

Throwing actual garbage on or into our tents," Jamilah said.

"Guys like Doug the Slug," Linda said, "thinking he's gonna ... I don't know what, *catch* homelessness? Just by being near us?"

Salina shrugged. "At least if we're in that room they gotta look right at us when they say shit."

"I mean, yeah," Erica said. "But they aren't the only ones who get to talk. We do, too. I'm going to speak, Claire's going to speak, and we're going to get other people to testify on our behalf. I'm also hoping a few of you will speak, too. This is our chance to help them understand."

Jamilah rolled her eyes. "I'm so sick of always being the one who has to explain. Why can't people who have everything make a little effort to understand without us having to explain it all the time? It's exhausting."

Marta nodded. "Homeless, drugs, brown skin, whatever. No offense to the white ladies here 'cause at least you're kind of trying. But I am so over this."

Erica met Marta's gaze, then looked over to Jamilah, and then to Salina. "I know. And I'm sorry. You all know me. You know I wouldn't ask you to do this if it didn't matter a lot."

Jamilah nodded. "I get it. I don't like it, but I get it."

"Yeah, me, too," Marta said. "I just needed to vent."

* * *

Erica looked over at Jamilah. She was so glad Jamilah had agreed to participate. Being Black in the lily-white Pacific Northwest is tough to begin with—being Black and unhoused and a woman and living with a mental health condition is a hundred times harder. Most of the Black and brown people Erica knew on the streets either hung together or stayed as separate as possible from anyone and everyone. Jamilah was the latter.

About six months ago, Jamilah had landed on Erica's client list, and they'd set her up with a recurring spot in a congregate shelter. But the shelter was just too chaotic for her, and the noise and activity aggravated an underlying anxiety disorder. Jamilah had grown increasingly agitated without knowing why. In her frustration, she had started acting out. She was kicked out of the shelter for getting in a fight with one of the other residents, and had been banned from all the other shelters as a result. She went back to living in a tent alongside a bike trail, tucked away where she hoped no one would see her. When Erica found her again, Jamilah was calmer and willing to get help on the anxiety disorder. But she also had more pressing problems because she'd lost her job as a dishwasher when she went through her crisis.

* * *

Claire cleared her throat and started to speak. "I, um ... Can I ask a question?"

Erica smiled. "You can ask ..."

"I don't want to say the wrong thing or offend someone," Claire said. "Since you just said you're tired of explaining, and I'm about to ask you to explain something."

Jamilah rolled her eyes and tugged on the ends of her short cornrow braids.

Marta tilted her head and gave a half-smile. "I'm easy to piss off, but not too easy to offend. What do you want to know?"

"Well," Claire said slowly, "I have a very different life from all of you ..."

"You don't say?" Wendi said.

"And so, I don't understand a lot of your experiences," Claire continued. "I've learned a lot just from being here with you and from seeing some of this from your perspective. But a lot of that has come from you explaining things to me. If you weren't doing that, I wouldn't know. So, I'm just wondering ... If you don't explain things to people who don't know, how do we learn?"

The women were quiet. Jamilah rubbed her chin, thinking about how to respond. Claire looked around the circle nervously.

Erica looked at Jamilah. "You want me to?"

Jamilah shook her head. "Nah. I'm just trying to figure out where to start." She leaned forward and rested her elbows on her knees, tenting her fingers. "Okay, so it's complicated."

Claire nodded and leaned in, too. "I want to understand."

"I get that," Jamilah said. "And that's part of what makes talking to you different. I mean, don't get me wrong. You're still exhausting."

"I heard that," Salina said.

Jamilah glanced in Salina's direction and smiled a little at the corner of her mouth, then turned back to Claire. "But you clearly want to help, you put your money where your mouth is and roll up your sleeves to help, and you legit want to know what's going on, what's wrong, and how to make it better and do better yourself."

"I do," Claire said.

"But a lot of people," Jamilah continued, "when they ask us to explain things, what they really mean is they want us to ... I don't know, to justify ourselves. They want to argue with us, or 'challenge our assumptions,' or prove they're 'different' than all the others, or some shit. They're asking, 'Why don't you fit into my neat little box and make this easy for me?' And when it turns out our story is too messy for them to understand or it makes them uncomfortable, they tune us out. Or blame us for the problem we are trying to describe."

"I can see that," Claire nodded. "That makes sense."

Marta interjected, "And there's a little more on that one, too."

Claire turned to her. "Tell me."

"Most people don't spend any time trying to educate themselves," Marta said. "When they ask us to explain things, that's just being lazy. They have Internet. They can read. Go learn some stuff and stop making us do your work, you know?"

Claire nodded, trying to understand.

Jamilah scooted closer. "Totally. And it's that way for being homeless and also for the race stuff."

Claire nodded but was clearly confused. "I'm not sure I understand."

"Okay," Jamilah said. "So, you're white. And you're rich and you're fancy, and you get whatever you want pretty much all the time."

Claire sucked the inside of her cheek. "I could argue I've had some big losses, but I get your point. In general, yes, you're right."

"I'm glad you said that," Jamilah said. "I know you've had some shit to deal with. And I'm not saying that wasn't hard and didn't hurt. But in the big picture, you're doing okay, right?"

"Yes," Claire said. "Put it like that and yes. I completely agree."

"Right," Jamilah said. "Thank you. Some folks don't get that."

"I try to be compassionate," Claire said.

"Not the same," Marta said. "Think about that first night we all slept here. So before then, because you are a compassionate but, sorry, kinda blind rich white lady, you knew we had it worse than you and wanted to help. But you didn't really know anything. And then after that first night? You knew more of what we all have to do every night. How we don't have like cashmere pillows or whatever. How the ground is hard. And the sun and any noise outside wakes you up. How you never realized how much you like a real flush toilet. You started to *kind of* understand what our life is like."

"Most folks like you," Jamilah said, "don't do that. Not just they don't try living outside, they don't ever try to understand our lives."

"And for me and Jamilah and Salina," Marta said, "and for anyone who looks a little different from—well, from you—we get to do that about our skin, too. We are always having to explain and justify our experiences."

"Yeah." Salina said. "And usually, even after we do, you people don't believe us."

Claire leaned back. "Thank you. I know I don't fully understand yet, and may not ever. But I'm glad to be a little closer. Thank you all for telling me this, and for taking the time and energy to help me understand."

"Thanks for taking it seriously," Erica said to Claire. "And for all of you," she said, looking at the rest of the group, "thanks for letting us in and for being a part of this project. We aren't going to get through this without doing some more educating. But if we succeed, we'll have a pretty rad place for everyone to stay."

The group sat quietly for a minute or so, until Sarah broke the silence.

"I can't believe you just said 'rad.' Are you, like, seventy?"

The group laughed and Erica tossed her pen at Sarah. "Fuck off."

"Is this meeting of the feelings society over yet?" Cheryl asked. "I'm hungry."

Claire laughed and looked at Erica. "Let's make it a working dinner, huh? I'll go get us some pizzas, if you all keep working on testimony and who we need to call to come out to support you?"

Jamilah shrugged. "I'm not saying having a rich white lady around is *all* bad," she said, and smiled at Claire. "Especially when she wants to be my delivery service."

CHAPTER 14

While work on the site progressed, Erica recruited supporters to testify at the City Council meeting. Many neighbors had enthusiastically welcomed them and volunteered to show up and say they supported the project. That would go a long way toward diffusing the blow of Doug's work against them. Erica wanted a bigger group, though, to show that there was support even outside the neighborhood.

One of the things she'd learned about Portland was that if you had a social justice cause and needed to rally a crowd, they would turn out. Holding signs and chanting seemed to be a particularly popular pastime for middle-class white people in the Pacific Northwest. It usually irritated her, principally because there was never any follow up. These folks may have the time and money to be able to hold a sign for a few hours, but they tended to disappear when it was time for real work. She usually rolled her eyes and ignored them, but this time she checked her assumptions and called two of the social justice organizers she knew who could turn people out. They agreed quickly and prepared a peaceful action outside City Hall, additionally encouraging their members to write letters of support to the city council and the news media.

She also recruited a few former colleagues from Portland Promise, one of the funders of her ill-fated tent project, and some of the service providers they'd been working with at the tiny home site.

She tried to get Jake the cop to testify, because a sympathetic cop would be a huge positive for the "law and justice" crowd.

"You know I can't do that, Erica," he said. "I'll help you however I can but that's one way I can't."

"You don't have to come in uniform!" she'd said. "You could just be a community member who also happens to have a day job as a cop."

"You know that's not how it works," he said. "We aren't allowed to have our own opinions. Not only would I probably lose my job and then my wife would murder me, but then she'd go to prison for killing me and my kids would be orphaned. Do you really want to make my kids wards of the state?"

Erica shook her head and rolled her eyes. "At least you're not being dramatic."

Jake smiled. "You think *you're* fighting a huge, intractable system that sees even the smallest critique as an assault on its very existence?"

Erica nodded. "Yes, I do. So?"

"Allow me introduce you to the institution of law enforcement."

Erica shook her head. "You seem like a decent human, Jake. I don't even know why you became a cop in the first place."

"I became a cop because I *am* a decent human. And it was a good job that can support a family. I *stayed* a cop because we need more people like me here."

"And I thought I was the one tilting at windmills," Erica said.

"We're an elite club," Jake laughed. "Look, I can't testify. But I'll be there at the meeting. Chief and the mayor were concerned there might be some altercations between protestors, so I made sure I got assigned to cover it. I'll be pulling for you, as long as you don't go punching anyone."

★ ★ ★

On the side of the opposition, Doug the Slug had also been busy. Not only had he been putting out his awful "Your Neighborhood is Next" signs, but he'd also been knocking on doors, sharing his flyers, and trying to get people from his side to write letters.

His main tactic, it seemed, was fear. He left his flyers underneath Claire's and Erica's windshield wipers one day. When she found the flyer, Claire brought it over to the group and did a dramatic reading. In it, Doug told people that if they didn't stop this one project, the next one would be across the street from *their* house. Their neighborhoods would become overrun with "the homeless," end up filled with trash, and "hoodlums" would descend on their quiet streets, turning a peaceful land into mayhem.

"I know I'm old," Claire told the group, "But 'hoodlums'? Seriously? People still say 'hoodlums'?

"Racists do," Jamilah muttered.

Claire balled up the flyer and tossed it into the trash.

★ ★ ★

After a meeting with some of the housing advocates to talk about their plan, Erica came back to the site and found Sam and Salina working on the platform for Marta's house. Hoping everything would go well at City Council and she wouldn't be needed, Sam had been attending to each of the platforms to make sure they were ready to have the houses built on top of them. Salina had taken to the work and was helping Sam rig the utility hookups.

"I think we have a good plan," Erica told them as she sat down in the grass next to the platform. "But this neighbor dude.

He's a piece of work with this whole 'you'll be next' boogie man stuff. It's just so Racism and Classism 101."

"Racists gonna racist," Salina said.

"True enough," Erica replied. "And it's just so obvious and coded. He's out there talking about us like we're one of those shitshow camps out at Delta. Like there's trash and needles and overturned shopping carts just pouring off this property and into the street. The picture on his flyer? It isn't even a picture of this place. It's of one of the camps under the Marine Drive overpass. Like, the worst one there."

She looked out at their site and shook her head thrusting her hands out in front of her with pride. "This place is so *nice.* You all—*we* all—have really made it something good. And we aren't even done. You should be proud."

Sam and Salina paused what they were doing to look out and see what Erica was talking about. The platforms were well-built and the tents on top of them were tidy. There was no garbage strewn around, and everything was in its proper place. Even the kids' toys were in their little box in the common area.

Salina nodded. "Amazing, isn't it? Don't treat people like trash and they don't act like trash."

Erica turned to gaze up at Salina. Tall and thin with deep brown skin and short hair pulled up into two little puffs on the sides of her head, Salina had this calm and steady presence that belied the chaos she'd been through in the last few years.

Salina had grown up just outside of Portland. She never knew her father and had a tough relationship with her mother. Most of her mom's family was back in Florida, so Salina didn't know them. She left home at seventeen and was able to get enough basic work to take care of herself. It wasn't a great life, but it was hers. She thought about saving up enough to go to Florida and see her grandmother and meet her cousins. Hard to do when you're making minimum wage, but she tried.

At eighteen, she and a couple of white friends were stopped in a car she was driving. The police said she'd failed to signal a turn, and when it turned out she was not the owner of the vehicle (they had legitimately borrowed it from the friend they were going to see, but that person wasn't there), the cops pulled her out of the car and searched it. One of her friends, who had been holding the pot and pipe they were planning to smoke later, stuffed it under a seat and it was easily found. The two white girls were allowed to walk with light probation. Salina was charged and went directly to jail.

There was no way she'd have been able to pay for her own lawyer, so a public defender was assigned. And while the lady seemed nice and sympathetic, she also looked tired and was too busy to even remember Salina's name. Before she knew it, Salina was convicted of a felony and sent to jail and then prison, with a sentence of just over three years. The prosecutor had compounded charges, for the possession as well as for driving with a suspended license. They'd initially also charged her with vehicle theft, but thankfully her friend came through and vouched for her, getting that charge reversed.

After she'd gotten out, when she met Erica and was telling her story, Salina said quietly, "I didn't even realize how lucky I was."

"What do you mean, lucky?" Erica asked.

"I didn't protest or put up a fight. I was so scared when that cop pulled me over, I just did what he said. When he pulled me out of the car, which he had no right to do, I just let him. When he shoved me up against the car to search me and cuff me, I let him. He hurt me, he violated my rights, and he yelled in this high little voice that told me he thought I was a threat. Me. A skinny Black bitch driving the speed limit and laughing with her friends. I wasn't even high yet and I'm so glad. If I'd done anything—anything—that made him think I was loaded, or had a weapon, or was a threat ... I don't think I'd be alive right now. I'm lucky because the guy with a hundred pounds on me, a gun, and body armor was afraid of *me* ... and instead of laughing at him for the coward punk he was, I just let him do it 'cause I knew that's the best way to stay alive."

She got out early, in just under a year, with a felony on her record. Even though Oregon employers aren't supposed to consider felony charges in the hiring process, everyone knows they do. Eventually she did find a job stocking shelves at a Walmart about an hour's bus ride from where she was staying with a friend. But her friend's place was full with her kids and extended family, and Salina knew she'd have to go soon.

About six months into the job, the court changed the day for her in-person check-in. Salina went to her boss to try to get her schedule adjusted so she could make those appointments, and it turned into a minor argument. The next day she was given the boot for poor conduct. She learned later this was common for people who were former inmates; employers could and did look for the smallest irritation and canned them "before it became a bigger problem." And, of course, getting fired makes it *so* much easier to get another job.

Unable to pay her friend the couple hundred bucks she was paying to stay on the couch, she found herself with nowhere to go and no job to pay for anything. She bounced around different shelters, sometimes staying for a while, and sometimes sleeping outside when the weather was okay. Thankfully, she had a probation officer who got it and allowed Salina to not have a permanent address, so long as she always let the P.O. know exactly where she was. Salina also knew she was lucky on that point.

Being young and strong, she was able to do day labor. During spring, summer, and fall, there was usually a lot of work cleaning up construction sites or working as a flagger. It was dirty, tiring work, but it usually gave her enough to keep her fed and to pay for a cheap gym membership so she could shower. But it still left her short of the huge pile of cash she'd need for a deposit and first and last month's rent.

She had finally made it onto a waiting list for subsidized public housing. "But they told me two years ago it's a three-year wait. I'm not crazy, I'm not a drunk or a junkie, I'm not sick, and I'm not old enough or young enough to be a priority. So I wait."

★ ★ ★

Erica was happy she'd found Salina. Staying here at the site, Salina could build up some financial reserves and make a stronger re-entry into the world. Erica hated that people like Doug looked at people like Salina and just saw a threat, instead of seeing a real person with real struggles.

"This guy Doug is out there saying if our project goes through, we're going to take over and colonize every other neighborhood in Portland," Erica said.

"Fuck that guy," Salina said.

"I hear you and I agree with you," Erica said. "But—"

"I know, I know," Salina said. "Don't take my potty mouth into City Hall."

"This just shows," Erica said, "how much they don't know about the work and time and money it takes to make this thing go. They're so afraid and are acting like we have some franchise plan to pop up in every open space. Like we're the McDonald's of homeless outreach."

Sam weighed in from under the platform, where she had crawled to re-attach a board they'd removed. "You should say that in your testimony," she said. But she was holding a couple of screws between her lips, so it sounded more like "meffimony."

"I should compare us to McDonald's?" Erica asked.

"No," Sam said, and tossed a screw out at Erica. It bounced off her knee and landed in the grass. "The fear thing. You should call that out."

Erica picked the screw out of the grass and turned it between her fingers. "Yeah, maybe. I mean, I'm not sure insulting them and calling them cowards is the best approach." She looked at the head of the screw. "This has spit on it."

"Give me that," Sam said, reaching her hand out from under the platform and grabbing for the screw. "It's going to have your blood on it in a second if you're not careful." She fake-jabbed it at Erica. "You kind of made a leap there. I didn't say insult them. Show them what they're doing and why it's wrong."

"Good luck with that," Salina said.

"Well, it's not like anyone else is going to do it." Sam said as she pulled herself out from under the platform. "Now move it. You're distracting us. Either go work on your testimony or pick up a screw gun and be useful."

"You know, you used to be nice," Erica said. She stood up and brushed grass and dirt off her backside, then started walking away.

Sam called after her, "I was never nice!"

"Ha!" Erica shouted back.

CHAPTER 15

Claire sat at the desk in Chris's study, working out a budget for the site. She used pencil and paper instead of the computer, but all the pieces were coming together. Back when Chris was alive and worked in here, she often came and sat on the window seat opposite him, reading. Now she imagined him sitting in her spot while she sat in his.

I should have let you do more of our books, he said. *You seem to be a lot faster at this than I ever was.*

"*Let* me?" Claire laughed.

He chuckled. *I just meant—*

"Oh, I know what you meant," she interrupted, and rested her elbows on the desk, cradling her chin in her hands. "This was always your domain."

She'd worked in marketing for a couple of years before they married, and managed all of her department's budgets. She knew how to do the work of business, and it came easily to her. She just hadn't found a passion for it, and happily let Chris handle all the household books. What she had really wanted was to be a mother and build the strong and connected family she always wished she'd had growing up. She had wanted to build a nest. However, an early miscarriage led to the discovery that she was unlikely to be able to bear her own children. They'd talked about the possibility of donor eggs, implantation, surrogates, or adoption, but never quite got around to it. Claire wasn't opposed to any of those options, exactly ... she just—well, if she were being entirely honest, she would admit that she'd just thought getting pregnant would be easier. She knew mothering was hard; every mother she knew said so. But it also seemed to her like the parents she knew who chose to adopt, or who struggled with fertilization treatments for years on end, had an added layer of difficulty that rarely got acknowledged. Simply getting pregnant and having a baby was—boop!—supposed to be easy. Since she'd never wanted or expected to work for it, she never put in any effort. And then, suddenly, it was too late.

Once it was clear that her childbearing years were behind her, she considered going back to work—but by that time she'd been out of the workforce so long, it just didn't make sense. The business and marketing world she knew had changed quickly and she didn't even know where to start, let alone how to keep up. So, she turned inward and dug into what she knew, which was being Chris's wife and managing their charitable giving. Claire the socialite and philanthropist became her permanent identity.

She gazed at the window in front of her, allowing the soft edges of the reflection to smooth out some of the wrinkles and show her a younger version of herself. She saw his face next to hers and thought back on the years that had led to this point. Claire had heard that you start to forget people's faces once they're gone, but so far she hadn't forgotten Chris. Just like his voice in her ear, she remembered his face clearly. The light caught the back of his hair and she tilted her head toward his so she could rest on his shoulder, but his image flickered.

She sighed. "Stop distracting me, mister."

Chris chuckled a little.

She shook her head and turned back to the budget. Financially, she had what they needed to get this project off the ground—which was good, because she'd essentially told Erica and Sam that if they needed something, she'd make sure they had it. They were so used to working on a shoestring that she trusted them not to overspend, but she also knew they needed to invest enough to make this thing sustainable. In addition to start-up funds, she planned to set up an endowed account to provide ongoing revenue from the earned interest. So many of these efforts, she'd learned, failed because they didn't have commitments for ongoing support. Her financial advisor also encouraged her to work with her attorney to set up a trust that would own and operate the site and ensure its healthy operation into perpetuity.

⋆ ⋆ ⋆

"I kind of hope we don't *need* it into perpetuity," she had told her attorney, after meeting with the financial advisor. "But I don't think this city is solving homelessness anytime soon. So I want to be sure the site's existence is protected as long as it needs to exist. And then if it's no longer needed or the needs change, the operators and residents will get to decide where to direct the funds in a way that will continue to benefit the community."

The attorney told her that was more complicated to do than she thought.

"Well, Alan," Claire replied, "that's why I'm paying *you*. Isn't it?"

He grumbled and continued to push back, telling her the complexity was more than she could grasp. The exchange put her on edge, but she pushed the feeling aside. Alan had worked with her and Chris's legal affairs since the very beginning. He knew her entire situation inside and out, but that was also part of the problem. Since he'd been with them from the beginning and Chris was the "breadwinner," as Alan said, Alan had always disregarded Claire and tried to gloss over important things with her because they were "complicated." It had become much worse since Chris died. Alan just couldn't seem to wrap his head around the idea that she was a competent, intelligent person on her own.

Looking over the desk at Alan, Claire remembered the last time she had been in the office, a few weeks after Chris died. They were finalizing some of the estate work, and Chris's voice in her ear confirmed her discomfort.

He's definitely treating you differently with me gone, Chris said.

"He's always treated me like this," Claire muttered.

"Did you say something?" Alan asked.

"Not to you," Claire said softly.

Alan narrowed his eyes.

Initially, he had told her she didn't need to concern herself with the estate, and he would go ahead and work on some asset transfers to make sure she had a nice "allowance."

"You seem to be forgetting," Claire said to Alan, "that Chris and I wrote our wills together. I know full well that there is no provision for you to parcel out an allowance while I remain oblivious to the rest."

"Claire, you know that's not what I mean," Alan said, and reached out to pat her hand.

She jerked her hand back and shook her head. "Then you're going to need to learn how to be more clear, Alan. And quickly. Because that is literally what you just said to me."

For this meeting with Alan about the tiny home site, Claire was more prepared for him.

You'll hold your own, Chris said. *Like always. He'll realize you aren't someone to push around, and he'll adjust.*

Then Chris laughed. *But you probably don't want to mention we still talk.*

Claire smiled and dipped her head so Alan wouldn't see. She stayed the course and they eventually worked out the language and technicalities to allow as much flexibility for the site as possible, while also trying to protect future operators from problems.

"It's very important that the site be self-governed," she told him. "That needs to be a part of the conditions. I don't ever want it to become something where some outside person or entity can tell them what to do."

Alan looked over his glasses at her.

"Are you sure that's a good idea?" he asked. "What if they make decisions that are ... less than optimal?"

Ugh. Here it was again. "Alan," Claire said, trying to summon her inner diplomat, "you're my friend. You were Chris's friend. We've known each other for years and you have been a lifeline at times when we—when I—really needed it."

"You're welcome, Claire," Alan said. "And I thank you for recognizing that."

"So please know I say this with love." She inhaled. "But you need to check your privilege."

He smiled and sat back in his chair. "You've been learning new phrases."

"I encourage you not to condescend to me right now," Claire said. "I appreciate your help and I want you with me to be sure we get this paperwork right. But please trust me when I say I know more about this project than you do."

He tapped his pen on the edge of his desk. "Well, that is true. You have indeed spent 100 percent more time sleeping in homeless camps than I have."

"*Excuse* me?"

"Tell me," he said, leaning in conspiratorially, "have you learned the secrets of their cuisine? Like cooking a can of soup over an open flame?"

Claire's eyes narrowed, but she stayed still. So Alan leaned in closer.

"Come on, Claire, tell me everything you learned from your time on the streets."

She tilted her head to the side, appraising him. She still didn't say anything.

"Well," he said, straightening up, "I was just trying to have a little fun. You and Chris really have a soft spot for these people, and I'm just glad to see it appears that even though you've gotten way too wrapped up with them, you're still going home to shower, so at least there's that."

Claire smiled. "I'm sure it's just a matter of time, Alan. You know, one of them did show me how to give myself a tattoo with a ballpoint pen, if you want me to show you."

"Seriously?" Alan's eyes widened. "Claire, you didn't!!!"

"Of course not, you idiot," Claire said, and pushed her chair away from his desk. "How dare you speak to me like this?"

"What are you talking about?"

"Alan, we may be in your office, but I'm your client and have been for many years, and your condescension is completely unacceptable."

"I was just having a little fun."

"At my expense. Literally. I pay you well, and not for this."

"You do pay me well, Claire," Alan agreed, and shifted in his chair to straighten his tie and reassert dominance in the conversation. "And as you know, I have several very satisfied clients who do, as well."

Claire eyed him silently for a few beats before speaking.

"So you'd be fine without my business, then."

"Now, Claire," he said. "Don't be irrational."

"Seriously, Alan?"

"What?"

"'Don't be irrational?' Do you have any idea what century it is?"

"Claire, don't get so worked up."

"Don't worry, Alan. I'm not 'getting the vapors.' Let me stop you before you call me 'hysterical.' I'm calm, I'm considered, I'm measured. I'm a client who pays you handsomely to give me good service. And you are failing—spectacularly—in that regard."

"Actually, Claire," Alan said with a low voice, "you pay me to give you good service and good advice. And with Chris gone, I'm just trying to look out for you and help keep you from making emotional decisions you'll regret later."

Claire stared at him for what felt like a very long time.

Finally, she simply said, "Okay."

Alan waited for a little bit more, but when nothing else seemed forthcoming, he smiled and said, "Great. So we'll put in some basic controls and restrictions, and—"

"No, Alan," Claire interrupted. "Not okay, you're right. Okay, you're fired."

"Pardon me?"

She gathered her papers and notes and stood. "Clearly, you are not the right person for this work. I'll let you know where to send my files, and your office can send a final bill to the house. This is our last meeting."

⋆ ⋆ ⋆

Claire trembled in her car in the law office's parking garage for a few minutes after leaving. She'd held it together in the room, walked down the hall and to the elevator with her head high and shoulders back, and strode proudly through the parking garage just in case anyone could see. But as soon as she sat down in the car, she found herself shaking with anger and frustration.

I've always thought he was kind of a prick, Chris said.

"*Now*!?" Claire shouted. "*Now* you say that!?"

Well, we never needed anything a prick like him couldn't do. In fact, sometimes, having a guy like that on your side helps you get a better deal.

"I am coming to hate everything about the world we live in," Claire said, and rubbed her temples.

Had she just tanked the whole project? This was going to be a complicated set of agreements and transactions. Even though Alan was a jerk, he might be the only one who could pull it off—especially in the timeframe they were working with. She needed to find a new lawyer immediately.

* * *

With no idea where to start looking, Claire called a couple of the charity lunch friends who were still speaking to her to ask for referrals. She got a few prospects from those calls, but even more importantly, she activated Portland's high-society gossip mill. The word that Claire was replacing Alan got around quickly, and soon she was swamped with calls from old white men who were looking to snatch up a high-paying client from their friend and competitor.

Those calls at least gave her somewhere to start. Rather than calling those guys back, though, Claire scoured their firms' websites to see who their younger female partners and associates were. She called a few of those women for phone interviews, then met in person with the standout at the top of her list.

Melanie Reyes had a few years' experience and a strong woman mentor at her firm, and she didn't hesitate for even a moment when Claire explained the project to her. She said she thought it was creative and resourceful, and she'd love to be a part of making it a success.

Melanie was a first-generation Filipina American, she told Claire when they met in person after their phone interview.

"My parents came here for a better life for me and my sisters," she said. "They struggled to put us through school and supported us all along the way. We were very fortunate to end up as success stories. But it was touch-and-go sometimes."

"It sounds like you have some experience that will help you identify with this project," Claire said.

"I do," Melanie answered. "But that's not why I want to take it on."

Claire arched her eyebrows as a question.

Melanie shrugged her shoulders. "You shouldn't need to have personal experience with struggle to help people," she said. "You should just help."

Claire hired her on the spot.

* * *

With a new attorney who was committed to the project and quickly getting up to speed, Claire was able to focus on the budget, as well as her task of talking to the City Council. For better or for worse, she'd already talked with the mayor. Moving on to the remaining four councilors, three of those conversations went well. They liked the idea, they liked the management plan, and they also liked that Claire wasn't asking for any money—she just wanted the variance and was handling everything else.

"I can't tell you," one of them said, "how rare it is to get a request that doesn't have a budget impact. So many people complain about paying taxes, but then also think the city has an unlimited piggy bank to take on whatever project they think we need to do."

The fourth councilor was tougher. He had been bankrolled and handpicked by the Portland Business Association, and he worked hard to defend the city's business elite at all costs. Claire had tried to convince him that, with business interests in mind, this should be a no-brainer for him. No public dollars being spent, and ten people who would otherwise be living on the street would be living in a quiet, well-managed place. She made her case as well as she could, but by the end of the meeting, she wasn't sure where he stood. A lot of people in town who called themselves "business-oriented" had simply adopted a "homeless people = bad" mentality. She wasn't sure if he'd give in to that lazy ideology.

⋆ ⋆ ⋆

Claire pushed back from her chair at Chris's desk. She wanted to go back out to the site and see everyone, maybe bring them something to eat. But she also didn't want to hover. She texted Erica to see what might be best.

How is everyone doing tonight? she texted. *Have dinner yet?*

Erica texted back quickly. *Just finishing up, and I'm about to head out. They decided to eat a little early since almost everyone worked through lunch.*

Need anything? Claire asked.

I think it's all good, Erica replied.

Claire looked at her phone and pouted just slightly. There was clearly no reason for her to go to the site. She sighed.

Great! she typed back.

⋆ ⋆ ⋆

With a little more time on her hands and her tasks accomplished, Claire checked the yoga schedule and found she could make it to the last class of the day, if she hustled. It would be good to move her body, and she could pick up something for dinner on the way home.

She checked online to make sure there was space in the class, booked it, and then went upstairs to change clothes.

As she walked up the stairs, she heard Chris's voice.

You okay? he asked.

"Yeah!" she answered. "Going to get a yoga class in. Why do you ask?"

You just ... I'm just wondering. It looked to me like you wanted to head out to the site.

Claire had reached her bedroom and began wriggling into her leggings. "I did. I haven't been out there in a couple days, and I miss it. I miss them." She reached for her sports bra and yoga top.

You've been doing good work for them here, Chris said.

"I know," she said, and grabbed a light sweatshirt before heading downstairs. She weighed walking or driving. Any time she saved driving she'd lose looking for parking, so she grabbed her keys and took off for 23rd Avenue at a brisk walk.

"I miss them, I miss you. It seems like I just need to get used to missing people," she said.

That's one way of looking at it, I guess.

"The way you say that, sounds like you have a different way to look at it."

Maybe.

She waited for him to say more and breathed heavily as she kept the fast pace down the hill, almost jogging.

"So?" she asked when he still didn't say anything.

Another way to look at it is that you're doing your thing. Sometimes that involves them, sometimes it's on your own. Of course, you like them and miss them. They're great. But their lives aren't your life. You're figuring out what's yours.

"But if helping them is part of what's mine, what happens when the project finishes? Who am I then?"

Someone who did an incredible thing.

Claire huffed and kept walking.

And that thing isn't over the day it opens, Claire. You've been more engaged in this project than I've seen you be with anything in a long time. I love seeing it.

"I love doing it, Chris," she said as she rounded the corner and the building with the yoga studio came into sight. "But they're not going to need me after it opens. I'm just sad in advance, I guess, for when I have to say goodbye."

As she passed the corner where she had met Wendi, she noticed a different tent in the same spot. She didn't recognize the person sitting outside but made eye contact and said hello.

You may not have to, babe, Chris said. *This may be a start, not an end.*

"I'm just so tired of it, Chris," she said in a whisper as she slowed her pace. "I'm tired of wanting something—or someone—having them, and then losing them and finding out when they're gone, there's nothing there to fill that space."

In front of the yoga studio, she smiled at a couple of other women rushing in at the last minute, and they all headed up the stairs together.

* * *

After yoga class, Claire waved goodbye to the relative strangers she'd just shared an hour with and was grateful none were walking in her direction. She didn't want to have to make polite small talk.

How was it? Chris asked.

"It was good ..." she said. "You know, it occurred to me that I'm talking to you more today than I have in the last week. Where have you been?"

No offense, babe, he said, *but I'm not the one who can answer that.*

"What do you mean?"

You do remember I'm not really here?

"Of course I do!" she swatted the air.

And you're not delusional or borderline or someone we need to worry about.

"Says you."

Says any medical professional who would examine you. I'm just here when and how you need me. And this last week, you didn't need me that much. So I left you alone.

"I need you all the time, Chris."

Demonstrably untrue. I love that you want me, but you don't need me. You've got everything you need right there.

She shook her head. "Doesn't feel like it."

Look closer. It's all there. You're all there.

"You sound like the yoga instructor tonight," she said.

"How so?"

"At the end of class we were in Savasana, the Corpse Pose, where you just lie there flat, with your palms up."

I'm familiar with it.

"During that part they always tell us to relax and let outside things go while we receive the benefits of the practice we just did. That's fine. It's nice, relaxing, you get out what you put in and all that. I usually kind of tune it out. But she said something different this time and it got my attention."

What did she say?

"It was something like, 'Let everything fall away. That's the beauty and purpose of Savasana. To show us that after everything has fallen away, after everything else is gone, we are still there. And we are enough.'"

That's a great interpretation of that pose, Chris said.

Claire nodded. "I agree. And it made me think ..."

You're still here?

"I'm still here."

She walked along in silence for a few blocks. At the foot of the driveway, Claire looked up at their house.

"I'm still not sure I'm enough and I'm still not sure where I fit, but I'm here."

CHAPTER 16

The day of the City Council meeting had arrived. In the late afternoon, the women piled into their assorted cars and trucks and headed downtown to make the early evening meeting. Some chose to stay at the site, including Wendi, so the kids could keep their bedtime.

As expected, neighbor Doug the Slug had turned out a group of angry opponents. About fifteen people stood in front of City Hall with Doug's "Your Neighborhood is Next" signs. He'd added a few new phrases to the mix, including, "Keep Our Neighborhoods Safe" and "Solve the Problem, Don't Enable It."

"Just ignore them," Erica advised the women as they walked past. "They can't bring those signs inside," she said. "And besides ..." she broke into a huge smile and pointed just ahead of them. "Look at *that*."

Coming down the street from the other direction was a much larger group of people holding signs of support. The signs were all handmade, not commercially printed. These folks had actually taken the time to make their own signs, which said things like, "Everyone deserves a home," "Be a YIMBY not a NIMBY," and "Shelter is a Human Right."

"What's a NIMBY?" Jamilah asked.

"Not In My Back Yard," Erica said.

"What does that even mean?"

Sarah interjected, "It means people like *Doug* don't want people like *us* for neighbors."

"Basically, yeah," Erica said. "Shelter is fine, just not near them."

Jamilah considered it. "So is YIMBY 'yes'?"

"Yeah," Erica answered. "Yes In My Back Yard."

"Or *yaaaaaasssss* in my backyard," Sarah sang.

"Are we really taking her in there with us?" Karyn asked as she flicked Sarah behind the ear.

Jamilah was still pensive. "They don't really mean their own backyards though, do they?"

Erica laughed. "No. They almost never do."

"But they're the ones on our side?"

"For now, at least, yes."

Jamilah considered this. "Well, let's use it while we got it."

⋆ ⋆ ⋆

Inside City Hall, the women craned their necks to look around. The building dated from the turn of the century ("The *last* century," Sarah made sure everyone knew she knew), and a restoration about thirty years ago left the Italianate building's red granite columns and floor tiles gleaming.

"I gone by this place all the time," Karyn said. "I even lived over in the park across the way for a while. I don't think I knew this was City Hall. I know where the jail is next door, but I didn't know what this was."

"I always kind of thought it looked funny at the top," Salina said. "Like someone cut the top off a cake or something."

"Well," Claire said, "it wasn't that. But you're right, something is missing. Back when they built it over a hundred years ago, they ran out of money for a fancy top. So, they just never added it."

"Huh," Salina said as they walked up the wide staircase to reach council chambers on the second floor. "Well, I guess it's nice we aren't the *only* ones they cut the budget on."

⋆ ⋆ ⋆

Inside council chambers, the Council of five sat against a flat wall, facing out at the audience area which sat in front of the rounded wall of windows. The central area was open to the second floor, and an overflow balcony had wooden bench seats. It was kind of impressive and imposing to walk in as an audience member and see the Council up there on the dais in this cavernous, elegant room. Erica and Claire tried their best to reassure everyone this building was made for the public, which also included them.

The seating on the main floor was split into two sections, with an aisle down the middle. As she signed them in to testify, Erica pointed the women to a couple of rows of seats in the middle. She'd arranged with some of the advocates to have their folks sit in front, so the women could sit a few rows back and not feel as exposed as they would if they sat in front. As they filled in, she noticed Doug urging his people to sit toward the front on the other side. Erica noted with some satisfaction that the group on her side was bigger. They spilled over a bit onto his side, and also filled most of the balcony.

⋆ ⋆ ⋆

The mayor banged a gavel and started the meeting. They ran through some routine business and then the mayor announced they'd be considering a housing variance in a residential area.

"This is us," Erica whispered.

The mayor looked out over the room with pressed lips and the corners of his mouth turned up slightly.

"Is he trying to smile?" Sarah asked.

"He looks like he has to throw up," Marta said.

"Both things can be true," Claire said.

The mayor cleared his throat. "Looks like we have a full house tonight." People on both sides of the aisle started clapping and hooting. "Okay, quiet down now," the mayor continued. "Let's remember some of our basic rules here. No shouting, please limit clapping so we can keep things moving, and be respectful of everyone. We are going to have staff present the case here, and then we will open it up for testimony. We'll call you forward, and you'll have three minutes to speak. After that, Council will deliberate and vote."

One of the city planners came up to the microphone at the heavy wooden table in front of the Council dais. He gestured toward a presentation displayed on a video screen, showing a map and photo of the property, and described the variance Claire and Erica were seeking for the project. After the presentation, the mayor spoke again.

"What I'd like now is to have the owner of this property speak and describe their project to us, so we can better understand it." He gestured to Claire. "Mrs. Anderson?"

Claire made her way up to the table, sat down facing the Council, and spoke into the microphone.

"Thank you for the opportunity," she said. "As you all know, I've spoken with you individually to help you understand our project. Before I tell you more about the specifics, I want to talk with you about the context and why we are undertaking this project."

Claire took a deep breath and continued. "I am a major donor to Portland Promise. I give large amounts of money on a regular basis, to support their mission to help end homelessness in our city. I don't say that to get your approval or to prove I'm a good person, but to let you know I am not new to this. I have been doing my small part to find a solution to the problem of people sleeping on our streets because they have nowhere else to go."

She swept her gaze across the Council in front of her. "At least, I *thought* I was doing my part. But as each of you sees, when you come to work here every day and pass dozens and dozens of people who have been forced to sleep on the street—literally, on the *street*—what we are each doing to 'do our part' isn't enough."

Sarah and Jamilah started clapping, and Erica reached over to gently shush them.

"There are people sleeping under overpasses," Claire continued. "In drainage ditches. In tents on sidewalks. Anywhere they can find a space, because we are not holding up our end of the bargain to help them. The things we are doing—the things I have helped privately fund, and that you fund with taxpayer dollars—are important, but they aren't enough.

"This project is an effort to do more." Claire looked behind her and gestured toward Erica. "With the expert management of a young woman who is experienced in delivering services and helping people reach self-sufficiency, we have designed a transitional housing program to help ten individual women get the support and stability they need to address the factors keeping them on the street."

She knew she was giving the councilors a lot of information to digest, so she paused to take a deep breath and let them catch up with her.

"We aren't asking for any public funding, only the variance needed to allow ten tiny homes instead of the two or three single-family residences the code currently allows. As you can see, this will be an attractive, well-managed site that integrates effortlessly into the neighborhood and helps move people out of homelessness and into self-sufficiency. This is a city in a housing and homelessness crisis, and this is one small step to move us toward solutions. We appreciate your consideration and urge you to approve this project. Let's work together to be a part of the continued solution, not the problem."

* * *

Claire returned to her seat and the women leaned in to pat her back and rub her arms, telling her she did a good job. Claire returned the squeezes and pats and settled in for the public testimony. The mayor started calling names on the list. Doug and his people had arrived early and filled the first page of sign-ups. He went first and tried to paint the project site as filthy and haphazard, filled with trash and noise.

"No one wants to help the homeless more than me, I assure you," Doug said.

Sarah rolled her eyes. "Give me a break."

"I truly care," he continued, "but I also care about my neighborhood and the children who will have to be exposed to this element. It's just not appropriate."

"I'll show you something inappropriate," Sarah said a little too loudly.

Erica shushed her. "Knock it off."

After Doug, another handful of speakers regurgitated the same thing: homelessness is bad, but a project to help end it, in their neighborhood, is even worse.

"I get the NIMBY thing now," Jamilah said.

"Do we really have to sit here and listen to this crap?" Sarah asked.

"I told you this part would suck," Erica answered. "Hang in there."

"The City Council is going to think we're a bunch of murderers by the time these people are done," Marta said.

"That's why I put us all last," Erica said. "These people are setting it up, but we are going to knock it down."

After a few more negative neighbors, the positive testimony finally began. People Erica knew from her outreach work spoke about the need for more programs and support. The service providers Erica had recruited described their specialized, targeted services. People she'd worked with on the tent distribution plan testified to her strong management skills and dedication to the work. Many of the neighborhood's residents also testified, noting that Doug did not represent the entire neighborhood, and that they supported the proposal. Erica looked down the row and saw her group loosen up as the testimony went more in their favor. Soon, it was her turn.

Erica made her way to the front and took a seat at the table, facing the Council. She took a deep breath. She and Claire had extensively debated whether or not she should speak tonight, given that the last time she was here she'd yelled at the Council and stomped out of the room. They decided they couldn't ignore it and instead should face it straight on.

Erica smiled. "Mayor," she said. "Council. Good evening." The council looked at her skeptically. "Not too long ago, I sat here before you to defend my actions distributing much-needed tents and supplies to unhoused people."

"Yes," the mayor said. "We recall."

"That conversation didn't go well, as I'm sure you also recall." She gritted her teeth for the next part. Claire had insisted she needed to apologize. Not because she was wrong, but because it was what the Council wanted to hear.

"While I don't regret serving this population with my full heart and ability," Erica said, "I do regret that I lost my temper with you. I care a great deal about this population, and I took it too far. I apologize."

She swallowed and waited. The Council didn't start yelling at her. Two of them nodded and one even almost smiled, maybe a little.

"That's why this project was so appealing to me," she continued. "It helps people who need help, but it takes a more productive approach. If you approve the variance, this project is entirely within the scope and bounds of city policy. It can work alongside other programs and service agencies. We will be helping ten women move off the street and into transitional housing, with all the supports they need to move toward self-sufficiency. And then, once they do move on, a space will open up to help someone else."

She looked up at them, and, to her surprise, they were listening to her.

"A small project like this one allows us to give individual support to each resident," she continued, "tailored to meet their specific needs while also giving them the agency to make important decisions for themselves. This approach is an established best practice, and brings good, long-lasting results. Even better, it frees up space in other public service programs, meaning the system you fund can help more people."

Erica paused again and scanned the council. It looked like they were still with her.

"I will be happy to answer any technical questions, but we also thought you might want to hear directly from some of the women who will be helped by this program."

She gestured for Marta, Jamilah, and Sarah to join her. "None of these women have ever testified at City Council before, so if it's alright with you, I'd like to stay up here with them as they share their stories with you."

Erica looked at the mayor, who nodded slightly.

"Thank you," she said, and showed the three to their chairs at the table facing the Council.

Marta went first, sharing that she'd been on the street for about ten years. She outlined how she'd been injured at work and an over-prescription of painkillers led to a bumpy road of addiction, petty crime to pay for the addiction, and spiraling decline.

"I'd been looking for treatment for five years," Marta said. "That wasn't who I wanted to be. It's not who I am. But it was, like, the only way I was finally able to get help was to go to jail. It shouldn't be like that."

Marta took a breath and continued. "Since I got into the medically assisted treatment program, I've been able to stay off the bad stuff," she said. "But I tell you it hasn't been easy without a regular place to stay. Since we've been staying at the site, it's been so much better. Erica's helping me get to my appointments, I'm getting regular sleep, and I have these other women around me helping me stay the course."

After she was done, their side of the room broke into applause. Marta, startled, looked behind her at the clapping crowd and smiled.

"Thank you," the mayor said. "We appreciate your story. Who is next?"

Jamilah was next up.

"For as long as I can remember," she started, "I had a hard time dealing with people and groups, especially when it would get loud. I'd get overstimulated and act out. I got kicked out of school and fired from jobs. But then when I was on the street, I couldn't even stay in shelters because I ended up ... losing it. I gave up and thought I'd just be living in a tent under a bush. By myself, forever. Not that it seemed like forever would be a real long time."

She shrugged. "It wasn't until Erica here helped me out that we learned I have what they called a sensory disorder and an anxiety disorder. Everybody—including me—thought I was acting out because I was just a bad person. But it turns out I just need to manage my environment real careful. I'm learning how to cope, I got some medicine that helps, and it's getting a whole lot better. But I can't stay in a regular shelter, or one of those big housing complexes. They send me right to the bottom.

"But this smaller thing? With my own place where I can close the door and get away, and where we don't have a ton of people and we have rules for noise and disruption, and I'm an active part of making it work? That works. I tell you it's just like the freshest newest start I ever had. If you let this project happen, you'll be helping me finally sleep all the way through the night, keep a job, and find my way. If you don't pass it ... I don't know what I'll do." Her voice faltered as she came to the end of her remarks. "It'd mean the end of all of it. Just ... the end ..."

Jamilah swallowed and looked around nervously. Marta squeezed her hand and Erica gently rested her hand on Jamilah's shoulder.

"Good job," Erica whispered. "Good job. You okay?"

Jamilah nodded. The advocates in the room clapped, a bit less raucous, trying to be sensitive to Jamilah's sensitivity.

The mayor smiled. "Thank you."

Sarah looked at him and back to Erica. "My turn?"

"Yes," the mayor said. "Your turn. Please go ahead."

Sarah nodded. "So, I ..." She looked at the women next to her and then back to the council. "My story's a little different from these two. I'm not a good person ... I'm not, like, someone who was on a good track and got knocked off it. I've always been trouble. Trouble for my parents, who ditched me, trouble for my foster parents, who also ditched me, trouble for school, trouble for bosses, trouble for boyfriends. I'm pretty messed up and even Erica here gets pissed off—" She looked suddenly at Erica. "Can I say pissed off?"

Erica shrugged and looked at the mayor inquisitively.

"You're okay," he said. "But try to keep it clean."

Sarah nodded. "Even Erica ... gets mad at me ... and she says it's almost like I like screwing up. Even now, I'm not saying the stuff I was supposed to say. We practiced a bunch of times and I can't remember what I was supposed to say and now she's getting piss—She's getting mad at me right now. You can't tell yet, because you're not sitting next to her like me, but I can feel it coming off her like heat waves 'cause it happens a lot when she's talking to me."

Erica rubbed the side of her jaw and whispered, "Pull it together, Sarah."

"But you see how she's, like, so patient with me even though I'm totally bombing this?" She looked at Marta. "I'm bombing this, right?"

Marta shook her head and lowered her gaze.

"But even when I screw up, Erica's there for me. She was there for me when I got pinched the first time, and she's there for me when I gotta get away from some guy, and she's there for me every single time. She told me once that's the whole point of a safety net—it's supposed to catch you when you fall.

"And I fall a lot. Like figural and also for real. I don't mean to, it just happens. But then whoop, there's this net. And that's what she said this place would be. A place where you get a second chance and if you need it a third chance and a fourth chance and even a seventeenth chance. I know I'm a pain in the ass—I mean butt—I mean ... I'm a pain. I don't mean to be but I am. I seriously don't know how she puts up with me because nobody else ever has."

Sarah stopped to take a breath and lowered her voice, slowing down, like she realized the truth of what she was saying.

"These ladies here today and the ones back at the site who didn't come? They're the first people in my life ever who it seems like ever wanted me to succeed. Marta here, Jamilah, Karyn back there—they got no reason to like me, especially the way I act sometimes. But they still got my back. And, like, Wendi, who's not here today cause she's back at the site with her two kids, she's so nice to me. And Sam, and Claire, and—this isn't some crazy, out of control campsite. I've lived in those places—we all have—and this is nothing like that. If you take this away, you're taking away all our second chances, and that's just not right. Even if you don't like me, do it for them."

Erica patted Sarah's hand.

"Was that okay?" Sarah whispered. "I'm sorry I forgot what I was supposed to say. That one on the end with the mean face kept glaring at me."

"You did fine," Erica said. "But shut up now, because the microphone is still live," she said, pointing at the microphone and nodding her head toward the councilor on the end who was frowning at Sarah.

The mayor thanked them all again for coming and for sharing their stories. He asked the three to return to their seats while Erica stayed, and invited Claire to join her.

"Now, we have some questions," he said.

Together, Claire and Erica fielded questions about logistics, operations, and how the site would be funded. They explained the site would be managed by Erica but self-governed. A councilor asked if the group would be willing to sign a "good neighbor" agreement and Claire glanced over at neighbor Doug. Keeping her eye on him, she said yes, as long as the agreement was reasonable and the standard for being a "good neighbor" went both ways.

Then it was time for the vote. One of the friendly councilors moved to approve the variance. After that motion, it was silent.

"Do I have a second?" the mayor asked.

The rest of the council was quiet, and Claire and Erica looked at each other nervously. Without a second, it could die right here and not even get to a vote.

The frowning councilor cleared his throat and leaned into his microphone.

"For the purposes of discussion, I will second," he said.

"What does that mean?" Erica whispered to Claire.

"It means he wants to vote against it but also wants a chance to talk about how bad we are first," Claire whispered back.

"Shit."

"Yeah."

"Okay," the mayor said. "We have a second. Councilor Hughes, you indicated you have discussion points, so please begin."

"Thank you, Mayor," the frowner said. "I appreciate the testimony and wish success to all of you who are trying to make better lives for yourselves. But I just have to say it, we can't let ourselves make bad decisions because we heard a tear-jerker story or two. We have to think about our taxpayers, about our businesses, about the people who elected us."

Erica gripped Claire's hand tightly. "Are you kidding me?" she hissed.

"Ssssshh," Claire squeezed Erica's hand back. "Hang in there."

Hughes sat up straighter and leaned in closer to his microphone. "Look, I'll just say it because no one else up here probably will. It's great that these women are here and trying not to be a drain on society, but for every single one of them, there are ten or twenty more out there who aren't. Just look at our downtown, at our parks, at our freeway ramps. These may be people who need help, but they aren't people we need to bring into our hardworking, respectable neighborhoods."

Doug and his crowd started whistling and clapping.

Erica turned to Claire, eyes wide. "Are we seriously not allowed to respond to this crap? Are you kidding me?"

Claire shook her head. "We had our time. This is their time. We just need to get through it."

Emboldened by the clapping from the NIMBY crowd, Hughes continued. "When people are sleeping on the streets in front of our businesses, our community is harmed. When people are living in our parks, our children cannot enjoy them. And when people are spreading trash and filth all over our freeways, no one wants to come here. We cannot allow this to continue."

"I'm dying here," Erica whispered. "All of that does suck. And it's not what we proposed!"

"Cognitive dissonance is part of his party's brand," Claire whispered. "But look at the other ones' faces, Erica. He's embarrassing them."

Erica looked around at the other council members, and saw Claire was right. One was rolling her eyes, and two were looking down at papers in front of them and shaking their heads. Even the mayor looked like he couldn't wait for this guy to shut up.

But he wasn't shutting up just yet. Hughes continued, "I am all for personal betterment, but we can't just give government handouts everywhere we go. This is a slippery slope. If we allow this variance, then what's to keep more and more of these camps from applying, and infiltrating our neighborhoods? Where does it end?"

He paused long enough for the mayor to interject, "Is that all, Mr. Hughes?"

"Yes, thank you, Mayor."

"Mr. Mayor?" The one who had been rolling her eyes raised two fingers.

"Yes, Councilor Finn. Please go ahead."

"I have a different perspective from my colleague," she began. "It strikes me as more than a little tone-deaf to blame people who have nothing for just trying to get by. If sleeping in a tent with the curb as your pillow is the 'choice' someone is making, then it stands to reason that a lot of things went wrong to get them to that place. Not the least of which is our city's—our country's—disinvestment in the public safety net."

"Oh, thank God." Erica breathed and relaxed slightly.

"Now don't get me wrong," Finn continued. "The situation in the unmanaged camps is appalling. And our businesses and residents need to be able to get to work without incident and enjoy our city's amenities. However, the way to do that is to help the people who have nowhere to go, not to punish and blame them and make things even worse."

Now a round of applause erupted from Erica and Claire's side of the room, accompanied by frowns and boos from Doug and his friends.

"Order!" the mayor said, and banged his gavel. "Councilor Finn, please finish."

"This is a good project," Finn said. "It is a good model for ways we can take small bites at the problem, and I appreciate that the only public assistance they are requesting is a zoning variance. This is not a government handout, but the provision of a tool to make our community stronger."

The other two councilors spoke next. They were not quite as positive as Finn, but they weren't over on the opposite side where Hughes was. The older one raked her fingers through her hair and sighed.

"I've been doing this long enough," she said. "I've seen plenty of good ideas come and go. We will be able to track this program's progress and see how they do. The city makes plenty of accommodations for developers who want to build luxury apartment towers; we can make one small variance for a well-planned project. That said, we also need to be sure we look out for the residents who were already in the neighborhood before this project decided to move in. Balance is everything."

"I'd like to follow up on that," the final councilor said. He was a younger Black man who had just been elected the previous year, having run on a platform of neighborhood involvement. He lived over on the east side, closer to the project site than any of the others. "Taking care of our neighbors and neighborhoods is very important to me. That's what I ran on, and my votes and actions to date have reflected that. I hear and understand the concerns of the neighbors." He made eye contact with Doug. "I know many of you are simply trying to do what you think is right, protecting your investments and looking out for each other. But the thing is, this project is also looking out for people. And the efforts they have made to integrate as seamlessly as possible into the neighborhood are admirable and worthy of respect. If things go south, there are mechanisms to bring them into line. But rather than presume something will go wrong, let's think about what can go right. By providing this variance, we can allow a project that will help ten women who need help. It won't end homelessness; it won't solve the problem. But it will help. And shouldn't every vote we take be an effort to help?"

Erica grabbed Claire's hand again, this time with excitement instead of fear. "Do you think we have the votes?" she asked.

Claire squeezed back and nodded slightly, holding her breath.

The mayor asked the clerk to call the roll.

Erica struggled to sit still. "I have never wanted a cigarette more in my life than right now," she whispered.

"Soon," Claire said.

A few rows back, all the women from the site were holding hands. "Come on, God," Sarah whispered. "Now, please. Do your thing now, please."

The young one voted yes. Hughes voted no. Finn voted yes. The older one paused before giving her vote. "While I don't support the negative arguments made by one of my colleagues," she said, "this does remain a difficult choice for me." She slowly took a drink of water.

Claire rolled out her neck and Erica started tapping her foot on the floor. "Are you kidding me?" Erica whispered.

The older councilor set down her water glass and swallowed.

"The potential rewards outweigh the potential risks. I vote yes."

"*Yes!*" Erica shouted and stood up. The mayor glared at her, and Claire pulled her back down.

"Order in the room," the mayor said, and banged his gavel. "We already have a majority, and I'll add my vote to the mix. I vote yes, and the motion passes. You have your variance."

The room erupted in applause and cheers. The women hugged and high-fived. Neighbor Doug kicked the seat in front of him, then ripped the "Your Neighborhood is Next" button from his polo shirt and threw it to the ground.

Tears streamed down Claire's face and she laughed with relief. She knew she'd been stressed about the decision, but didn't realize how much. She and Erica rushed back to hug the women and congratulate them.

* * *

The mayor banged the gavel again.

"Quiet, please. Congratulations Mrs. Anderson, Ms. Ford, and all the rest of you. You have your zoning variance."

"Thank you, sir," Erica said.

"We did have one more question for you," he said seriously, bringing a hush over the room. "And it's an important one."

"Sir?"

"All this time, you've been referring to this project as 'the project' and 'the site.' Do you have a name for it yet?"

Erica shook her head no. "We've just been trying to make it happen, we haven't thought of a name yet."

"Well," he said, "you all had better get on that."

"Yes, sir," Erica said. "Thank you, sir."

"Meeting adjourned!" the mayor said loudly, banging his gavel. The City Council left the room and everyone on Claire and Erica's side of the room cheered as they poured out onto the street in front of City Hall.

Sam held up her phone as she stepped away from the group. "I need to text the others!" she called over her shoulder.

"Holy shit holy shit holy shit!" Sarah said and jumped up and down on the sidewalk. She jumped onto Erica's back and hugged her from behind. "You're amazing!"

Erica reached around to grab Sarah's arms and get out of her embrace. "What are you doing?" she asked, also laughing. "Get the hell off of me!"

Sarah headed toward Salina, who put up one hand to stop her. "No," Salina said. "We're all happy, but you do not get to crawl on me."

Sarah gave up and threw her arms around her own shoulders to give herself a hug. "This is so amazing!"

"It is," Marta said. "I didn't think they'd do it. When that one Council guy started talking shit about us, I thought it was over."

"Me, too," Jamilah said. "I was totally getting ready to follow him after the meeting and jump him while he was walking to his car."

Claire's eyes widened. "Really?"

Jamilah rolled her eyes and shrugged. "Not really-really, but it was a nice fantasy for a minute."

Claire exhaled.

"Don't worry, Rich Lady," Jamilah smiled. "We wouldn't do you like that."

★ ★ ★

As everyone else hugged and cried tears of joy, Sam came quietly to Erica's side.

"We need to get back the site," Sam said softly.

"Yeah, I can't wait to see everyone else!" Erica said.

"We need to go *now*," Sam said.

Erica realized Sam was not speaking with the same happy excitement as everyone else.

"What's up?" Erica asked.

"Wendi just texted me."

"Did you tell her it went great?"

"Erica, *look*." Sam said and held her phone up for Erica to read the texts.

Help some guy from the state just came and took my kids he took my kids I dont know where they went

Come back

Help me

Erica grabbed the phone. "What the fuck?!"

"I know."

"Get everyone together. We gotta go."

CHAPTER 17

When they arrived back at the site, Wendi was curled into a ball inside her tent. Cheryl, who'd also stayed behind, sat next to her. When Erica entered the tent, Cheryl shrugged her shoulders.

"This is a huge improvement over the screaming," Cheryl said.

"How'd you calm her down?" Erica asked.

"A couple of Xanax."

Erica turned her head sharply to Cheryl.

"The fuck are you doing with Xanax?"

Cheryl held very still and tilted her head just slightly.

"… Helping … Wendi?"

"What the hell, Cheryl?"

"Can we just focus on Wendi here? This is a crisis!"

Erica sighed. She extended her hand. "Give me the rest."

"I don't have any more."

"Bullshit."

"I swear."

"You lie."

"Fine." Cheryl pulled a plastic baggie out of the pocket of her hoodie and gave it to Erica.

Erica looked at the bag's contents: about two fistfuls of colorful, unlabeled pills.

"Christ, Cheryl. Opening a pharmacy?"

"Just doing some spring cleaning."

"Are you sure what you gave her was Xanax?"

"Pretty sure," Cheryl lifted and dropped one hand.

"We're going to deal with this later," Erica said. She stuffed the bag into her own pocket and knelt down by Wendi.

"Hey girl," Erica said as she touched Wendi's shoulder. "Hey, we're back."

Wendi reached her hand up to grab Erica's and pulled it in toward her chest, sniffling. Erica adjusted her position to sit more comfortably while letting Wendi keep her hand.

Claire approached with Sam and the others peeking around behind her. "What happened?" she crouched down and asked through the opening in the tent.

"We were just getting to that," Erica said, settling in next to Wendi. "Cheryl? Why don't you go out there so we aren't so crowded in here, and start telling us what happened. The tent walls are thin enough we can all hear."

Cheryl crawled out of the tent and stood up next to the others who surrounded it. She jammed her hands in her pockets and rocked back and forth on her heels.

"I was just chilling in my tent like the others," she said. Wendi and the kids were over in their area. "They were coloring or drawing or something, and they had some show on her phone they were sort of half-watching. I yelled over they should use headphones or turn it down. It wasn't that loud, but the lady's voice in it was super annoying. You know how sometimes there's just these voices that really bother you and you don't know what it is, but—"

"Fast forward, Cheryl," Sam said.

"Right," Cheryl nodded. "Some lady and some guy showed up and started talking to her. I was in my tent and mostly ignored it till Wendi started yelling. I stuck my head out to tell her to keep it down, but she looked super upset, so I came over to check it out."

Still not opening her eyes, Wendi reached into the pocket of her hoodie and pulled out a crumpled business card, thrusting it into Erica's palm.

"They took them," she whispered.

Erica scanned the card. The man and woman, it turned out, were from Child Protective Services. Wendi cried and clutched Erica's hand. Erica stuck the card in her own pocket, squeezed back, and stroked Wendi's shoulder with her other hand.

"We'll get them back," Erica said softly. "Not tonight, but we'll get them back." She leaned over out of the tent and beckoned Marta to come in.

"You take care of her for tonight?" she asked Marta, who nodded. Erica placed Wendi's hand inside Marta's, exchanged places with her, and crawled out of the tent.

"Everyone else, let's give them some space." She led the group over to the other side of the lot.

Child Protective Services doesn't just show up out of nowhere, Erica explained to them. When they know a kid's homeless, they usually act quickly to get them off the street. But if Wendi was mostly mobile and staying off their radar, it was probably hard for them to keep track of her. At least, until she settled in at the site and stopped moving.

"But still," Jamilah said. "Someone would have to tell them she was here and where to find her, right?"

"Oh my God!" Sarah cried.

"What?" Erica asked.

"It was me!" Sarah yelled. "Oh no! Stupid, stupid, stupid!" She started punching herself in the hips.

"Stop it!" Jamilah yelled, and grabbed Sarah's arms to get her to stop hitting herself. "What is wrong with you?"

"I did it," Sarah sobbed. "It's my fault!"

"You reported Wendi?" Sam asked.

"No, but I talked about her tonight! At the City Council! I mentioned the kids! They heard me and came to get her!"

Erica shook her head. "It wasn't your testimony that did this, Sarah."

"What do you mean? I totally called them out. Stupid!"

Erica paced. "It wasn't you. You mentioned them, what—less than two hours ago? Child Protective Services is a lot of things, but fast is not one of them. Someone called this in a while ago."

She looked across the street at Doug's house. He had arrived home while they were clustered around Wendi. Now he stood next to his front door, arms folded, glaring at them.

"Congratulations on your big win," he called. "But too bad, looks like you lost a couple people along the way."

"You did this, didn't you?" Erica yelled back.

"I don't know what you're talking about," Doug said. After a beat, he added, "But I do know that's no place for children."

"Fuck you!" Jamilah yelled.

"Nice 'good neighbor' language," he called back, and went into his house.

* * *

It took a lot, but somehow Claire and Erica managed to convince the rest of them not to rush Doug's house and tear him to pieces.

"Look," Erica said. "It's after eight o'clock. There's nothing we can do right now. They have the kids and we're not getting them back tonight. Wendi's being taken care of, and we all had a big night. Let's turn in and get some sleep.

With mutters of "Fine," and "I guess ..." the women scattered to their individual tent platforms. Sam, Erica, and Claire stayed behind and walked over toward their cars, parked at the street.

"We were having such a good night!" Claire sighed as she leaned against her car door.

Erica nodded. "We had a good victory."

Then she added, less convincingly, "We can handle this."

"Are you sure?" Claire asked. "Those poor kids! They must be so scared."

"Those kids are tough," Sam said. "They'll be okay. Wendi's going to be a mess for a while, but the kids will be okay."

"I knew she shouldn't be putting those kids through this," Claire said. "Carting them around in the backseat, living in a tent. It's no good. Of course they were taken away."

"Hold up," Sam said, standing up straighter and moving closer to Claire. "What are you talking about?"

Claire shook her head. "I just knew, from the first moment I met her and saw her on the street, and with those kids in the backseat—this is a terrible life for children."

"Claire," Erica said, "you're tired and I think—"

Sam interrupted. "She thinks you should check yourself. First of all, it's not like Wendi had a choice. Like, 'Oh, I just think I'll just go live in my car with my kids for fun, that sounds like a hoot!'"

"Sam—" Erica said, trying to slow her down, and positioning herself in between the two women.

"No, lemme finish," Sam said.

Erica shook her head but stayed in between them, putting her hands up as Sam moved in toward Claire.

"Second of all, they aren't living in a car anymore, Claire. Look around you. Remember this project we are all working on? Remember that?"

Claire stiffened and sucked her her teeth. "I'm well aware," she said slowly, "of what we are doing here. I simply ..."

"You simply think you could do it better than her," Sam said. "Is that it?"

Erica was fully holding Sam back from Claire now, though Claire didn't seem to realize it and just pressed her lips together in response.

"Of course you could, Claire." Sam lunged once toward Claire but then backed off and stepped away, rolling her neck and looking up toward the sky. "Wendi has had to make choices you've never even had to consider in your life. She's doing the best she can, and those kids are loved. It's a total piece of shit for you to be judging her now that something awful happened."

Erica cleared her throat. "Okay, you guys, let's cool it down here."

Claire folded her arms across her chest and swallowed to hold back tears. "It just kills me to see it. Some people can't even have children, and then there are women who can, and their kids have to live like this."

"Don't make this about your shit, Claire," Sam said.

"I'd appreciate you not speaking to me that way," Claire said.

"Look," Sam said, "I'm sorry, and I know you're my boss and you can fire me if you want, but they—we—don't need you judging us like this."

"I'm not—"

"You are."

"Erica?" Claire asked.

Erica looked at Claire, then Sam, and back to Claire. She took a deep breath.

"It feels like you are, Claire," she said. "And it's not a good look."

Claire couldn't hold her tears back any longer and started crying. She put her face in her hands. Sam and Erica looked at each other, unsure what to do.

"You're making this about you, Claire," Sam said.

Erica agreed and said softly, "I know you feel bad. We all do, and we are all stressed out." She put her hand on Claire's shoulder. "But this isn't about you. This is about Wendi and her kids."

Claire sniffled and stopped crying, but kept her head low.

"We all just had a big night," Erica said, "and it's been a long few weeks leading up to it. This is a lot to come back to. Since we can't do anything more about it tonight, we should all just try to get some sleep."

"I'm sorry I cried," Claire said, and avoided their eyes. "I should go."

"Are you okay to drive home?" Erica asked.

Claire wiped her eyes. "Yes, I'm fine."

"Okay," Erica said. "And just to be sure—do we still have jobs?"

Claire sniffled and sort of half-laughed. "Yes, you have jobs. Like I could finish this on my own."

"Go home and get some sleep. We'll talk tomorrow."

"Okay."

They put her in her car and watched her drive away. Sam looked at Erica after Claire was out of sight.

"Did you ever think you'd be in a position where *you're* the one who was the grown-up?" Sam asked.

"Never," Erica said. "This job is so weird."

Sam half-snorted in agreement. "You heading home?"

"Nah, I'm going to stay here overnight. I need to talk with Cheryl first thing."

⋆ ⋆ ⋆

Whenever she stayed at the site, Erica was always the first one up. She crawled out of her tent and started a pot of coffee in the makeshift kitchen. When it was ready, she poured two cups and took them with her over to Cheryl's tent.

"Hey, knock knock," she said softly. She heard Cheryl make some noise and roll over, so she spoke a little louder.

"Hey, Cheryl," she said. "Time to wake up. I made you some coffee, and we need to talk."

She heard Cheryl flop over and pull a pillow over her head.

"Now?" Cheryl said through the pillow. "It's barely even light out."

"Yes now," Erica said. "You going to let me in?"

Cheryl groaned and crawled toward the tent flap, unzipping it halfway. Erica passed a cup of coffee through the opening.

"Coffee for you," she said. "Extra sugar, right?"

"Yeah." Cheryl's hand reached for the cup.

"Can I open this the rest of the way?" Erica asked.

"Fine."

Erica squared herself up with the opening to Cheryl's tent, sitting on the ground cover just outside the tent.

"Nice personal wake-up call," Cheryl muttered.

"I think you know why," Erica said.

"I told you I was just doing some cleaning up and found those pills," Cheryl said.

Erica looked around Cheryl's tent, which was nearly empty except for a stack of clothes and couple small boxes of personal items.

"Not a whole lot here to clean," Erica said.

"I'm real efficient."

"Uh huh," Erica said. "You know we have very few rules here. And the ones we do have were agreed on by everyone, including you. Two big rules were no using and no holding."

"I'm not using!" Cheryl said.

"You're not high right now," Erica said. "But last night I made you turn over this big bag of candy. You telling me you never took a piece here and there?"

"I just found them!"

"I'm kind of insulted by how lame your story is here."

"I'm not bullshitting you," Cheryl said. "I was going through my things and I just found them. I didn't have the chance to get rid of them yet."

"Spring cleaning," Erica said.

"Spring cleaning."

"You realize, of course, that what you had in that bag is a felony, right? And having it here on the site puts every single person here in jeopardy."

Cheryl shrugged. "I was going to get rid of it."

"Yeah," Erica said. "I'll take care of that."

"Seriously, I was going to flush them!"

"You can't flush them; we have porta-potties."

"I know, that's why it was taking me a long time!"

"Did you happen to find anything else I should get rid of for you? While you're spring cleaning and all."

Cheryl avoided Erica's eyes. "No."

"Sure?"

"Yeah. No."

"According to the rules," Erica said, "using or holding means you have to go."

"I know."

"Knowing the bag I took last night is not in your tent right now, are you currently breaking any of our rules?"

Cheryl shrugged. "No."

"Are you positive?"

Another shrug. "Yeah."

"If I learn you're lying to me now, or something new comes back to the site with you," you're going to have to leave."

"I know."

"I want you to stay here, Cheryl. I want you to be a part of this group and help us make it successful."

"Me, too," Cheryl mumbled.

"Other people are starting to wake up," Erica said. "Why don't you get up and start making some breakfast?" She moved to the side.

"Fine," Cheryl said, and crawled past her to get out of the tent.

Erica sighed and stood up, brushing off her seat with one hand and holding her coffee with the other.

"Just hold it together a little while longer, Cheryl," she whispered, then followed behind to get another cup of coffee and have a cigarette. This was going to be another long day.

CHAPTER 18

Over the next hour, everyone at the site except Wendi started to rally. They all agreed to let her sleep as long as she could, and tried to keep the noise down in the common area as they drank coffee and ate breakfast. The quiet didn't last long, though. Sam's truck pulled up on the street in front, then turned and started backing up onto the lot, hopping the curb and reversing slowly toward the central area.

Everyone scattered, grabbing their cups and chairs.

"Stop freaking out!" Sam yelled out her window. "I'm not going to run you over!" She stopped and turned off the ignition.

"Calm down, people," Sam said as she hopped out of the truck. "We've got—well, *you've* got—a lot of stuff to unload here, so I thought you'd appreciate not having to carry it as far." The back of her truck was stacked with lumber and hardware. She reached in behind her front seat and grabbed a cardboard box full of work gloves.

"Grab some gloves, make sure you have closed-toe shoes on, and let's get to work." She opened the box and walked around, tossing a pair of gloves at each woman.

Sarah tossed her gloves back at Sam. "Um!" she called. "We are in the middle of a emergency! What are you doing?"

Sam stopped and looked around. "We can do two things at once, you all. It's—" she pulled out her phone and looked down at it. "Nine fifteen. Protective Services just opened, and if I know Erica, she's already made like four calls to different people who can help Wendi with her kids."

"Okay!" Karyn said. "If they just opened, then we better get down there!"

Erica interjected. "Actually, Sam's right. I made a bunch of calls, and I'm on it. Going down there right this second won't help us."

"So ..." Linda said, "you're just trying to keep us busy?"

Sam snorted. "Whatever. This isn't busywork. We got real work to do. The thing with the kids sucks, but you do remember they gave us our variance last night, right? I ordered the modular unit before I left home this morning. The foundation work starts tomorrow, and the building should be here in less than two weeks. And I stopped at the yard and picked up as much lumber as I could fit, so we can get started on the houses before the main order arrives."

She looked around and slapped a pair of gloves on the cardboard box for effect. "Come on! That truck isn't going to unload itself!"

Slowly, and with no small amount of grumbling, the women started pulling on their gloves and heading toward the truck.

Erica walked over to Sam and smiled. "Thanks," she said. "I know it's not busywork, but we did need something to keep them occupied."

"I know," Sam grinned. "*That* I can help with. We have plenty of work to do."

She looked over at Barb and Heather chatting as they carried one 2x4 board together.

"Especially at that rate."

* * *

Near lunchtime, the truck was unloaded and everything was sorted into piles.

"It's time for me to hire the extra folks I need to get this done," Sam told Erica. "Do we still have budget for that?"

"Yep," Erica said. "We planned for that, and even though Claire isn't here to confirm, she did tell us if we needed it, we could have it. So, yeah. Let's get this thing built in a few weeks, not a few years."

"Agreed," Sam said. "And hey—would it be okay if I offered Salina a job on the crew? She's been awesome and even though she doesn't have the experience, she's learning fast."

"Yeah," Erica said. "If she wants it. We just need to be sure when she's working, she's working and when she's off, she's off. Clear expectations and all."

"Totally," Sam said. "If she likes this and is as good as I think she'll be, she might be a great candidate for the apprentice program I did."

"I love that. Talk to her about it and let me know how I can help."

Sam went to find Salina and start making calls, and Erica went to check in on Wendi.

* * *

Wendi had woken up, groggy, in the middle of the morning. Since Marta's back exempted her from hauling things out of the truck, Erica had asked her to stay with Wendi.

As Erica approached Wendi's tent, she heard them talking softly.

"Hey, it's Erica," she said gently. "Can I come in?"

"Yeah, come on in," Marta said.

Erica knelt at the tent opening and sat just her rear end inside, leaving her feet with shoes on outside.

"How we doing?" she asked.

They were sitting side by side at the back end of the tent, propped up on a huge pile of pillows. Marta had her arm around Wendi's shoulders and Wendi rested her head on Marta, who was rocking gently, almost imperceptibly, side to side.

"We're doing okay," Marta said. "Right, Wendi?"

Wendi was silent.

"A little talking, a little water," Marta said. "A lot of crying, but that seems to be slowing down."

"It's about lunch time," Erica said. "Why don't you come out and join us? I made some calls and found out some stuff. Everyone else wants an update, too. We all love Ella and Theo, *almost* as much as you do."

Marta looked down at Wendi and squeezed her shoulder. "What do you say? Your butt's gotta be sore from sitting here all morning."

"I guess." Wendi rubbed her face and sat up. "They all sound happy out there."

"They're working to keep their minds off the kids," Erica said. "And they're worried about you. Come on. Let's go out there and get you some fresh air."

Erica backed out of the tent and stood up. As Wendi and then Marta emerged, she helped them to their feet.

"I can't tell you how ready I am for a real house," Marta said to Erica as she stood. "I was too old for this shit like fifteen years ago."

* * *

The group's meals were usually staples that were easy to prepare in large quantities without a real kitchen, like pasta or soups or pots of rice and beans. But nobody had remembered to start cooking today, so they kept it simple with sandwiches, apples, and chips. They ate in a loose circle around the common area. Some were on lawn chairs, others sat on the ground.

"Where we're sitting," Sam said, "is going to be the backyard of our common building in less than two weeks. I can't wait till you all have a kitchen and bathrooms and a dining room."

"*You* can't wait?" Jamilah said. "That line starts over here."

"Right behind me," Heather said.

"No, I think you're behind me," Salina said.

"Whatever," Marta said. "*All* of you behind *me*."

They laughed, and someone tossed a plastic knife at Marta, who deflected it with her paper plate.

Silence settled in, and then Sarah spoke up.

"Are we ever going to talk about it?" she asked. "About the kids? About that shithead across the street and the people who came and stole the kids in the middle of the night?"

Wendi started crying again and Marta pulled her close, rocking her and cooing gently.

"We are," Erica said. "I wanted to be sure we all talked together."

"So what do we do?" Sarah asked.

Erica set her plate down and cracked her neck as she assembled her thoughts.

"Here's what I've got," she said. "My people at the state said Child Protective Services doesn't just come and take your kids away on their first visit. They wouldn't tell me more specifically about Wendi's file, but they told me that."

"Apparently they do!" Wendi cried and stood up. "They just grabbed them last night!"

Marta reached for Wendi and brought her back down to the chair.

"This is a such a mess," Karyn said. She rose to her feet and started pacing back and forth. "Why do we even think we can open this place? This whole thing is going to fall apart."

"Hey, now," Erica said. "Not necessarily."

"What are you talking about?" Salina asked. She pushed herself back into the grass, resting on her forearms. "Of course it is. They. Took. Her. Kids."

Karyn nodded. "We might have got the permit or variation or whatever, but they are going to shut us down! They're going to take this away just like they take everything else away!"

Salina pulled out her phone and started scrolling through it for a phone number. "You know, it's early in the day. We can probably get most of us on a list for some of the shelters."

Sarah sank back in her chair and groaned. "Uggggggghhhhh, I don't want to go back to a shelter! But I also don't want to go back to Delta Park. This place spoiled us, Erica. You let us think this would work and we'd be able to get out and now we're going back worse than before. We lost good spots in line at the shelters, we lost good spots at the camps, Wendi lost her damn *kids*." Her voice got higher and higher. "The only person you can trust is yourself, and I totally forgot that and *now* look where we are!"

Jamilah was leaning forward in her lawn chair, resting her elbows on her knees with her head in her hands. "Hold up, hold up. You guys are freaking each other out and it's making me freak out, so just shut up for a minute."

"Come off it, everyone," Erica said, clearly frustrated. "I say this with love, but could you please just shut up and pull it together for a minute." She stood up and walked around behind her folding chair, putting her hands on the seat back and leaning into it.

"Salina, put down your phone for a sec. Sarah, Karyn, come back over here. Wendi ..." She looked at Marta, who was stroking Wendi's hair as she cried. "Wendi, stay where you are but listen."

"Look, you all," she continued. "CPS taking Wendi's kids is huge, I know."

Wendi lifted her head to take a breath and then sobbed and buried her face deeper into Marta's shoulder.

"But this isn't the end of the line," Erica said.

"Psh," Salina objected and shook her head.

"It doesn't have to be, at least."

Karyn rolled her eyes. "Tell that to the two kids locked up in some foster dungeon right now."

Wendi cried harder and Marta tossed her empty plastic water bottle at Karyn's head.

"What?" Karyn asked. "I'm not wrong."

"I blame the rich lady," Sarah said. "She's the one who got our hopes up." She looked around. "Where is she, anyway? Everything falls apart and she splits? Typical."

"Come on," Erica said. "You know she's not always here. *You* live here, not her."

Salina made a sucking sound against her teeth. "No offense," she said, "but trusting you, and her, is what messed us up in the first place." She sat up. "Thanks for the charity, but I'll take care of myself from here."

Karyn nodded. "Yeah, I think I got this. I mean, I'll keep the new sleeping bag, but I don't need anything else that'll just get taken away from me."

"Maybe *you* don't, but I could use like fifty bucks," Sarah said.

Jamilah laughed and rubbed her forehead. "Sarah," she said.

"What?"

"Nothing," Jamilah said. "Everything. It's just ... You're very *you*."

Sam stood up. "Oh, for fuck's sake, you guys!" She banged her hand on the closed metal lid of the cookstove. Everyone stopped to look at her.

"This situation sucks," Sam said. "I know it, you know it, and that dillweed Doug is over there across the street laughing his wide load off because he knows it, too. But *this* woman," she pointed her empty soda can at Erica, "this woman has done everything in her power and some things totally not in her power to get you here today. And she's trying to give you some kind of inspirational speech to get through this, but you keep interrupting her by freaking out. Knock it off!"

Sam ran her hand through her hair and sighed. "Look, it hasn't been that long since I've been exactly where you are."

Sarah smirked. "Um, you *are* where we are right now. We're all in the same place."

"Shut it, Sarah," Sam continued. "I know something about every single one of you that not many people know."

"What, my Social Security Number?" Sarah asked.

"Seriously, Sarah. I will throw. This can. At your head. And I have very good aim."

"Sorry."

"You all have been through the worst shit," Sam said. "You've dealt with things most people never have to even think about."

"Except the rich lady," Sarah said.

Sam crushed the can and held it overhead.

Sarah put up her hands. "Okay, okay."

"Even the rich lady," Sam answered. "She's been through some shit, too. And going through hard stuff makes you hard. It makes you put up walls and barriers and build your muscles and get smarter and get faster and learn how to survive it. You. All. Survived it."

She looked around and kept going. "But here's the thing I know that most people don't: being that strong and that tough is exhausting. And it's scary. And it doesn't leave you with much left to work with. And that's part of why, sometimes, we go back to what's comfortable. We go back to the drugs, or the drinking, or the bad boyfriend, or the being an asshole to everyone we know. Because we know it might not help, but it's how we survive. It's what we know."

Sam looked over at Erica and Erica nodded, *keep going.*

"But I'll tell you what," Sam said. "You have a 100 percent track record for surviving even the worst day. This, right now? This is hard. And it's hard in a different way from the last hard thing you had to deal with. And what makes this hard thing right now different is none of us will be able to get through it alone. We all need each other to get through this one. So you can take off if you want, and go back to the hard thing you're comfortable with. Or you can stay here and fight for yourself, and for all the other people you see here."

The women were silent, looking at Sam expectantly.

Sam looked back at them.

"So now would you all just shut up and let Erica give her inspirational talk?" she asked.

Jamilah started cracking up and everyone else joined.

"What!?" Sam yelled.

"I, uh ..." Erica said. "*My* inspirational talk?"

"Yeah," Sam said.

"I think you just gave it for me," Erica smirked.

Salina put her phone down and slumped back. "Fine," she said. "I'll give it a couple more days. It's better here than some nasty campsite or shelter."

Wendi lifted her head and wiped her nose with the back of her hand. "How are you going to help me get my kids back?" she asked.

"First we need to figure out what happened," Erica said.

"*CPS took them!*" Wendi cried.

"I know," Erica said. "But I mean before that. They don't just come and take your kids on the first visit. Had you ever seen them before? Not those exact people, but people from Child Protective Services?"

"No, never," Wendi said. "I mean, a year or so ago when we were staying in a church parking lot, someone came by. But I moved the next day and then went all the way to the suburbs and stayed there for a while, and I haven't been back to that church since."

"But nothing recent? Here at the site? They had to have come by sometime."

"No, never."

Sarah raised her hand. "Um ..."

"Sarah?" Erica asked.

"Well, remember last week when you all went to the food pantry and the clothing warehouse on shower truck day?"

"Yeah ..."

"And I stayed here and watched the kids?"

"Yeah ..."

"I forgot to mention it, but someone came by while you all were gone."

Wendi screamed, "Seriously?" and started to lunge at Sarah. Marta held her back.

Sarah also screamed. "I forgot! And it didn't seem like a big deal!"

"Oh my God," Wendi started sobbing and buried herself in Marta's shoulder again.

Jamilah glared at Sarah and threw a water bottle at her. "How did you think CPS visiting was not a big deal?"

"I didn't know that's who they were! It's not like they wore T-shirts saying, *I'm here to take your kids.*"

"Tell me what happened," Erica said.

"They're going to keep throwing things at me."

"Maybe," Erica said. "Tell me anyway."

"So, the kids and I had the ball and were playing out on the lawn there," she said, and pointed toward the area in between them and the street.

"We were just kicking it back and forth and there was a car parked at the street, watching us. When they saw me looking at them, this man and woman came out and said hello. I said hey and they asked if they could ask me a couple questions. I said no, because that was weird. But Theo kept looking at them, and they didn't go away.

"They asked if I was the kids' mom, and I said none of your business, but Theo said no, my mom's at the food pantry. I told him to shut it, and then they asked if we lived here. I said none of your business, but then Theo said yeah and asked if they wanted to see his sleeping fort. I told him to shut up—"

She looked quickly at Wendi. "I mean, I didn't, like, yell at your kid to shut up, I just told him to be quiet. And then I said no, they're strangers and they're not invited and then I took the kids around to the back and made them get into the tent.

"While we were in there, I told Theo not to talk to strangers. And I want to point out that when I said don't talk to strangers, he said to me 'Well *you're* strange,' and that was very rude.

After a little while I looked back out at the street, and they were gone. You guys didn't get back for another couple of hours and I figured it was just weird neighbors or friends of Doug the Slug, and I forgot about it."

Erica nodded. "That had to be them."

"I can't believe you didn't tell me," Wendi said.

"I'm sorry! I didn't know. They looked like weirdo creepers, not the kid police."

"Okay, look," Erica said. "Here's what I think happened. Doug the Slug called CPS and told them to come check it out. That was the visit when Sarah was here. They saw the kids and got confirmation you're living here."

She thought back to that day. During that time, they were building the platforms. "They must have also seen it was an active construction site and could be dangerous for kids."

"But we were always so careful!" Wendi moaned into Marta's shoulder.

"They can't take your kids away just because you're homeless," Erica said.

"Apparently they can!" Linda said.

"No," Erica continued. "They can't take kids away for being homeless, but they *can* decide that where you are staying isn't safe—and take the kids away for that. This is good. I needed to know this. I'm going to make some more calls and see if I can figure out who came out here and get ahold of the social worker they assigned to your case. We may be able to work this out. We're building real homes here. And it may not be safe right now, but it *will* be."

Wendi wiped her eyes and sat up. "Wherever they are, they must be so scared."

"We'll figure it out, okay?" Erica said. "Now what you need to do is get yourself cleaned up, and help Sam. Keep yourself busy. Same for all of you. Let's keep working on the site and get it done."

She paused and looked at Marta, whose shoulder and chest were damp with Wendi's tears and snot. "You may want to change your shirt before you do anything else."

Marta looked down and laughed, "Truth."

CHAPTER 19

Erica didn't love what she learned from her friend who worked for the state. She also didn't love that Claire wasn't returning her calls. Claire had been shaken up when she left the site two nights before, but it was weird for her not to be in touch. She always responded quickly. Yesterday, though, she was radio silent all day. Erica texted, called, even tried emailing that night, thinking maybe Claire had lost her phone or something. This Wendi situation was bad enough, she did *not* need to be dealing with an AWOL Claire now, too.

After fuming for a while about Claire's absence, she eventually settled down and thought maybe it would be okay, at least for now. She checked the bank; Claire may have disappeared, but she hadn't cut them off. It felt a little mercenary to say, but as long as she still had access to the bank account, she could manage.

Erica left yet another voicemail for Claire, texted her, and emailed again. As soon as she could break free, she planned to drive over to Claire's house to see what was up. But for now, she had too much else to do from her makeshift office inside the cab of her truck, parked at the site.

Her phone rang with a State of Oregon number, and she answered immediately. Her friend at the state had connected her with a woman named Dara at Child Protective Services. This personal referral was huge; talking to the wrong person about the wrong thing at CPS could do more harm to Wendi and her kids than help. Even on a good day, CPS was understaffed and under-supported, and the staff were often exhausted and prickly. Dara, Erica's friend assured her, was like Erica: someone who went above and beyond to help clients.

"For privacy reasons, I can't talk with you about specifics of Wendi's case," Dara said. "But if you describe a current situation to me, I can give you my best assessment of what I think a normal CPS operating procedure might be, and how someone might navigate it."

Erica explained that while Wendi had previously been living in her car, she was now a resident at the site. The residents were currently living in tents, but they were in the process of building tiny homes. Wendi and the kids would have their own place and be connected to a supportive community with direct services to help her find stable employment while the kids were in school, and the plan was that they would eventually move to their own apartment.

"That's all great," Dara said. "I mean seriously, this sounds like an awesome project."

"Thanks," Erica said. "I'm excited about it."

"But the court isn't going to see a tent as safe and stable housing."

"We can build her house first," Erica pleaded. "We just got started on the build, and I know we could have it done in like a week. Would that help?"

"You're building all of them from scratch, right now?" Dara asked.

"Yeah," Erica said. "I mean, we have the platforms done so now we just need to build the houses on top."

"So ... even after you finish Wendi's place, it'll still be an active construction site while you finish the other houses?"

Erica looked around, taking in the lumber and tools strewn around the site. It was well-organized under Sam's direction, but there was no way anyone would call it "kid-safe."

"Shit," she muttered.

"Sorry," Dara said. "I don't want to give you false expectations."

"No, I get it," Erica nodded.

"Do you think you'll be totally complete and done within a month?"

"We're trying, but it'll be tight."

"So here's what I think will happen. I'm going to assume you won't be done within a month, because when you said it just now, I didn't believe you."

"Gee, thanks."

"No offense. I do this every day, and wishful thinking doesn't get kids back to their moms."

Erica sighed. "Fair."

Dara's keyboard clacked as she looked up Wendi's case. "There's going to be an initial hearing to determine foster placement. It should be within a few days, but hard to say when."

"Where are the kids now?"

"I can't tell you where specifically, but kids in a situation like this generally go with one of our emergency foster families. They take kids during this time right after they are picked up, temporarily before they either go back to the family or go to a longer-term foster placement."

"So what's this hearing for?"

"To determine whether they should go to a longer-term foster. If Wendi weren't unhoused or it wasn't a construction site or this was some kind of clerical error, it *might* be possible to intervene at that hearing and possibly get them back. But that happens like literally maybe once a year. And given what you've told me, it's not worth spending our time on."

"Wonderful." Erica sank lower in her seat and massaged her forehead with her fingertips.

"At this first hearing they'll get the assignment to go to a new foster place. Then thirty days after that, there's supposed to be a check-in hearing. That's why I asked about the month. If you thought it could be totally fixed up and ready to go, and Wendi could be stable by then, it'd be long-shot possible to get them back at that time. And I'm not exaggerating when I say long shot."

"So we should try for that."

"Girl," Dara said flatly. "You can try for it, but seriously if it's not a realistic possibility, I wouldn't get everyone's hopes up. Again, no offense. I just don't want to bullshit you."

"Good point," Erica said. "But say we try for that. Then what?"

"Well," Dara said, "the next landmark is ninety days. During the first few weeks, Wendi will get a social worker assigned. They'll develop a safety plan, with all the things she needs to do. That ninety-day hearing will judge how she did with the plan."

"So if she gets it all done, she could get them back then?"

"Yes."

"And is that realistic?"

"It's plausible. Not the most common, but I've seen it happen. It depends what's in the plan."

"What kinds of things are in the plan?"

"It's always really specific to the family—but some of the things, based on what you're telling me, would be things like no physical dangers at the site, checking backgrounds, making sure their house is safe, and documenting that Wendi has additional supports to help her succeed. Given what you've described, that should all be fine. Then there'll be stuff like getting any treatment she might need, and starting to earn steady income. Also, I imagine they'd want the kids to get into trauma treatment as well. Even if they're good kids, they've been through a lot and that's pretty standard now ..."

Dara's voice trailed off like she was a little distracted. Erica waited, but when Dara didn't keep talking, she jumped in.

"Alright," Erica said. "This sounds like it might be a little overwhelming to Wendi, but yeah, we have a good community here and we can help her out. Thanks. You've helped ease my mind. Now I just need to figure out how to tell Wendi and everyone else."

"Erica?" Dara asked with an edge that wasn't in her voice before.

"Yeah. What's up?"

"Does Wendi have an ex-husband?"

Erica froze. "She has ... I think technically he's still her husband."

"So ..." Dara swallowed. "I need you to be really judicious with this information because I am *not* supposed to be sharing this file."

"What is it?"

"Seriously. I could lose my job and it could hurt Wendi's case."

"Shit, what is it, Dara?"

Dara exhaled. "They, uh, they found him and contacted him since he has right to custody."

"*What*?"

"Yeah. Looks like staff have left him messages but haven't connected yet."

"He beat the shit out of her, and she ran away. She miscarried he beat her so bad. Those kids can't go to him, Dara."

"I hear you, but they are technically still married, and there is no formal complaint, restraining order, or proof of abuse. On paper, she's the one at fault."

Erica sank further into her seat and banged her fist against the truck door. "I hate this system."

"You and me both," Dara said, and took a breath. "Look, do what you need to with that info to keep Wendi safe. But also know you did *not* get it from me. I can't help you if I get fired."

"So is the court going to give him custody?"

"It could happen."

"Shit."

"But …" Dara said and sounded far away again, like she was looking up more information. "It looks like he hasn't replied to them yet. That's good. If he hasn't turned up by the first hearing, then you have a little time. Maybe not long, but a little time to breathe."

Erica rubbed her forehead. "This keeps getting better and better."

Erica could hear Dara typing.

"Let me see what I can do here," Dara said. "The sooner we can get her hearing scheduled, the less chance the husband will have to show up. I think I can get her moved up without bumping anyone else or breaking rules."

"You're amazing," Erica whispered.

Dara typed some more, and Erica heard her murmuring to herself.

"Hey you know what?" Dara asked abruptly. "Let me go do this. You don't need to listen to me type. Make sure Wendi is ready to go the hearing soon. I think this'll work. It may not be tomorrow, but I bet I can get it the next day. I'll text you when I know anything, but expect to get a call from the system scheduler soon."

"Oh my God, thank you," Erica said.

"No sweat," Dara said. "What good is knowing the system if you can't use it to help people? Now get busy."

★ ★ ★

Erica tossed her phone into the passenger seat. She straightened herself up and then knocked her head against the headrest a few times. Bracing herself to get out and talk to Wendi, she looked down at her phone. A couple texts had come in while she was talking to Dara. One was from Claire.

So sorry, Claire's text said. *I got wrapped up in a few things here. I'll be by soon. Keep me posted!*

Erica shook her head. Glad you're alive and all, but way to bail when things get hard, lady. She sighed and typed a reply.

We are going to have a hearing for Wendi's kids tomorrow or the next day. Will be at least a month, more like 3, before she gets them back. Wld be nice if you were here to support.

★ ★ ★

Claire inhaled sharply when Erica's text came in. She was sitting at the desk in Chris's study. She felt bad for ignoring most of Erica's texts and calls, but she knew they'd be fine without her. She needed to put all her focus on those kids.

They did not belong in foster care. They needed a real home. She imagined seeing them playing in the living room or running through the backyard. Who knew what the foster system would bring? She had the space right here.

In the time she'd been gone from the site, she'd been busy. She'd contacted her new attorney, Melanie, and worked out a plan to get Claire qualified as "friend of the family" foster parent for Ella and Theo.

When she finally replied to Erica's calls and texts, she had just received confirmation she'd been approved. Melanie had advised her not to appear for the preliminary hearing, but to be there right afterward to get the kids. Claire knew she should tell Erica. She almost made the call and sent the text a few times, but she just couldn't bring herself to do it. Erica would tell Wendi, Wendi would want to either get the kids or come here to be with her and the kids, and ... for at least a little while, she just wanted to get them alone and give them a taste of the life she thought they deserved. So she sent the upbeat, content-less text, and lied by omission.

"I know she thinks I'm blowing them off."

Then tell her you're not, Chris said.

"I don't want to tell her until we know it's for sure and those kids are safely here," Claire said.

Don't you think the kids' mother should know?

"Maybe," Claire said. "But not if it doesn't work. We don't know how the court will react."

Not a good reason to keep it from them.

"It'll be fine."

Claire.

"It's better this way."

Claire.

"What?"

You're not thinking those kids can stay with you permanently, are you?

"Of course not," Claire huffed.

You sure about that?

"I just want to know they're safe."

Their mom is Wendi.

Claire nodded.

Not you.

"I know that."

Claire nodded again and started to make a list of kid-friendly groceries to pick up.

"I know that."

CHAPTER 20

Erica was walking over to Wendi's tent to tell her what she had learned. She stopped when she saw Heather frantically pacing back and forth, with most of the women from the site clustered nearby, trying to talk to her.

"Great," Erica muttered. If Heather was freaking out, it was probably about Cheryl.

Heather rushed over to Erica and grabbed both of her hands.

"Let's go to Delta Park," Heather begged. "I'm sure she's there. Or maybe at the camp off Irving by the freeway, she likes that one a lot, too. Come on, it's going to get dark soon."

"Whoa," Erica said, removing her hands from Heather's grip and placing them gently on Heather's shoulders to steady her.

Heather let Erica's hands rest there for a moment, then shook them off. "Come on!"

"Heather," Erica said kindly, "slow down." She put a hand on Heather's elbow and gently steered her back toward the waiting group of women.

"Tell me what's going on," Erica said as she guided Heather into a chair and took a seat next to her.

"She's gone," Heather said.

"Who's gone? Cheryl?"

Heather rolled her eyes like, *Obviously.*

"How long has she been gone?"

"Since yesterday morning," Heather said.

"Did she tell you when she left?"

Heather pressed her lips together and tilted her head. "Sort of."

"What does 'sort of' mean?"

"It was after you took her stash. She was pissed."

Erica nodded. "I was pissed, too."

Heather nodded. "She didn't tell me, but you know she was going to sell or swap that stuff to upgrade."

"That's what I figured, too," Erica said.

"After breakfast yesterday she said she was just going to visit a friend."

Erica nodded.

"I offered to go with her," Heather continued, "and she said no. Which was weird, because we have all the same friends."

Salina interjected, "So you knew when she left, and you knew what she was probably going to do."

Heather half-nodded and avoided making eye contact.

"You could have said something then, you know," Linda said.

"It's not against the rules to leave and go see friends!" Heather bolted upright and shouted.

"Yeah," said Barb. "But you knew that's not what was going on."

Heather slowly slumped back into her chair.

"I know." She took a ragged breath. "I know. I was just hoping she'd get it out of her system and come back."

Erica gave her sort of a half-smile. "Because that's how it works? People just 'get it out of their system' and things are fine?" she asked.

Heather shoved Erica. Not too hard, but enough to move her. "Fuck off."

Erica scooted closer. "No, I'm serious. Is that how it works?"

Heather's eyes hardened as she looked at Erica and she pushed again, harder.

"I'm serious, too. Fuck. Off."

Erica didn't move, and held Heather's gaze.

"No."

They stared at each other for a couple of seconds that felt like minutes, and then Heather grabbed her chair and scooted back about a foot. She pulled her knees up under her chin and hugged her arms around her legs.

Erica eased back in her chair. They may have lost Cheryl, but she didn't want to lose Heather, too. In conversations like this one, finding the balance of pushing just hard enough but not too hard was always tricky, and the target was constantly shifting.

"Has anyone heard from her since she left?" Erica asked.

"No," Heather said, and hugged her knees in tighter. "Right?" She looked around the rest of the group. "Has anyone heard from her or seen her?"

The others shook their heads.

Erica nodded. "Has anyone else tried to reach her?"

"Yeah," Salina said. "We all tried calling or texting."

Erica took a deep breath and let it out slowly, and took Heather's hand. "And she hasn't replied, or reached out to anyone herself? She hasn't called to tell you where she is, or to ask for help?"

Heather shook her head and started to cry.

"So we have no idea where she is or what she's doing," Erica said.

It was a statement, not a question.

Heather shook her head again. "But I'm sure I can find her. I know her favorite places. She probably needs our help! What if her phone is dead? What if she's hurt? What if she O.D.'d?"

Erica squeezed Heather's hand and stood up. She went over to the women who were gathered and spoke with them quietly, then they all came back and gathered in a tight circle around Heather.

"You guys, it's getting dark," Heather said. "We need to start now. If we take both your trucks," she pointed to Sam and Erica, "we can get to more places."

"Heather, hon," Marta said gently, "that's not something we are going to do tonight."

"Okay, fine," Heather said. "I get that it's getting dark. So tomorrow morning. We can get up super early and get started."

Sam shook her head. "She knows where we are, Heather. She knows how to find us."

Heather pushed them away and stood up, overturning her chair as she backed up.

"What the hell!?" she yelled. "She needs help and you're seriously going to just sit there?"

Karyn started to go to Heather, but Erica and Marta gestured for her to stay put.

"Heather," Marta said evenly, "I know you're worried about your friend. We are, too. But she left on her own."

"I knew you were bitches," Heather said, "but I didn't know you were totally heartless."

"Heather," Erica said, "what would you do if you found her? Say you go out and you walk all over town and you finally find her. What then?"

"If she's hurt, I'd help her! We could take her to emergency, or to detox, or bring her back here!"

"And what if she's not hurt?"

"I—"

"You know you can't just drag her back here."

"But we can help her!"

"Not if she doesn't want it," Erica said.

"Not if she's actively using," Marta said.

"Not if she's not ready to come here on her own," Sam said.

Heather shook her head and looked at the ground.

They sat together in silence for a couple of minutes, then Salina spoke up.

"That's one of the hard things about recovery, isn't it?" she asked. She looked straight in front of her, asking the question of no one in particular.

She continued. "These problems are bigger than us. That's the whole 'unmanageable' part of this. I can't manage this problem on my own. I need help ..."

Erica and Marta nodded softly to encourage her.

"But ..." Salina continued, "if I'm not ready to take that help ... If I'm still going around thinking I got this on my own ... then I'm just still stuck in my own mess."

Heather shook her head. "She doesn't want to use anymore. She doesn't want to be stuck anymore. I know. She told me."

Marta sighed. "It's a powerful force," she said. "That's why we say we're powerless. But ..." She paused and waited for Heather to look up and catch her eye. "Until you really admit it, you're never going to be able to move through recovery. If Cheryl isn't there yet, then maybe this isn't the place for her."

Sam and Salina nodded sadly.

"It hurts to lose someone," Salina said. "But if they don't want to be found, that's on them, not on you."

Erica leaned forward with her elbows on her knees. "You need to focus on your own recovery. You can't help her if she doesn't want it, and you can't help her if you're not clear on your own stuff."

Marta smiled. "What's that thing they say on the airplanes?"

Heather shrugged. "I've never been on a plane."

"You've seen it in movies or on TV," Marta said. "When they're in turbulence and it's all bumping around and the masks drop from the ceiling, they say you need to put on your own mask before you help anyone else."

Heather rocked her head back and looked up at the sky, which was getting dark. A few stars were popping out.

"I don't have a plane or a gas mask or whatever," Heather said. She stretched out her arms and legs and stood up. "I hear what you're saying. I do. But I need to go find my friend."

Marta shook her head and Salina ticked her tongue against her teeth.

Erica said quietly, "I wish you would stay here."

"I know," Heather said. "But I've got to look. I've got to try." She looked around the small circle.

"I'll come back," she said. "I know I got a good thing here. I don't want to mess it up. I just want to see if I can find my friend and help her."

"You've been doing so good on your drug court plan," Erica said.

"And I'm going to keep doing good," Heather said.

"A lot easier to do good on your plan from in here than out there," Marta said.

Heather stuffed her hands in her front pockets. "I know. But I'm coming back, so it's okay. I'm just going to grab a sweatshirt and take an energy bar in case she's hungry when I find her."

Marta shook her head and they all watched Heather head to her tent. They sat silently until she emerged and came back over to them.

"Anyone want to give me a ride?"

They all just looked at her.

"Alright then," she bristled and stood up a little straighter, "I guess it's the bus for me."

"Heather—" Marta started.

"I'll be back tomorrow," Heather said. She started walking toward the street, pulling her hood up and stuffing her hands into the front pocket of her sweatshirt.

"I hope so," Marta whispered after her.

"Doubt it," Salina said at the same time.

"Alright you all," Erica said and stood up. "Let's pack it in." As she stood, she remembered she still had to talk to Wendi about Child Protective Services. She looked over and saw Wendi talking quietly with Jamilah. She held Marta back as Sam and Salina walked away.

"Wendi looks like she's doing better," Erica said.

"For now," Marta said. "She's still pretty dazed, but the tears dried up for at least a little bit."

"I found out more about protective services and what's going to happen," Erica said to Marta.

"Anything urgent, like she has to know right now?"

"No. I wish there was good news, but it's mostly all still waiting."

"If it can wait till morning, I say you do," Marta said. "Let her get some sleep, and you go home and get some, too. You look like shit."

Erica gave Marta a side-eye glance. "I thought you were like the mother figure for this group."

Marta laughed. "I am. And Mother says you look like shit. Go home. We got this for tonight."

Erica stopped walking and Marta stopped next to her.

"What, now you need a hug?" Marta asked.

Erica considered it. "Actually, yeah."

"Come here." Marta leaned in and whispered as she hugged Erica tightly, "Tough guy."

Erica laughed and they released the hug. "Thanks."

"Shoo," Marta said. "Get out of here and take a break while you can."

CHAPTER 21

The next morning, Erica came back to the site to brief Wendi on what she'd learned. It didn't go well. The crying started up again, along with screaming and trying to rip her tent apart with her hands. Sam and Jamilah managed to hold her back, and Karyn and Barb stuffed a sleeping bag with pillows, towels, and clothes to give Wendi something soft to punch. Erica was glad she'd taken Marta's advice and waited until morning to tell her.

Between Wendi's situation and Heather taking off to find Cheryl, the vibe around the site was prickly. Sam and her crew worked on the houses, and a few of the residents distracted themselves by working in the garden beds.

Finally, shortly after lunch, Erica received the automated call that Wendi's hearing would be the next day. She immediately called Dara and thanked her, and asked if Dara would talk with Wendi for bit about what she should expect. Once Wendi was set up on the phone, Erica left her alone in the tent and went across the site to check in with Sam.

"Is this really what you do all day?" Sam called out to Erica, teasing her. "Just wander around talking to people while everyone else works?"

"You know it," Erica said.

"Look at her, not even breaking a sweat," Sam teased.

"You need me to remind you about all the hours I spent walking around talking to people to help you fix *your* hot messes?" Erica asked, and plopped down on the ground next to where Sam was working.

"But look how I turned out!" Sam said and flexed her arms, pulling the trigger on her power drill so it revved a few times.

Erica laughed, pulled out a fistful of grass from the lawn, and threw it at her. "I created a monster."

Sam nodded solemnly. "You only have yourself to blame."

Erica lay back, resting her head on the ground and looking up at the sky. She sighed heavily.

"But you're kinda right," she said. "All I've been doing today is talk to people. The day's barely half over and I am fried."

She lay there for a while like that, and Sam continued to work. A few minutes later, Sam stopped working and cleared her throat.

"Hey, Erica? I don't think you're done just yet."

Erica raised her head and opened her eyes, and Sam nodded toward the road. She followed Sam's gaze and saw Heather slowly walking toward them. From this distance she didn't look high or disoriented, but she did seem preoccupied. Heather had come back, which was good—but she had come back alone.

"Speaking of hot messes," Sam said.

"Shut it," Erica said to Sam. "You know this part's hard." She stood up and brushed off the seat of her pants, then headed toward Heather. She wanted to get a good look at Heather's eyes and get her talking, to make sure she was both generally okay and specifically sober. She also figured Heather hadn't eaten or had any water since she left, too.

"Hey girl," Erica said. "I'm glad to see you."

Heather looked up. "Hey." Her eyes were clear.

"You eat?" Erica asked. "We had lunch a little bit ago, there's plenty left."

Heather shrugged like she could take it or leave it.

"Come on," Erica said, and steered her toward the kitchen area. "Let's get you a sandwich. Sarah tried to make sloppy Joes, and they were kind of a disaster. But we've always got peanut butter and jelly."

Heather sat at one of the tables. Erica poured a cup of water from the jug and set it in front of Heather.

"Knock that back for me," she said.

"I'm not thirsty."

"Do it anyway."

Heather took a sip from the cup, paused, and then drank the whole cup. Erica nodded and refilled it for her.

"We have as much of that as you want," Erica said. "PB&J?"

Heather shrugged. "Sure."

Erica made her up a sandwich, cut it in half, and put it on the plate. Then she grabbed a bag of potato chips and shook a few out onto the plate next to the sandwich. Heather pulled her knees up under her chin.

"Don't you want to know?" Heather asked.

Erica took a few chips for herself, then sat in a chair at the other end of the table. "About what?" she asked lightly.

Heather jerked her head up. "Seriously? I thought you cared."

Erica leaned back in her chair. "Of course, seriously. If you want to tell me something, you'll tell me, right?"

"Yeah, I guess."

Erica held up a chip and used it to gesture toward Heather before popping it into her mouth. "Then we're good. I'm just going to sit here and eat a few chips."

She brushed her hands off on her jeans, and got up to pull a soda from one of the tiny fridges. As she sat back down, she reached forward and grabbed a single chip off Heather's plate.

"I forgot how much I like these kettle cooked ones," she said as she reached.

Heather smacked the back of Erica's hand. "Get your own."

Erica smiled. "Fine, fine." When she went for the bag, Heather took a bite of her sandwich. Erica settled into her chair. All she wanted to do in this moment was hug Heather. Even though she didn't know what had happened, it was clear Heather was hurting. Erica wanted to ask what was going on, but she'd been through this enough to know she needed to let Heather go at Heather's pace. It didn't even matter what had happened—in this moment, Erica needed to back off and allow Heather to approach.

It didn't get any easier, no matter how often she did this.

They chewed in silence and Erica looked out over the site. Sam caught her eye and Erica nodded slightly to let her know it was all good. Everyone was working on whatever they needed to be working on, and Wendi was still in her tent talking to Dara on the phone. Erica looked back at Heather, who had her head down but was slowly eating her sandwich and some of the chips.

Heather finished one half of the sandwich and then took a sip from the water cup. She held onto the cup with both hands and stared down into it.

"I found her," she said into the cup.

Erica barely heard her but was expecting that answer. She nodded slightly but otherwise stayed still. "Yeah?"

She waited.

Eventually, Heather looked up and met Erica's gaze.

"She's not coming back."

Erica nodded again and waited.

"Don't you care?" Heather asked and raised her voice. "I went out and found her and you don't even want to know how she was doing?"

"You're the one who's here," Erica said. She spoke slowly and gently. "Of course I care about Cheryl, but she left. You're here. How are *you* doing?"

"I'm tired," Heather said.

"Did you sleep anywhere?"

"No," she shook her head. "When I found her I stayed there for a while but then I left. I just been walking back."

"Where did you walk from?"

"That Rose Quarter camp over by the Broadway Bridge."

Erica nodded. If Heather had walked here from there, that meant she'd just walked at least ten miles.

"That's where she was?"

"Yeah, I figured it'd be the first place she'd go cause it's just one bus ride. And," Heather added, "'cause there's like three guys there who'll always hook up a girl for a trade."

"Yeah," Erica said. Heather didn't have to explain what she meant by "trade." There was always one thing a woman on the street with no money could trade. It got way too many women in trouble over and over again. And a lot of them got hurt very badly.

"How did you do there?" Erica asked. "Tough place to go if you're trying to stay straight."

Heather raised one shoulder like, *What can you do?*

"It's not like anywhere else is different."

"This place is," Erica said.

"Well, duh," Heather said and rolled her eyes. "Of course, this place is."

"Just making sure we're on the same page."

Heather sighed and splayed her legs out in front of her, slouching back in the chair. "This place is different and it's clean and it's safe and there aren't any drugs ... well, I mean, except for what Cheryl brought in I guess." She looked around the site. "It's real nice here. It makes me want to keep going."

"That's the idea."

"I think a lot about going back. I mean, serious. I think about it all the time."

Erica nodded.

"But then," Heather continued, "I'll remember. And I'll go to a meeting or grab the others and have a small meeting right here, and it helps me not want it so much. And then I come over here to the kitchen and there's all this food that's good and I can have however much I want. And I'll go in my tent and smell my clothes I was able to wash at the laundromat. And we can go to the shower truck anytime, and the porta-potties aren't disgusting. And pretty soon we'll have real bathrooms and real showers and man it has been a *long* time since I had that. And ... I remember I don't want to mess this up. So I just try to get through today without screwing it up."

"What was it like where she was?"

Heather shook her head. "It was nasty, and it was a mess, and it was loud. I saw some peeps hadn't seen in a while and I kind of missed them, but they were all gone. Like they were there but they were *gone*. It seemed like everyone was high. I know they weren't *all* high."

Erica smiled. "No, some were drunk."

"Shut up," Heather smiled. Then she said seriously, "But yeah. Some were drunk, some were high, some were crazy, and the ones who weren't, were sad and angry."

Erica nodded.

"I used to live like that," Heather said.

"Yeah," Erica said. "And I remember you yelling at me more than once, telling me how I was just a dumb bitch who didn't know."

Heather shrugged again. "Maybe you did know." She paused and looked sideways at Erica. "Doesn't mean you're not a dumb bitch."

Erica didn't flinch. "I love you, too."

Heather shifted in her seat and sat up, sitting cross-legged in the chair.

"So you found her," Erica said.

"Yeah."

"How was that?"

Heather smiled sadly. "It was kind of like old times."

Erica waited.

"She was out of her mind, feeling no pain. She was all happy to see me and hugging on me and tried to pull me in and this one guy started to grab on me. When I pulled away, he started cussing me out and she crawled all over him and then started cussing at me, too, like I was trying to steal him from her or something. It was so dumb. I tried to talk to her, but she didn't want to hear it."

Heather took a breath to say more, then stopped. She closed her mouth and sank back into her seat.

Erica leaned forward. She'd been waiting, not wanting to appear too eager to grab Heather and pull her tight, not wanting to scare her away. There was clearly more that happened last night, but this was where Heather was going to stop.

"I'm glad you came back," Erica said softly.

Heather looked at her for a couple of seconds. "Me, too," she whispered.

They sat like that for a couple of minutes. Erica had let Heather know she was here for her, but now she needed to back off again. This dance was exhausting but so important. Soon, Heather spoke again.

"In the recovery classes and stuff, they talk about how you need to change your whole life. Where you are, what you do, who you see."

Erica nodded and leaned back.

"I was never able to do that till we came here. Everything changed all at once, but we were so busy it's like I didn't even notice. Even though I thought about going back all the time, I didn't really miss it, you know?"

"I do," Erica said.

"I been away from it now long enough, I guess," Heather said. "When I was back there it was weird. It was like seeing something I used to want. Like, I don't know, you see your old boyfriend who you were ready to die for and you missed him so much ... but then life goes on, and you run into him later and you see he's really just a broke down loser."

She paused to reflect. "And you're looking at him and you realize ... Oh shit, it's not him who changed, it's me. He was always that dirtbag ... I just didn't see it before. And now even though you miss that old feeling from before you realized it, you can't go back. You do realize it, and you don't want nothing to do with him."

Erica nodded. "It's a perspective shift."

Heather wrinkled her nose. "Sure, college girl. But, like, I went back and saw that life like it really was ... but she didn't. Cheryl went back and she was all, 'Yes, please.'"

"I bet that didn't feel good for you," Erica said.

Heather shook her head. "It felt like shit." She noticed she was still holding the empty water cup and set it down on the table. "What if she wants to come back?"

"Well," Erica said, "that's up to her, and it's up to the group. You know the rules—the whole group decides on whether someone can stay or has to go."

Heather nodded and kept looking at the ground.

"It'll probably be a tough sell. She'd have to stop using, and she'd have to be present and stay here. She's got to actually want to be here and make the change. You can't have it both ways."

"Yeah," Heather said.

"If she decides she's ready to try again, I'll hook her up the best I can, like I always do," Erica said. "There's no such thing as a last chance on that."

Erica paused. "But as for living here? We can't hold that bed. We're going to have to find someone else to fill it. There's a lot of people who need help and who want to be a part of their own recovery. But if there's space in the future, and she wants to come back, then everyone who lives here needs to decide together. This community belongs to all of you."

Heather sighed again. "Okay, I need a break from all this touchy-feely stuff."

Erica laughed. "Don't worry, I won't tell anyone."

"Better not." Heather stood up and stretched. "I need to sleep for a little bit."

"Get to it," Erica said. "You're on dinner duty so you've got a few hours."

Heather looked at Erica and held her gaze. "Thank you," she said.

Erica didn't break the look. "Always," she said.

★ ★ ★

With Heather in her tent, Erica realized she also needed a break, and had better take it now when there was time. Marta making her go home last night reminded her it was so easy to run ragged in this job. There was always someone who needed more help, always something else that needed more time. If she'd learned anything at all during her time in recovery, it was that she needed to listen to her body's and her mind's own signals. She went over to where Sam and Salina were working.

"Hey, you guys okay if I take off now, and miss dinner? I think we're settled till the hearing, and I want to get a meeting in and then get to bed a little early."

Sam looked her up and down. "No offense, but after the last few days you've had, I can't believe you're even standing here talking to us. Get out of here. We got this."

Salina nodded. "What she said. We don't need a zombie running around here."

"Thanks for the support," Erica smirked.

"What?" Sam said. "We're telling you to go do your thing!"

"And also telling me I look like death warmed over!"

Salina shrugged. "You don't want us to lie, do you? What if you try to eat our brains?"

Erica turned and smiled on the walk back to her truck. Even hard days had their bright moments.

At the street, she heard Salina yelling "Braaaaaaiiiiiiiinns!" back at the work site. She loved these people.

CHAPTER 22

The determination hearing went so fast it was almost uneventful, and everything else went down exactly how Dara had described it would. They'd had to wait nearly two hours for Wendi's case to be called, sitting in orange molded plastic chairs in an antiseptic waiting room.

"I think they use the same floor cleaner as the shelter down by the river," Wendi said.

"Yeah?" Erica asked, bemused.

"Yeah, it smells totally the same in here. The stuff comes in these huge five-gallon buckets and it's like bright green."

"I bet the county gets a deal on it in bulk or something."

"Theo always called it the 'green monster sauce' when he saw it," Wendi said. "It's this sticky, gooey gel until they mix it with water."

"He's a funny kid," Erica said.

"He is," Wendi agreed, and hugged herself tightly.

When it was finally her turn, Wendi's public defender didn't challenge the state's custody. He also looked exhausted and overworked, and accidentally called her Wanda. The judge had to correct him.

After that, Wendi had to go wait in another line at the court clerk's office to get instructions about what to do next. Then she had to stand in another line to get a bill for all of it.

"Don't worry about the court bill," Erica told Wendi. "We'll cover it. You don't need that hanging over you, too."

"Oh my God, thank you," Wendi said.

"No, we know how it is. I just wish I could do it for more people here today. Most people don't realize how expensive it is to be poor."

"It sucks so much," Wendi said. "I've met so many people who got ticketed for something a regular person wouldn't even get noticed for. But then they couldn't get to court because they had to work, or needed a ride, or I knew one guy who didn't have a phone to set an alarm to wake him up on time, and he missed his hearing and got a fine."

"Yup," Erica said. "But of course, you can't pay the fine, so you get more fines, and then probably also get a Failure to Appear notice, and then that leads to even more charges and fines."

"I'd pay it if I had the money," Wendi said. "I'm not trying to be a freeloader."

"I know," Erica said. "I know. Hopefully helping you here is part of how we get you out of this cycle."

⋆ ⋆ ⋆

Because Dara had said not to expect to get the kids back at this hearing, they weren't surprised when it turned out that way. They were hoping to at least see them, though, and it was a blow when they were denied. Wendi had been holding it together, but she broke down when she wasn't able to see the kids.

Erica guided Wendi to the parking lot and sat her in the truck's passenger seat. With the door open and her legs dangling over the side, Wendi alternated between sniffling and straight-up sobbing. Erica let her get it out while she read through the paperwork Wendi had received. There was a number to call in two weeks to get a date for the next hearing. There was a different number to call to get assigned a social worker. There was yet another number to call with questions—which Erica tried calling, and it went straight to voicemail.

At the very end of the document, Erica found a section about what happens next to the kids. Parents who are "relieved of custody" are not initially told where their children are being placed. Eventually, apparently, the social worker Wendi was yet to be assigned would be able to tell her where her kids were.

Erica tried calling the social worker number right then, even though the instructions said to wait until "at least twenty-four hours" after the hearing. The person who answered looked for Wendi's file, and then told Erica she couldn't find it.

"Well, it has to be there," Erica said. "She just got out of the hearing, so we know you have her in the system."

"She just got out?" the woman on the other end of the line asked.

"Yeah. Like twenty minutes ago."

"Well, ma'am," the woman said, "she needs to wait at least twenty-four hours. I can't help you."

"You seriously don't have the information?"

"It will not be available for twenty-four hours."

"Look," Erica said. "I used to work for a big agency. Not as big as yours, but big. I get there are controls. I mean, maybe she's dangerous and you need to protect the kids. But I assure you she is not dangerous. She just wants to get started on the process of getting her kids back."

"You *know* she's not dangerous."

"Yes!"

"Well, ma'am, *we* don't know that. And my computer definitely doesn't know that. I'm sorry for the inconvenience, but you'll need to call back in ... twenty-three hours and forty minutes."

Erica stuffed her phone in her pocket and looked up at the sky, trying not to look as frustrated as she was.

"They have this info locked up tight. We can call back this time tomorrow."

Wendi started crying again. "Their whole lives I've always known exactly where they were. This is the first time I've ever not known where my kids are!"

"I know," Erica said. "This sucks." She tapped Wendi's legs to get her to pull them inside the truck so she could shut the door, then walked around to the driver's side.

"But they're okay," she continued as she buckled in. "They're okay. They have to be."

"They have to be," Wendi repeated with a whimper.

Erica backed the truck out of their parking spot and headed for the site.

⋆ ⋆ ⋆

While Erica and Wendi were in the hearing, Claire had arrived at the state building through a different set of doors and sat in a different waiting room. She looked around at the others in the room, whom she thought must also be waiting for foster assignments. A lot of them were older, like her—grandmother or aunt age. A few middle-aged people. All women, except for one older man who was there as part of a couple. Were these people who were relatives of kids who needed placement? Friends? Or career foster parents? She wondered what they thought about her.

In the order the day's hearings were completed, names were called and people were ushered behind a closed door. Since they didn't come back out, Claire presumed they were paired with their foster kids and then sent out a different door. She tried to get a look behind the door when they opened it, but all she could see was a gray hallway.

She sat and waited. In the corner of the room, one of the fluorescent lights was struggling to stay on. It flickered and went out, then popped back on again. Claire counted the seconds in between flickers.

Finally, they called her name. The woman who called her pointed to an open door down the hall, where she told Claire to take another seat. Ten minutes or so later, the woman walked back in with Ella and Theo.

Claire stood and smiled broadly when she saw the kids, then crouched down and opened her arms. The kids looked relieved to see someone they knew, but they were clearly disappointed it wasn't Wendi. They walked slowly into Claire's arms.

"Where's my mom?" Theo asked

"Are you taking us back home to Mom?" Ella asked.

She hugged them and eased back to sit in the chair, taking their hands.

"Your mom is okay, and she misses you. We're going to go to my house for a little bit."

The social worker, still standing at the door, cleared her throat. "Can you all come with me now? We need this room."

Claire stood and took the kids by their hands. "Of course," she smiled. "Let's go, superstars."

On the way out she signed yet another form, and then they were released. They walked toward her car in the parking lot, and Ella asked again if they could go see her mom. Claire had been so excited to get them assigned to her and out of the main foster system, so happy to see them, she hadn't thought about how much more they'd want to see their mom than they'd want to see her. She quietly buckled them into the back seat of her Mercedes and got into the driver's seat.

"Where's my mom?" Theo asked again.

"Where is she?" Ella asked.

Claire eased the car out of the parking lot and said gently, "Your mom is at the site with the tents."

"I want my mom!" Theo cried.

"We're going to my house for a while, Theo," Claire said. "You'll like it."

"I want to go home!" Ella yelled.

"My house will be home for a bit," Claire said, trying not to let her voice break.

The kids burst into tears and called for Wendi. As they wailed in the back seat, Claire tried to focus on navigating the car toward home. She'd never had kids, and knew she'd missed out on a lot of things she'd wanted. At a particularly piercing scream from Ella, she gripped the steering wheel and realized there were other parts of parenthood it wasn't all bad to have skipped.

* * *

The kids exhausted themselves on the drive home and were finally quiet by the time they pulled into the garage—for a little while, at least. Claire brought them into the house and showed them their room. She'd tried not to go overboard on gifts, but had bought them each a new stuffed animal and a new outfit, as well as a couple new games for them to play together.

Ella eyed all of it cautiously and kept her distance, though Claire noticed her eyes linger on the pink T-shirt laid out on her bed. Theo carefully reached for the stuffed bunny on his bed and looked back at Claire doubtfully. She nodded.

"That's for you," Claire said. "I thought you could each use another friend."

Theo took the bunny by one paw and pulled it close.

Claire felt herself wanting to hug them both tightly, but held back.

"Are you two hungry?" she asked.

Theo hugged his bunny and Ella shrugged.

"Let's go down to the kitchen and get a snack."

They followed her back downstairs. She noticed she was holding her breath. She exhaled and glanced at the clock in the kitchen. It had almost been one hour since they'd been brought to her. One hour that felt like twelve.

* * *

She decided it was late enough that instead of a snack they'd have an early dinner, and she made them grilled cheese sandwiches. She knew that was one of the things they liked best for dinners at the site, so she decided to stick with something familiar. The kids sat on the stools at the bar and watched.

Waiting for the sandwiches to brown, Claire washed an apple and cut it into slices, placing the slices in a bowl in front of the kids.

"Go ahead and get started on these," she said.

Theo reached for an apple slice and Ella gave him side-eye. Claire noticed that when she did, she looked exactly like Wendi. The resemblance made her laugh a little.

"What?" Ella asked.

"You look just like your—" Claire started, then thought better of it.

"It's okay, Ella. You can have some apple. I know you're probably hungry."

Ella folded her arms across her little chest and looked so adult as she glared at Claire. Claire turned to attend to the pan, and Ella quickly reached for an apple slice. Claire pretended not to notice.

"When can we see our mom?" the little girl asked through a mouthful of apple.

Claire kept her eyes on the pan. "Soon."

"When?"

Claire checked to make sure the sandwiches were brown on both sides.

"Soon."

"When is soon?"

She pushed the sandwiches onto two plates and put them in front of the kids.

"Be careful, those are hot," she advised.

Theo reached out to grab his immediately, and then dropped it with a howl.

"Owwwwww!"

Claire came around the bar to scoop him up, and carried him around to the sink, to put his hand under cold water. "I told you it was hot."

"I want my mooooooooommmmmmmmm!" he wailed.

Ella slipped off her stool and ran out of the room.

"Ella!" Claire shouted.

"Put me down!" Theo wriggled and squirmed so much, Claire was worried she'd drop him. She set him down gently on the floor and he ran after his sister.

"God damn it," Claire whispered. She started to go after them and heard their feet pounding up the stairs. At the foot of the stairs she looked up, and heard them run down the hall to their room and slam the door.

She leaned against the newel post and blinked back tears. At least they were safe. At least they were upstairs safely in the room, and they had each other. Right? That's what's important, right? She wasn't sure, but she hoped so.

She made her way back into the kitchen and kept an ear out for any activity upstairs. She put the sandwiches on a paper towel and cleaned up the dishes and pan. After washing up, she went back to the staircase and listened. Nothing. They had to still be hungry, she thought. But those grilled cheese sandwiches were cold. She went back and made a couple of peanut butter and jelly sandwiches, poured two cups of milk, and put all of it with the rest of the apple slices onto a tray. She walked it up the stairs and down the hall, standing outside their room. She couldn't hear what they were saying but she heard their voices.

"Hey, you two," she knocked gently on the door. They stopped talking immediately. Claire could have opened the door—none of the bedroom doors had locks—but she thought better of it and stayed outside.

"I know you are probably very tired and hungry and scared," she said. "I made you some new sandwiches. Can I bring them in?"

"No!" Ella shouted.

"Tell you what," Claire said. "I'm going to leave them here right outside the door, and then I'm going to go downstairs. If you want them, you can open the door and get them." She paused and there was no answer.

"Come and get me if you want anything," she said. "I'll be right downstairs."

Still nothing.

"When you want to go to bed, there are pajamas and toothbrushes in the bathroom."

Quiet.

"Okay, you two. Good night."

She stood there a little bit longer, hoping they'd open the door. But they didn't, so she made her way back downstairs.

* * *

In the kitchen, she poured herself a small glass of wine and took the paper towel with the cold grilled cheese sandwiches into the living room. She sat in her reading chair and took a bite of one of the sandwiches, following with a sip of wine.

She had known they'd want their mom.

She had known that bringing them back to the house and giving them a couple of presents wouldn't automatically solve all the problems and erase all the traumas.

She also knew that eventually she'd have to tell Wendi, Erica, and all the rest of them how she'd used her leverage and connections to work the very same system that had taken Wendi's kids away, to make it so they could come home with her.

But she'd still kind of hoped that just for one night, it could have been easy, and the kids would have wanted her.

CHAPTER 23

In just over a week, Sam's crew had been able to frame out and put together two entire houses and halfway finish a third. Although the crew did most of the real building work, she found important tasks for the residents to do, too, so they had ownership and were a part of the process.

"You're a good teacher, Sam," Jamilah said afterward when they were checking in and Sam told them they'd done a great job.

"You told us exactly what to do and what we'd need to do it, and then you let us do it and ask you questions if we had them."

Sam raised an eyebrow like, *yeah, of course.*

"Most of the time," Jamilah said, and gestured to herself and Heather, "people don't tell us what's expected. Then they yell at us when we don't do it, and then we get punished."

Heather nodded and Sam eyed them both.

"I remember how it feels to be someone no one expects anything from," Sam said. She paused and it looked like there was more she wanted to say, but she stopped herself. "We're not playing that here."

Jamilah smiled. "I feel like you almost got a little sentimental there, Sam."

"Psht," Sam said, raising her chin. "There's a lot of dust around here. Got something in my eye."

"Right," Jamilah said. "Right."

"Stop slacking, you two," Sam said and clapped her hands. "We got all that prep work for the pre-fab done last week, and it's supposed to be getting here tomorrow morning. Grab your checklists, and let's make sure we are all set."

"Aye, aye," Karyn said. She and Jamilah stood up straight and made exaggerated saluting motions. "We're on it, Cap'n!"

Sam smiled and waved her middle finger at them as she walked away.

⋆ ⋆ ⋆

At first, no one noticed the red Suburban truck circling the block; but this block never saw a ton of traffic, and when the truck came around a third time, Jamilah nudged Salina with her elbow.

"You see that guy come around a few times already?" Jamilah asked.

"Wasn't really paying attention," Salina said. "Maybe?"

Jamilah stood up and located Sam on the site. "I'm going to go talk to Sam," she said. "It's probably nothing."

Jamilah went over to Sam and mentioned her concern about the circling truck. Sam nodded and it came around again, a little slower this time. Sam and Jamilah tried to see inside but the windows were too dark. Erica was working on her laptop over by Wendi, who was tending one of the garden beds. Erica noticed the women standing and talking, and caught Sam's eye. Sam gestured slightly to the truck and tipped her head like, *It might be nothing, but ...*

Erica glanced over at Wendi, who was engrossed with separating sections of young lettuce plants.

"I'll be right back," Erica said, and Wendi nodded, not looking up. Erica left her laptop on the seat of the chair and tucked her phone in her pocket as she walked over to Sam and Jamilah.

"What's up?" she asked quietly once she was close.

"That red truck has come around a few times now," Sam said. "Jamilah noticed it first. Don't know how many times he's been around, but at least two we just saw."

"Haven't seen that truck on this block before," Jamilah said.

"Could you see who it was?" Erica asked. Since the City Council meeting, they'd occasionally get lookie-loos. Irritating, but generally harmless.

"No," Sam said.

"Tinted windows," Jamilah added.

Wanting to calm both her own nerves and theirs, Erica offered, "It's probably just another gawker."

"Maybe," Jamilah said. "Felt different though."

They stood there a while longer, and when it seemed like the truck wasn't going to come by again, they started to disperse. Just then, the Suburban pulled up slowly one more time, stopping right in front of the site. The driver put it in park and the engine kept running. No one got out, and the windows stayed rolled up tight.

Erica, Sam, and Jamilah looked at each other and back at the truck, unsure what to do.

"I'll go see what's up," Jamilah said. She started walking toward the idling vehicle.

She knocked on the passenger window and gestured for them to roll it down. The window came down about two inches. Sam and Erica couldn't hear the conversation, but Jamilah talked through the window to the driver for a minute or so, and pointed toward the main road. Then she looked over her shoulder at the site, turned back to talk to driver some more, and shrugged.

The driver turned off the truck and they heard the door on his side open. Someone hopped down. He stood there for a while, blocked by the rest of the truck. Jamilah looked back at the others with her hands bent at her sides, trying to communicate, *I tried to tell him not to come over.*

Finally, the guy walked out from around the truck. He was a big, relatively young, white guy. He wasn't fat, but was broad, and wore tan work pants, a T-shirt with some energy drink logo on it, and an unbuttoned flannel with the sleeves rolled up. He had a trucker hat jammed down on his head with the bill pulled low. Bushy, dark hair stuck out from underneath.

Jamilah tried to keep a step in front of him, and spoke to the others before he did.

"This guy said he was lost and needed directions. Then he asked what we were doing here, and said it sounded interesting and he wanted to know more." Her voice was flat, and her effort to sound completely neutral showed the rest of the women that she thought he was going to be a problem.

He nodded and smiled thinly at the three of them but kept his hands jammed in his pockets as he looked around them at the site.

"I do some construction, and it looks like you're building something, so I just wondered what it was," he said.

"And I told him we were building transitional housing," Jamilah said. Her voice took on a harder tone. "*And* that the site was private property."

He lifted and then dropped his shoulders. "I'm into this stuff, so I just wanted to know more."

Erica looked him over. "You're interested in a transitional housing development to help people coming out of homelessness?"

He shrugged. "Sure."

Erica shook her head. "Well, this is private property and we are all private citizens, so thanks for your interest, but I'm going to ask you to head on back to the street."

"What's the problem?" he asked, puffing up his chest and getting an edge to his voice.

"No problem," Erica said and started walking toward him with her palms up to communicate that she wasn't a threat. "No problem at all." She gestured toward the street, trying to direct him that way. "Just wanting to maintain the privacy of our residents."

He snapped at her and raised his voice, getting louder with each sentence. "Are you sure all your 'residents' respect other people's rights? Are you sure everyone here doesn't take what isn't theirs and then disappear?"

When he started yelling, it drew the attention of the rest of the women at the site. Erica scanned the area and saw Wendi at the garden boxes, frozen, her eyes wide with terror.

Shit.

The husband.

It had to be.

This wasn't just some redneck harasser. This was Wendi's husband, Chad.

Chad hadn't seen Wendi yet. The garden beds were sort of blocked by one of the housing platforms. You could see the street from the garden but couldn't really see the garden from the street unless you knew it was there. Erica walked toward him and took his focus back. She circled around in the other direction, so he was facing her and his back was to the garden beds.

Sam saw what Erica was doing and didn't totally understand but followed her lead. She leaned in to Jamilah and told her to stay close to Erica, and she moved toward the houses where the crew had stopped working and the rest of the residents were gathered, watching.

Two of the women on the work crew came toward her and asked what was up. Sam told them there was a guy they needed to remove from the site and sent them to help Erica. Then she headed toward Wendi and beckoned Marta to come with her.

Sam knelt down next to Wendi, who was repeating, "Oh no, oh no, oh no," under her breath.

"Wendi," Sam whispered. "Hey girl. Hey. Look at me."

Wendi turned her head slightly toward Sam, but kept her eyes on the scene out front.

"So this is someone you know, huh?"

"Oh no, oh no, oh no."

"It's okay, hon. He hasn't seen you yet. You need to stand up and come with me."

Wendi didn't move.

"Wendi," Sam snapped her fingers in front of Wendi's face and spoke more sharply. "Now."

Sam put her hand on Wendi's arm to help her stand, but Wendi stayed put.

Marta was confused but recognized Sam was trying to get Wendi inside the completed tiny house that was closest to them.

"Wendi, *mija*," she said and moved to Wendi's other side so she and Sam had her between them. "Get up now. Let's go."

Wendi responded to Marta's voice and slowly stood up, and Sam and Marta steered her to the house, opening the door as quietly as possible and getting her inside.

"Can you stay here with her?" Sam asked.

"Of course," Marta answered. She had started to put together what was happening. "That's the ex?"

"Seems like it," Sam said. "Keep her here and we'll come back as soon as he's gone." She pulled the door closed and turned around once she was back outside. Everyone else had migrated to the front of the site, where Erica had the guy from the Suburban in conversation.

"My *wife* took my *car* and she took my *kids* and now I *found* them and you can't keep me away," he shouted.

"There are no kids here," Erica said. "And if your wife is here, that's her business, not yours."

"You can't hide them."

"No one's hiding anything, man," Erica said. "You need to go."

From the group that had gathered behind them, Sarah shouted, "Get the hell out of here, you wife-beater!"

He wheeled around toward the direction the voice had come from, and pulled a handgun out from his waistband, pointing it in that direction. Sarah, ready to fight, lunged for him but stopped abruptly when she saw the gun

"Whoa, dude!" she screamed. "Not cool!" One of the women from the crew grabbed Sarah and held her still. Everyone else froze and looked at the guy with the gun.

"Not so tough now, are you?" Chad asked, and gestured with the gun.

Sarah spat on the ground. "Big talk from the big man who needs a gun to feel tough. Fight me unarmed, motherfucker."

Sarah started to jump forward again and everyone around her held her back.

Erica made her way over to Sarah and put her hand on her shoulder.

"Cool it, okay?" she said calmly.

Sarah shrugged off Erica's hand but stepped back.

"Hey!" Chad yelled. "I'm not leaving till I get my wife and my kids."

"You're trespassing right now, and there's no one here for you. Do you see your wife? Do you see any kids?"

"You lie!"

Erica tried to keep her voice low and calm and walked slowly toward him with her palms out.

"You really should go," she said. "Why don't you head back to your truck, and we'll—"

"Stop moving," he said, and trained his gun on her, stopping her cold.

Just then, a police cruiser pulled up, popping the siren a couple times and swirling the lights once.

"Who called the cops?" Chad yelled.

Everyone shook their heads and looked around, bewildered.

"Hell. This day just keeps getting better," Erica said under her breath.

The cruiser door opened and Erica braced herself for the police to make everything worse. Then she realized the officer exiting the car was Jake.

"Oh, thank God."

Jake took in the scene and pulled his own gun, pointing it at Chad as he slowly advanced.

"I'm going to need you to drop your weapon, sir," Jake said.

"They are harboring a fugitive," Chad yelled. He kept his gun aimed at Erica and looked back and forth between her and Jake. "My wife stole my kids and they're hiding them here."

"That really sucks," Jake said. "Let me help you figure it out. You're going to need to put down the gun for me to do that, though."

Chad looked uncertain.

"Seriously," Jake said. If you don't drop the weapon you're going to have much bigger problems than the ones you came here with."

"Fine," Chad said, and pointed the gun away from Erica and toward the sky, taking his finger off the trigger.

Erica hadn't realized she wasn't breathing until she suddenly exhaled and bent over, putting her hands on her knees with relief. Sam and Jamilah rushed up to her and helped her sit down on the lawn.

"Okay, sir," Jake called. "Good choice. Here's what we'll do. You gently lay the gun down on the ground. Yep, just right there. Now take three steps back."

Chad did as he was told.

"Excellent. Now come on down to your knees and put your hands behind your head."

The guy seemed a little confused but followed directions. Jake moved up behind him quickly and in one swift motion brought Chad's right arm and then his left down behind his back and handcuffed him there. He paused and noticed a second gun in the guy's waistband. Jake held the guy's hands still.

"Double-fisting it, huh?" Jake asked.

"I don't know what you're talking about."

"Uh huh. Hold still, sir. I'm going to lift up the end of your shirt here and remove this weapon."

"What the fuck?" Chad called out.

Jake lifted the gun out, checked the safety, and kept it.

"Just making sure we all stay on the same page here, man," Jake said. He went over and grabbed the guy's other gun and walked back over close to him.

"You could have just sent me an invite to the party, Ford," Jake said.

"Ha," she replied flatly from where she was sitting.

"So I heard *his* story," Jake said. "What do you have to say?"

Erica started to stand. "This guy stalked our site and then came onto the property and started harassing us and wouldn't leave."

"Sounds like we have a couple very different stories," Jake said. "Is anyone hurt?"

Erica shook her head.

"Why am I the one in cuffs?" Chad yelled, and started struggling against them. "They're the ones took my kids!"

Jake grabbed the guy's arm to hold him still. "You got a concealed carry permit you forgot to show me?"

Chad just shrugged.

"Right this second," Jake said, "you're the only one here who has clearly broken a law. Stand up now, and we're going to walk over to my car."

Jake helped Chad stand up from where he was kneeling, then steered him over to the cruiser, reciting his Miranda rights. As he shielded Chad's head and tucked him into the car's backseat, Jake explained, "I don't know the details of your argument, but what I do know is this is private property. Unless they sold it just this afternoon, these women live here and you're the one trespassing."

"This is bullshit!" Chad yelled.

"Could be," Jake said. "But better safe than sorry. Some of those women look pretty tough and I just want you to be safe while I check out your story. Okay?"

"Bullshit," Chad repeated.

"Language, man," Jake said. "Language. And while I check you out, a word of advice: that's a dangerous—and stupid—way to carry a gun. Just because you saw it on TV doesn't mean it's a good idea."

CHAPTER 24

Claire was trying to get the kids settled with coloring books for Theo and reading books for Ella, and her phone was going nonstop with texts and calls from Erica. She finally just turned it off, and then just for good measure put the phone in her purse, put her purse in the hall closet, and put two coats over the purse.

Things with the kids had improved. They hadn't stopped asking about their mom, but they were less upset about it. They had started to get into a bit of a routine, with quiet time right after meals and naps or playtime right before.

Claire wasn't sure where they were on a school timeline—at six, she imagined Ella should be in kindergarten. At a bare minimum, they should both be in preschool. Ella wasn't reading yet, but she was sounding out letters and words, and Claire had picked up some early-reader workbooks. She had started calling around about programs at nearby schools but stopped herself when she remembered she was in a totally different school district from the site.

She didn't know why she was keeping her custody a secret. She needed to tell Erica, and Wendi needed to know her kids were safe. But she couldn't bring herself to do it.

The kids didn't need more disruption, she justified. They just needed a little more time to get settled.

* * *

With the kids occupied in the living room with their books, Claire sat at the table in the kitchen where she could see them without hovering. She thought about her phone in her purse in the closet. Not only did she need to get back to Erica, there were a lot of other pieces moving around. It was irresponsible to be unavailable.

She thought this, but she stayed in the chair. She drummed her fingers on the table and looked up occasionally at the kids. Something felt off, and when she tried to figure out what it was, she almost laughed.

What's off? How about everything? How about nothing feels normal anymore, everything is off, and I'm completely unsettled?

Suddenly, she knew what it was.

The voice in her head just now was her own.

She was used to it being Chris's voice.

He hadn't come and talked to her in so long.

"Where are you?" she whispered.

Silence.

"Chris?"

In the other room, the kids had started to fight. "Stop, Theo," Ella whined.

Claire startled to attention and went over to the kids. Theo had started to color in one of Ella's reading books and she was pushing him away. He was retaliating by pulling her hair.

"Hey, hey, now," Claire said. "Hands to yourselves. What's going on?"

Ella explained, Theo protested, and Claire worked out a settlement that involved apple slices and twenty minutes of approved edutainment videos.

* * *

The kids were at the kitchen counter, eating apples and watching the tablet screen with a blue dog singing and counting. Claire was cleaning up, and the doorbell rang. All three of them looked up in surprise.

"It's just the door," she told the kids.

She stayed at the counter. She wasn't expecting anyone or anything, and decided to ignore it.

Then the bell rang again. And again ... And again.

Ella paused the video on the tablet.

"I can't hear my video over the bell," she said, and looked at Claire expectantly.

The bell rang again.

Claire sighed. "I'll go stop it. You two stay here. Ella, watch your brother."

The bell rang again, followed by persistent knocking. Claire pulled back the curtain and saw Erica. Of course. Even better? Wendi was standing behind her, eyes red and face puffy.

Shit.

Erica pounded on the door again. "I know you're there! I just saw you! Open up!"

Claire glanced back at the kitchen. The kids weren't visible from this angle, but she heard Theo laugh at something in the video. She unlocked the door and opened it just enough to step outside, closing the door behind her.

"What are you doing here?" she asked.

"If you'd answer your damn phone, you'd know," Erica said.

"What's going on?"

"We need your house."

"What do you mean, you need my house?"

"Look I don't know what's up with you or why you went AWOL," Erica sighed, sounding exhausted. "I don't know if someone hurt your feelings or what the hell is going on, but we've been dealing with a lot of shit over at the site, and we need you right now."

Claire furrowed her brow and looked confused.

Erica clarified, "Well, to be more specific, we need your house."

As Erica explained the short version of the protective services visit to the site and taking Ella and Theo, it dawned on Claire that they didn't know she had the kids. They were mad at her for leaving, but were totally unaware Ella and Theo were just thirty feet away. She could explain everything right now, but ... where to begin?

"I, uh ..." Claire said. "I have guests right now."

Erica folded her arms across her chest and pursed her lips like she'd tasted something rotten.

"I'm sorry, what?" Erica asked.

"I ... I have guests in the house."

"You've been ignoring our calls and texts because you're ... *entertaining*?" Erica spat.

"Well, it's not exactly—"

"Look, I really don't care," Erica interrupted. "Sorry to bother you while you're hosting a garden party or whatever, but Wendi needs to stay here for a few days."

"What?" Claire asked, her voice a little too high. "Why?"

"Well, if you'd bother to interact with us, you'd know we got an unexpected visitor at the site this morning."

Claire looked quickly at Wendi. "Your ex?"

Wendi nodded.

Erica interjected, "Fun fact: not her ex. Still her husband, and thus even more of a problem."

"Where is he now?" Claire asked.

"County lockup for the moment," Erica said, "but it probably won't hold. We're working on that part, but we need a safe place for Wendi to stay just in case, while we sort it out."

Claire just stood there, trying to figure out her next move.

Erica plowed ahead. "We're still trying to figure out where the kids are, too. The social worker still hasn't told us. But the only good part is if we don't know where they are then he doesn't, either ... so at least for now, that's a good thing."

She started to push past Claire and reach for the doorknob, but Claire stepped to the side and blocked her.

"Well like I said, we're pretty full up here ..."

"Oh, come off it, Claire," Erica spat. "I've been inside this house. Unless you've invited a small city to come and stay here, I know you have room."

"I just don't think—"

As Claire spoke, tiny hands pushed back the curtain next to the front door and two small noses pressed against the window.

"Mommy!" Ella cried.

"Mama!" Theo echoed.

Erica and Wendi looked down at the sidelight window.

"Mother. Fucker," Erica said, and glared at Claire.

"Oh my God!" Wendi shrieked and reached toward the window.

Claire looked down at the window and back up at Erica and Wendi. Realizing there was nothing else she could do, she opened the door. The kids pushed past her and ran to their mom, who dropped to her knees, arms outstretched.

"My babies," Wendi sobbed, and hugged them tightly, collapsing with them onto the ground.

Erica looked past Claire into the otherwise empty house. "*They're* your company?" Erica asked.

* * *

Now that there was no reason to keep Erica and Wendi out of the house, Claire ushered them inside. The children dragged Wendi upstairs to show her their room and their new toys and clothes. Claire and Erica stood in the living room, in awkward silence.

Well, Claire's silence was awkward. Erica's silence had a lot of visible rage.

"I'm trying to understand what's going on here," Erica hissed. "But I could use a little help."

"I don't know if this is the right time ..." Claire started, and then trailed off.

"Oh, this is the Right. Damn. Time," Erica said in a carefully measured tone that made it clear she was trying not to explode at Claire.

"I don't know where to start."

"Let me help," Erica said. How about ..." she put her finger to her lips and tapped them. "Hm, oh, I don't know, how about we start with CPS taking those kids, you going dark, us having no idea what's going on, and now you somehow, mysteriously have the kids in your house? And you can't return a phone call, but you *can* hook them up with coloring books and new shoes? How about we start there?"

Claire blinked. "That's not really a starting point," she said softly.

"We are going to start with me choking you if you don't start talking," Erica said.

Claire sighed and noticed she was wringing her hands. She separated them and wiped her palms on her pants.

"Fine. Come in here."

She led Erica into the kitchen and started preparing a pot of coffee to keep her hands busy while she talked. She explained to Erica that the day after they found out about the kids being taken, she worried about what would happen to them.

"I mean," she whispered to Erica, "I think Wendi is wonderful, but foster care is so uncertain and that's no life for kids and I was worried they'd be taken away forever."

"We are *all* worried about that, Claire."

"Well, I wanted to do something about it."

Erica stared at her in disbelief. "You wanted to do something about it. Unlike the rest of us?"

Claire placed a cup of coffee in front of Erica, who reached for it then shook her head and pushed it away like it was poison. She held her hands up and shook her head back and forth like she was trying to clear it.

"We live in entirely different worlds," Erica finally said. "I mean, I knew we were different, but I—"

"Is it wrong for me to use the tools I have to try to help?" Claire asked.

Erica stuttered. "You—you think stealing Wendi's kids is *helping* her? You think putting them up in your Barbie Dream House here and hiding out is *helping* things?"

Now Claire yelled. "Better than some foster home with strangers where anything could happen to them? Yes, yes, I *do*." She banged her coffee cup down on the counter. Coffee spilled over the edge and she reached for a towel to wipe it up.

"Claire, I just—can you even *begin* to understand how insanely privileged it is for you to just snap your fingers and get a lawyer and fix everything the way you want it? And how messed up that is in comparison to the lives of everyone else we are working with? You could have gotten Wendi a lawyer, but instead you got *yourself* one?"

"I shouldn't have to remind you, Erica," Claire said tersely, "that everyone else we are working with has something to work on and a place to go precisely *because* of my 'privilege' and the fact I wanted to share it."

Erica stared at Claire for a beat.

"Well, Claire, you shouldn't *have* to remind me. But you sure didn't waste any time doing so, did you?"

They glared at each other.

Claire broke the silence. "I am just trying to help."

"Claire," Erica placed her hands on the counter to steady herself and bring the temperature back down.

"I believe you think you are helping and that you genuinely do want to help. But I need you to understand that if your help is simply trying to force other people's lives into a structure that works for you, your 'help' may not actually be helping."

Claire swallowed and blinked back tears.

"What's your end game here, Claire?" Erica asked. "You're helping these kids, you say. But you're not trying to help Wendi. What if Wendi doesn't get them back?"

Claire didn't say anything.

Erica tilted her head to the side. Another thought hadn't occurred to her until now. "Are you ... trying to *keep* them?"

Claire swallowed. She really didn't know, but it wasn't off the table. "I don't know. I really don't know. But ... wouldn't living here be better for them? I could give them a life they'd never be able to have otherwise!"

"Can you *really* not see how you're making this about you instead of about them?"

"It's about me helping them!"

"I need you to stop saying that," Erica said. She pushed away from the counter and started pacing.

"Claire, your willingness to pay for this project, to make it happen, is incredible." She stopped and made eye contact with Claire. "It really is. But—" She looked at the ceiling to try to find the words. "But we have talked from the beginning about how just jumping in and 'fixing' things doesn't actually fix anything."

Claire glared at Erica, sucking in on her cheeks in a way Erica had seen before and knew it meant Claire was hearing and understanding.

"If your solutions and help are about trying to cram other people into your worldview and make them do what you think they should ..." Erica softened her voice to speak with as much kindness as she could muster. "If they are about you and not about them, then they aren't solutions and help."

"Self-determination," Claire said quietly.

"Self-determination," Erica confirmed.

More silence.

"Claire," Erica began. "Who are you really trying to help here?"

"Wendi and the kids, of course."

"Are you sure?"

"Of course I'm sure."

Erica bit the inside of her lip and chose her words carefully. "Then why did you disappear for over a week?"

Claire paused and fiddled with the bag of coffee beans.

"It was very busy here," she said, and unfolded and re-folded the closure on the bag of beans. "Hectic."

"There was no time, in the span of *days* since that hearing, when you could have replied?"

Claire remained focused on the coffee beans.

"Maybe your phone was broken," Erica said. "Was your phone broken?"

Claire kept looking at the bag.

"How about your car?" Erica asked. "Car in the shop and you don't know how to use the bus, phone's broken so you can't

Uber, so it was impossible for you to tell us you had the kids and everyone was okay?"

"I didn't want to make anyone upset," Claire said weakly.

"You didn't want to make anyone upset, or you didn't want anyone to get in the way of the kids staying here with you?"

"No, that's not it," Claire said.

Erica shrugged. "That's sure what it looks like."

"You know," Claire said, putting up more defenses, "you probably shouldn't even be here. If the court hasn't told Wendi where her kids are, there's probably a good reason."

"It sounds like your story is changing, Claire."

Claire shoved the bag of coffee beans and grunted in frustration.

"I don't know, okay!?" she said, and banged her hand on the counter.

Erica waited.

Claire shook her head and rolled her eyes to the ceiling. "I wanted to be sure they were safe. But ... yes, maybe, after getting them back here, it did cross my mind that it might be better for them to stay here than to go back."

Erica stayed silent.

"You know," Claire said, "in the long run."

"In the long run," Erica repeated softly.

Suddenly, the tension was broken by a sob from the doorway.

"I don't believe you!" Wendi cried.

"Oh, Wendi ..." Erica said, moving toward her and shooting daggers at Claire with her eyes.

"You want to steal my kids?" Wendi said, shaking off Erica's attempt to reach for her. "That's why you did this whole thing? You're sick!"

Claire put up her hands in protest. "Wendi, no, I just wanted—"

"You've wanted to steal my kids since the day I met you!" Wendi said. "I should have known you weren't just some lonely old lady. You're sick! You're trying to take my kids!"

"That's not—! I'm not—!" Claire started but couldn't finish.

"You're not going to get them! You're not going to keep them!" Wendi shouted. "We're leaving right now!" She looked at Erica expectantly. "We are going to take them back right now!"

Erica hesitated.

Wendi headed for the staircase and looked back when she saw Erica hadn't moved. "What are you waiting for?"

Erica exhaled. "Wendi, we can't take them."

"What do you mean? She took them, we'll take them back!"

"Wendi, the court assigned her temporary custody. You probably shouldn't even be here."

"So now you're on *her* side? I don't believe this!"

"Wendi, no," Erica said, and went to her. She looked up the stairs and saw the kids sitting at the top of the stairs, listening. "Let's go back into the kitchen."

"No!" Wendi shrieked. Immediately after, Theo and then Ella started crying. Wendi ran up the stairs and sank down next to them on the top step, hugging them.

Erica looked up at them and then over at Claire.

"Nice job," she said, and folded her arms, trying to figure out what to do next.

CHAPTER 25

Erica put Wendi and the kids upstairs in the kids' room so they could reconnect, then stomped down the stairs and pulled Claire into the kitchen.

"Look," Erica lowered her voice to speak to Claire. "I know enough about the system to know I need to get her out of here. According to the court, she can't be near these kids right now. I'm still trying to figure out what the hell is going on with you, but we're going to go so we don't screw up her chances with the courts."

Claire nodded and folded her arms across her chest, looking worried.

"I hope you're not trying to take these kids from her, Claire," Erica said.

Claire shook her head, opened her mouth, and closed it again.

"I'm not," she finally said. "I mean, I ..." She looked at Erica and her eyes started to well up with tears. She thought about Chris, and about the kids she thought she'd have but didn't. Then she thought about Chris again, and missing him so much and wondering why he hadn't been talking to her. Then she thought about awful charity dinners with awful rich people, and how much she preferred the company of the wonderful women she'd met through Erica. She didn't want to ruin this. She'd missed out on having kids, but this was not the way to fix that.

She sniffed back the tears and simply said, again, "I'm not."

Erica looked Claire up and down, seeing she'd just gone through some kind of very thorough, very fast, thought process.

"I don't know how I can say this more directly, Claire." Erica took Claire by the shoulders and looked her directly in both eyes. "Wendi's kids are Wendi's kids. Our goal is not to have you become a foster mom, but to get Wendi back on her feet and get them back."

"I know."

"And you're on board?"

"I'm on board."

"Good." She released Claire and stepped back, gesturing toward the staircase. "Now you need to go upstairs and convince Wendi."

"What? There's no way she wants to talk to me."

"*You're* the one who needs to talk. You need to convince her you're not stealing her kids. And I need you to do it right now, because I need to get her out of here. And then once we're gone, I am going to need every ounce of your privilege to get us through this."

* * *

Claire went upstairs and knocked softly on the door to the kids' room.

"Wendi? It's Claire. Can I speak with you privately, please?"

The door cracked open and Theo peered out, his face just below the doorknob.

"She doesn't want to talk to you right now," he said.

"I bet she doesn't," Claire said, and sank down to her knees so her face was even with Theo's. "Do you think if you and I talk here, she can hear me?"

He looked back inside the room, then back to Claire. "Yeah, I think so."

Theo was holding the door with one hand and his stuffed bunny with the other. One of the bunny's legs stuck through the opening in the door, and Claire reached out and stroked the bunny's leg with one finger.

"I want your mom to know I'm really sorry. She's mad at me right now, and she has every right to be."

"Why is she mad at you?"

"Because I did something very mean. I didn't realize it was mean when I did it, though. I thought I was making things better. I thought I was doing something very nice for two people I like very much."

"But it was mean, not nice?" Theo asked.

"Yes, it turned out that way. It turned out I wasn't being nice, I was being very, very selfish."

"Our mom says it's bad to be selfish."

Claire caught a sob in the back of her throat and a tear rolled down her cheek. "That's because she's the best mom."

"She is," Theo nodded. "She's the best mom."

"You two are very lucky, and I want your mom to know I know that. Even though you can't be all together yet, I promise I'm going to do everything I can to get you all back together again as quickly as possible."

Theo looked back into the bedroom, then popped his head back to the crack in the door. "I think she heard that."

"And I want her to know I'm deeply sorry for being mean before. I made a mistake, and I'm not going to do it again."

Theo looked back. "She heard that, too."

"Good."

"Are you done now?" he asked. "I didn't know this would take so long and I have to go pee."

* * *

When Claire came back downstairs, Erica filled Claire in on the husband situation. She explained that Chad had shown up because Child Protective Services had contacted him.

"Thankfully," she said, "he's about as bright as Wendi made him out to be. Instead of replying to their calls and securing the kids for his custody, he just tried to find Wendi."

"How did he find the site?" Claire asked.

"Our address was on her paperwork. But lucky for us, he also didn't bother with a permit for his guns, so when he went all cowboy in front of a cop, he made it even worse for himself."

"All of that happened this morning?" Claire asked.

"I told you it's been a long day," Erica said. "And since you apparently have the ability to find any lawyer to do anything you want, I need you to use your power for good to keep that jackass locked up."

"I'll do what I can ..." Claire said, sounding unsure.

"No," Erica insisted. "You *will*. This isn't optional. The whole thing falls apart if he gets out. If you're a woman who's trying to protect herself and her kids from an abusive, dangerous guy," she said, "there are so many holes in our legal system that you're pretty much on your own. Unless, you know, you've got a Claire to help you out."

Claire asked about restraining orders, and Erica explained how they're necessary for documentation but unfortunately for most women, if he violates the order, by the time the cops get there it's already too late.

"In its own sick way," Erica said, "it's a good thing he showed up this way. I mean, it's only good because Jake got there before anything bad happened. But still."

Erica tasked Claire with getting the necessary restraining order against Chad, and also getting him on the "red flag" list.

Since he'd been waving his gun around right in front of the cop, they could prove he was an "extreme risk." They also needed to make sure a copy of all these orders made it to the court for the custody hearings, to ensure Chad wouldn't be able to get custody when he was eventually released.

"And speaking of release," Erica continued, "that's where we need your lawyer to work some magic."

Even with the gun incident, Chad would likely be released with just a small fine and only a few hours in jail. Erica was hoping that with Claire's fancy, expensive lawyer on their side, they could find every past violation, unpaid fees and fines, and whatever else they could to push the court to hold him longer. It still might only get them a couple more weeks or months, but anything helped.

Erica and Claire made a list of all the questions and points Claire needed to work on with the lawyer, and Claire nodded enthusiastically when they were done with the list and ready for her to get started.

"This guy is going down!" Claire said excitedly.

Erica sort of half-laughed. "Yeah, kind of," she said.

"What do you mean?" Claire said. "We are going to bury him!"

Erica smiled in the sort of half-sympathizing, half-pitying way she'd gotten used to doing with Claire. "Yeah, kind of," she said again. "With your fancy lawyer we're probably going to get a lot further than Wendi would on her own. But—" and here she lowered her voice again, "odds are, he's going to be out and hunting for her again within a year. She's going to be looking over her shoulder for the rest of her life, and she's not going to have nearly as much support then as she does right now."

"How can we do something about that?" Claire asked.

"We do as much as we can now," Erica said, "and we help her get stable and prepared to deal with the future. She's not the first woman who became homeless running from a shitty man, and she won't be the last."

"You really know how to rain on the hope parade," Claire said.

"Hope isn't what's going to help Wendi here," Erica said. "You making those calls while I somehow peel her away from her children and drag her kicking and screaming to my apartment, however, will."

Claire raised two fingers to her forehead and saluted.

Erica rolled her eyes.

"I'm sorry I disappeared," Claire said.

"You should be."

Claire nodded and looked down at the notes in front of her. "I am."

Erica stood up from the table and scooted her chair in. "Everyone deserves a second chance. Or a fourth."

"Or a seventeenth," Claire said.

"Or a seventeenth," Erica echoed. "Even you."

"I'll take it," Claire said.

"Good," Erica said. "Now turn your phone back on and get to work."

* * *

After Erica and Wendi left and Claire settled the kids down for a nap, she took her purse out of the closet and pulled out her phone. She eased into Chris's chair in the office and called her lawyer.

"I want to be sure I have this right," Melanie said to Claire. "Now you *don't* want to negatively impact the mother's case?"

"Correct," Claire said.

"You do know that for us to ensure the kids stay with you, it'd be best to demonstrate neither parent is fit."

"I know that's what we talked about before," Claire said. "But now I don't want to harm Wendi's case."

"So ... now you *don't* want to keep the kids?"

"I need you to bear with me here," Claire said. "I want to support Wendi. We need to be sure the husband is not only deemed unfit as a parent, we need to find everything we can to keep him in jail for as long as possible, and then keep a tight rein on him if and when he gets out. Restraining order, ankle bracelet, whatever we can do. Within the bounds of the law, of course, but ..." and she hesitated here, but then decided to go for it. "... within the bounds of the law as it applies to me. I know there are different standards of justice, so push the system as far as it will go to help Wendi and keep him away from her and the kids."

Melanie understood, and said she knew the person who could help them.

"But now what about *your* case?" she asked.

"I want to help Wendi get her kids back," Claire said. "She's first priority. I'm second."

"You do know that's different from the last time we talked. It's different from what I've been working on."

"I know," Claire said. "It is. Things have changed. I want to help Wendi now. Okay?"

"Got it," the lawyer said. "Is that it?"

"I think so. For now, at least," Claire said.

"Okay Let me get to work. I have a lot to do between now and when the courts close in two hours. And Claire?"

"Yes?"

"I'm glad you're going this direction."

* * *

Claire leaned back in the chair and gazed out the window into the front yard. She closed her eyes, then inhaled and exhaled slowly.

Good work, Chris's voice said in her head.

"Where the hell have *you* been?" she said softly.

I'm proud of you.

"For what?" she asked. "For doing the right thing and not trying to keep a woman from her children even though I could give them a far better life than she ever will? For using my money and privilege to manipulate the legal system to achieve a desired result?"

She visualized him smiling kindly at her, felt him stroke her hair and run the edge of his hand down her cheek.

All of that, he said. *Look at where you are now and think about where you were two months ago.*

"I'd rather go back two years ago," she said. "Before any of this, when you were here. When none of this had happened, When we still had plenty of time."

I'm serious, he said.

She opened her eyes just slightly and said with an edge, "So am I."

Claire, Chris said.

"Chris," Claire responded.

Seriously, look at everything you have done. It's incredible. You're this close to opening a transitional housing site for ten women, and two kids, who were living on the street. You are helping a woman who was about to lose everything keep her kids and move forward. You helped Erica show the leadership and drive she was always capable of and never had the opportunity. You used the resources you had to create something good.

She sighed, grudgingly accepting his points.

I think you may have also found some of the feeling I used to have when I was helping others.

"My heart isn't nearly as good and clear as yours, Chris."

You're giving me too much credit, he said. *The reason I got so involved and spent the time and money to volunteer—that was about me. It was about how helping people made me feel, and how it helped me reconcile the differences between what I had and what others had. It was rather selfish, actually.*

"Just going to rip away the last shreds of everything I was hanging onto, huh?" Claire asked.

CHAPTER 26

Erica settled Wendi in at her apartment, even though there wasn't much there for anyone to "settle in" to. Not only was the place tiny, Erica spent so much time at work she didn't have much in the way of furniture or creature comforts.

Once she had Wendi set up on the couch with some snacks and an iPad to watch videos, she climbed into her truck to head back to the site. As she pulled away, her phone started ringing. Since she was expecting about ten different calls, she just answered without looking, and put it on speaker.

"Yeah, hello?"

"Erica? Is that you?"

"Mom?" Her mom usually texted. She never called first unless something was wrong. "What's wrong?"

"What are you doing, sweetie, where are you?"

"I'm driving, Mom."

"Is it on speaker? Both hands on the wheel!"

"It's on speaker, Mom. Both my hands are on the wheel. What's wrong? What happened?"

"Nothing. Why do you ask?"

"Because I can literally count on my fingers the number of times you've called me out of the blue that weren't because someone had died or gotten hurt."

"Your dad's here, too, sweetie. Say hi to Erica."

"Hey Little Bear!" her dad called into the phone. "Why's it so loud? Where are you?"

Erica rolled her eyes. "I'm driving, Dad."

"Ten and two, baby, ten and two."

"I know, Dad!" she groaned. "Seriously, you guys, I'm about to have a heart attack. What's going on? Who's in the hospital?"

"She's so negative," her mom said to her dad. "She gets that from you. We saw you in the newspaper," she said to Erica.

"In Olympia? What, did they run an article about people from Oly High who still live within two hours of their parents?"

"Oh, Lord," her dad said. "That article would be like thirty pages long, and so boring it'd make you cry."

She'd get there faster on the freeway, but talking to her parents was distracting so she decided to stay on surface roads in case they did finally drop some bomb like her favorite cousin had died or one of them had cancer. Erica grimaced as she turned onto Burnside to take it all the way east to the site. "Dad, you do know you just insulted me along with every other Oly graduate?"

"Nah, Little Bear, You're different."

"I don't mean to sound impatient, you guys. It's nice to hear from you. But ... seriously ... what's up?"

"You really were in the paper, sweetie," her mom said. "We just read all about your homeless camp. This is a nice change from that tent situation with the city."

Erica shook her head to try to figure out what the hell was going on. The *Oregonian* had written a small blurb after the City Council meeting, but she hadn't seen anything major. As her mom told her more about the article, she realized that little blurb must have been expanded and picked up on the wire. Everything her mom was citing was pulled directly from their presentation.

"Must have been a slow news day in Olympia," Erica said.

"I thought you were working at Portland Promise," her mom said.

"Well ..." Erica said, "I *was* ..."

"Oh, Erica," her mom said. "You didn't end up getting fired after all, did you?"

"Thanks for the vote of confidence, Mom," Erica said.

In the whirlwind of the last few weeks, she had never told her parents about leaving Portland Promise and starting up with Claire and the project site. In her defense, there was a lot going on ... but she also hadn't been super excited about giving her parents yet another opportunity to question the sustainability of her choices.

"Well, sweetie," her mom said, "I wish you'd told us, but this new job sounds very interesting. It sounds like you're running the show there."

Erica blinked and wished she could rewind the conversation. Did her mom sound proud of her without reservation?

"Well, it's a small operation," Erica said.

Now her dad jumped in. "But you're doing some serious hands-on work, it sounds like. Really having the chance to make a difference?"

"I hope so ..."

"Well, tell us more about it," he said.

Since she was taking the slower route, Erica had about twenty minutes to talk with her parents. She told them about meeting Claire and developing the plan. She carefully omitted the part about sparring with Bruce, so her mom wouldn't freak out. Then she described each of the women. Her mom, with all her work in the courts, had some input on ways to help the women who were justice-involved. She also gave Erica a couple more tips on ways to handle Wendi's husband through the legal system. Her dad praised her approach and said he'd been reading a lot of studies about peer support.

She couldn't believe it. This was the most in-depth, professional conversation she'd ever had with her parents.

"We're just so proud of you, sweetie!" her mom enthused. "We've never *not* thought the world of you, but it was just so disappointing to see you in these low-level, subordinate roles. You've been a leader since you were just a little girl."

"With a little time-out there for a few years," Erica said dryly.

"You came out even stronger after all that," her dad said. "You have a gift for helping people, Little Bear. And it sounds like now you're going to be able to help those ten women and so many more after them."

Erica beamed as she pulled up in front of the site, but it quickly turned to a grimace when she saw Sam in the middle of the street, having an animated conversation with Doug the Slug.

"I've got to go, you guys," she said, turning her attention back to her phone for one more moment with them. "This was exactly the call I needed today. Thank you."

"Go get 'em, Little Bear," her dad said.

"We love you," her mom added.

"Love you both," Erica said. Then she hung up, took a deep breath, straightened her shoulders, and jumped out of her truck to see what the hell was going on now with Doug.

CHAPTER 27

Erica checked the time on her truck's dash before getting out of her truck. How could it only be early afternoon? This day had already lasted four years. As she approached, she saw Sam's arms raised in frustration.

"Seriously, man, *what*?" Sam yelled. "I know you think harassing us is your full-time job, but you really need to find something else to do."

Erica stepped in between them to intervene, and held them each at arm's distance.

"How's it going, you guys?" Erica asked. "Nice neighborly conversation here, huh?" She glared at Sam to try to remind her to calm down. She didn't know what was going on, yet, but did know that yelling at neighbors, even one as irritating as Doug, wasn't in their best interest.

"Someone want to tell me what's up here?" Erica asked.

Doug adjusted his shirt and stood more upright. "I don't know why your friend here is so upset," he said archly. "I just saw her at her truck and came out to ask if everything was okay after that visit from the cops this morning."

"And I *told him* that everything was fine," Sam said.

Erica looked back and forth between them. That interaction didn't sound like something that would lead to a face-off in the street.

"Is that it?"

"It should have been," Sam said. "But he wouldn't let it go. He just kept pushing me for more information." She closed her hand into a fist, sticking out her index finger and jabbing it toward him. "And I *told* him it was *fine* and I had work to do and to Leave. Us. Alone."

Erica looked over at Doug and raised her eyebrows.

He shrugged and folded his arms across his chest, resting them on his little pot belly.

"As the neighborhood association chair, I feel I should know the circumstances of any altercations in the neighborhood."

"I *told* you, we took care of it," Sam yelled, and walked away to pace in little circles. "This guy, E."

"Doug," Erica said calmly, "I'm sorry if anything that happened this morning, with the police and all, disturbed you. It was an unfortunate miscommunication with someone who came to the site, and it won't be happening again."

"Well probably not from him," Doug said. "I saw them take him away. But I can't be watching out for you at all hours, calling the cops whenever some unsavory person drops by."

Sam stopped pacing and stared. Erica dropped her hands and turned to face him.

"What?" Erica asked.

"Huh?" Sam echoed.

"*You* called the cops today?" Erica asked.

"You watched the whole thing?" Sam asked.

Doug rolled his shoulders back and lifted his chin. "Yes, I called them. None of *you* were doing anything productive."

"I don't understand," Erica said.

He cleared his throat. "I was at my window keeping an eye on you all, like I do," he said.

"Of course, you were," Sam muttered. "Creeper."

Doug tilted his head just slightly and opened his mouth. He caught himself and started over.

"Yes," he said. "I watch you all a lot so I can report any bad behavior. And it's a good thing for you I was watching, because I saw him circling. And then I saw him pull up. And then I also saw something you *didn't* see, which was when I called Officer Jake."

Erica's brow wrinkled. "What did you see?"

"Right after he got out, when he was standing there before he came over to you, he reached back into the truck to get a couple of guns, which he put in the waistband of his pants. His door blocked you from seeing what he was doing, but I saw the whole thing."

Erica waited for more. "So you ..."

"He had a gun—well, two guns—and looked like he was planning to use them," Doug said. "So I called the cops."

Sam shook her head like she couldn't put the pieces together.

"I called Officer Jake directly," Doug said. "I had his card from that first day and I thought he'd be able to get here quickly."

"I was wondering about that," Erica said. "Cops showing up—when you want them ..." she trailed off.

"That isn't how it usually works for us," Sam finished.

"I may not be happy about all this," Doug waved generally toward the site. "But there is no call for a weapon. He was clearly only here to cause trouble."

"True that," Sam agreed. "But I still don't ..."

"... Understand why I did something to help you?"

"Yeah," Sam said.

Doug shrugged slightly and looked at the ground. "Me, neither. I still think your site isn't good for our neighborhood. But you're here. You're my neighbors now, whether I like it or not."

"Huh," Sam said. "Unexpected."

"I was just ..." Doug started, and struggled to finish. "I was just hoping everyone is ... okay. I saw you," he nodded toward Erica, "leave with the one lady who had the kids."

"Things are okay for now," Erica said, noting that he said *had* the kids, past-tense. Thanks to him, Wendi did not *have* her kids, present-tense. Just because this guy had done one good thing, he still wasn't a friend. She didn't want to tell him too much.

"Thanks for calling the cops." She paused and gave him a wry smile. "That's not something I ever thought I'd hear myself say. But I'm glad Jake was here when we needed him."

"I am, too," Doug said.

They looked at each other uneasily.

"We, uh," Erica said, "we're supposed to be getting the main commons building tomorrow. It's going to come on a truck and there'll probably be some disruption for a little while."

Doug nodded.

"But we'll try to keep it to a minimum, and not disturb the neighborhood too much."

"Thank you for letting me know," Doug said.

Sam smirked. "It should be pretty cool, actually," she said. "But you'll know that, since you'll be watching."

CHAPTER 28

The pre-fab commons building was going to arrive in just a few minutes. Sam had been getting text updates and sharing them with the group, and the most recent text said they were turning off from the main road. When the truck with the container building turned onto their street, everyone stopped what they were doing and stared. Neighbors came out to watch and Doug opened his curtains wide, no longer even trying to hide the fact that he was staring from his living room window.

It was a slick operation. There were two guys in the truck with the building on it, and they were followed by three guys in another truck carrying a huge crane. These five guys and the crane were going to put the whole thing into place.

The guys backed the truck with the building up onto the property, as close as they could get to the spot where it was going to go. They'd instructed Sam and Erica to have the whole area in front clear, and now it made sense why. If there had been any landscaping, it would have gotten crushed.

Then they pulled the second truck up on the street directly in front and used hydraulic levers to stabilize it and anchor it onto the road. Three guys clambered on top of the building to set up straps and hooks, while the other two secured the crane. They cleared everyone away, and then ... the crane lifted the entire building up, so it hovered off the truck. Four of the guys used long rods to help guide it as the guy in the truck maneuvered the building so it was directly above the foundation. Everyone took a breath, and then as the crane lowered the building down, the four guys on the ground got up close and used the long rods to help guide it into position. They used headsets to talk to each other the entire time, and Sam was amazed at how smooth the whole thing was. It was done in less than two hours.

After the building was placed and all the connections made, they came over to Sam to talk through the final checklist and asked Erica to sign off on payment.

"Looks like you guys have done this before," Sam said.

The guy who handled the crane nodded. "Once or twice," he said, and smiled.

A different guy, who had driven the truck with the building, looked around at the tiny houses.

"This is really cool," he said. "What are you all doing here?"

Sam explained the site concept and gestured around to some of the women who'd be living there.

"And you're building all the houses yourself?" the driver asked.

Sam nodded.

"Now *I'm* impressed," he said. "You're building all those yourself, and just have this one container that's prefab?"

"Yeah. We wanted to do the houses by hand for customization, but it was just easier to go prefab for the building with the major plumbing and electric and all."

He nodded. "No, no, I get it. It's great. It's a smart plan."

Sam smiled. "Thanks. I thought so, but then sometimes you see something like this," she gestured at the container building, "and you wonder if you actually know what you're doing."

The guy shook his head. "Can I tell you something?"

"Sure ..." Sam said.

"This is the tightest setup I've seen in a long time."

"Seriously?"

"Seriously. Everything is organized, you left all the space we needed in front, our utility guys said they had no problems getting everything ready, and those houses you're building look amazing. I can't tell you how often we get to a job site and it's a mess. We have to either wait around for them to be ready for us, or we have to take out fences and bushes just to get where we are going, or who knows what. Makes it turn into a real long day."

"Wow," Sam said, and nodded. "Thanks."

* * *

Once the guys and the trucks had left, the women from the site stood at the road, admiring the building. A few neighbors also came around and stood with them. A few said it looked nice, and they couldn't believe how fast it all went in.

"Makes it look like a real ... place, you know?" a woman from down the street said to a friend of hers.

"It's always been a real place," Salina said from behind them.

Startled, the two women turned around nervously. "I didn't mean—" one of them said.

Salina interrupted her with a smile. "Nah, you're right," she assured her. "I get it."

The building was about 800 square feet. More than four times the size of the individual tiny houses, but still only about half the size of the smallest houses on the rest of the block. To fit the look of the neighborhood, Sam had worked with the designer to give it the look and feel of a ranch-style house like the ones all around them. It had the same kind of low-pitched roof and the longer overhang in the eaves, which made the one-story building feel more settled into the ground. The front door had a small stoop with an overhang, where a couple of chairs could be set up, and there was a large picture window in the front living/gathering space, looking out onto the road in front.

Inside, the building had a wide, open-plan feel. The kitchen was designed to offer a little more room at the counters and the island, to accommodate more people, and it opened directly onto the main commons space. At the back of the building, a specially-designed accordion door opened fully onto the patio pad in back. There was a small bedroom/office room on this side of the space. They'd have a computer set up in there for common use, and they'd keep a cot in the closet in case they ever needed an emergency space for someone to stay. There was a full bathroom connected to this room, and a half bath in the hallway.

The most exciting part for everyone was the shower/bath unit that took up the space where the garage would be on a "normal" ranch house. There were three showers and three toilet stalls, all with their own locking doors. There was a common sink area with four sinks, and ten tall lockers for all the women to keep their own supplies and personal items. Off to the side were two stacked washer/dryer sets, both large enough to take bedding. This side of the building could be accessed directly from outside, and also from a door through the kitchen.

Erica and Sam had the women who'd be living there walk through so they could see it first, before anyone else. They smiled at all the "oohs" and "aahs" that came from the group.

"All right you all," Erica said. "Time to test it out! We'll set up a regular schedule, but since I bet everyone is going to want a shower, let's start with fifteen minutes each and we'll go alphabetically for now. If it's not your turn yet, you can start moving stuff from the camp kitchen into the new kitchen."

"My middle name is Anne," Sarah said. "I just decided I'm going by my middle name."

"Nice try," Sam said. "You're showering with 'S.' You and Salina go grab the coolers and start putting the stuff into the fridge."

"Not fair," Sarah said.

"100 percent fair," Sam replied, and wrinkled her nose at Sarah. She walked over to Erica to compare notes on next steps.

"Sam, this is freaking amazing," Erica said.

"It really came together."

"I knew you were the right person for this," Erica said.

Sam arched one eyebrow. "Um, you okay?"

Erica realized her mouth was open and closed it. Then she opened it again to speak, and closed it again. "I'm trying not to gush," she finally said.

Sam beamed. "Go ahead and gush. It's goddamn spectacular."

"Remember us little people when you go off and become a famous developer."

"Not a problem," Sam said. "And of course, I wouldn't be a famous developer if you hadn't had the brilliant idea."

"I guess we're both pretty brilliant," Erica said.

"We are," Sam nodded.

"Definitely," Erica said. They both smiled and laughed.

Sam stuffed her hands in her front pockets. "And, uh ... not to dwell, but we wouldn't have been able to be so brilliant if we didn't have Claire."

Erica nodded. "True."

"Where is she, by the way?" Sam asked. "Haven't seen her in days, and I want to show this to her."

"She will definitely want to see it," she started. "It's been a wild few days. Wendi, the kids, custody."

"Things got kind of wild here, too, you know," Sam said.

"Hey," Erica said. "I have an idea."

* * *

Erica pulled out her phone and called Claire for a video chat. Now that Claire had turned her phone on and might actually answer, this was a great way to connect them all. There were a few tedious minutes while Claire tried to figure out which direction to hold her phone, and then Erica and Sam telling her they could hear her just fine and she didn't need to yell. Once they sorted it out, they had a video chat going where the three of them were able to all talk together, like they had early on.

"It's not the same as sitting at your kitchen counter, eating your food and drinking your coffee," Sam said. "But it'll do for now."

Claire laughed. "I've missed you, Sam. I'm sorry I was out of touch, and you are welcome at my kitchen counter any time."

"Okay, you two," Erica said. I wanted to get us all on at the same time partially so you could remember what each other looks like, and partially because we have a lot to catch up on. Claire, most of all we wanted you to see this."

She flipped the view on the camera so she could slowly scan the site. She and Sam talked Claire through what she was seeing. Houses almost finished, the new commons building in place, the portable toilets and tarp soon to be removed, the container gardens that were going to start producing fruits and vegetables any day now. She flipped the view back to their faces, and jerked her thumb toward neighbor Doug's house, visible over her shoulder.

"Even Doug the Slug said the new building made a huge difference," Sam said.

"I can't believe it, you two," Claire said. "It's so ..."

Sam grinned. "Real?"

"Yes."

"That's what *we* said!"

Claire made them show her the site again, and then after she'd promised to get there the next day to see it for herself, she and Erica filled Sam in on all that happened with Wendi and the kids. Claire then updated them on her calls with the attorney. There was still more to do, but things were looking reasonably positive for making Wendi's husband her ex-husband, and making sure he'd be in jail for at least the next few months.

"I can't believe how difficult it is to keep dangerous people away from the people they want to hurt," Claire said. "I never realized ... well," she said, catching herself, "I guess there's a lot I never realized."

"Claire," Erica said, "you're doing fine. We are literally here because of you, and against all odds and predictions it looks like we might possibly pull this thing off."

"I've learned so much from you ... from everyone," Claire said.

"Ditto, Rich Lady," Sam said. "You want to say hi to everyone?"

Claire's face lit up. "Oh yes! If they're not too busy or doing other things!"

"Everyone's had a long day," Sam said. "A couple may be sleeping or checked out, but the rest will be happy to see you. Let's go see."

Erica walked the phone across the site, turning the view so Claire could see it all again as they walked. Sam went ahead to the commons building and poked her head in.

"Hey, you all want to talk to Claire?" Sam called.

"Who?" someone called back.

"The rich lady, dumbass," someone else said in response.

"Oh! Sure!"

"Where's she been?"

Erica brought the phone into the room and panned around the living area space next to the kitchen.

"Hey Claire," Jamilah called.

"Hi everyone," Claire said back. "You look great, and so does that place."

"It's sweet, huh?" Karyn said.

"I've taken, like, five showers since it got here," Sarah said, "and I'm never going to stop."

Claire laughed.

"No, she's serious," Barb said. "We had to create a Sarah Rule for the shower. It's like for seconds—you can't go back till everyone else has had firsts."

Jamilah shook her head. "Every rule exists because there's always one person ..." She smirked at Sarah. "I'm teasing, but also serious."

Erica turned the view back to her face and took the phone outside.

"Can you show me one of the houses?" Claire asked. "The inside?"

"Nope," Erica said. "You're going to have to come see the rest for yourself, in person."

"Is Wendi there?" Claire asked.

"No. Just to be safe I took her to my apartment," Erica said.

"When you go back, can you let her know the kids are settled down and doing great?"

"Of course," Erica said.

They chatted a little longer, and talked about what they each had to do to get the site finished and get the Wendi-and-kids situation squared away. Just as they were about to hang up, Claire's eyes welled up with tears and she choked up a little.

"Thank you both so much," she whispered.

"What are you talking about?" Erica said back. "We should all be thanking you."

"No," Claire sniffled to keep the tears at bay and shook her head. "It goes both ways."

Erica nodded. "Good night, Claire."

"Good night."

CHAPTER 29

The site had been finished for about three weeks now, and it looked better than Claire could have ever imagined. She sat on the little porch just outside Wendi's tiny house, enjoying the warm sun on this crisp early-autumn day. The kids were off playing with Wendi, and Claire had stowed her purse and the kids' bag of toys just inside the door of the house. Everyone else was bustling around, getting ready for the party.

The houses were all the same style, but with individual details that made each one unique. Porches, loft areas, fold-down tables and desks that made the space more useful. Seeing all the houses together, it really did look like a tiny little neighborhood, with mulched paths and the central commons building to connect them all.

Look what you did, Babe, Chris's voice whispered into Claire's ear. *Look at these houses, this place, these people.*

Claire smiled. "It's not like I did it alone, Chris." She looked around and drank in the sight of all these women who had put so much effort into changing and improving their lives.

"They all worked so hard. They have been working harder to get here than I ever had to work in my life. All I did was pay for it."

You think that's all you did? You think you're just the checkbook?

"Well ... yes."

I don't think that's true. I don't think you'd still be here if this was just about writing a check.

* * *

As the site approached completion, the women had decided they wanted to celebrate with a Grand Opening. Not something huge, but something to make it special. Claire and Erica fully supported the idea, and liked that it allowed them to grow the connection with the neighborhood. The neighbors had been coming around wanting to get a look at the houses, and this would give them a chance to snoop around—and, more importantly, to meet these incredible women.

The group decided they would only open a couple of the tiny homes up for tours. A few of the women didn't want to let strangers in, and that was okay. They opened up the house that had been intended for Cheryl, and Linda and Marta also decided they'd open their houses so people could see.

"You know they're gonna want to look, and they're going to ask," Linda had said. "I'll let them look in my house, as long as I can stay close to keep an eye on things and make sure they don't snoop in my stuff. It'll give me something to do."

"Same, same," Marta said. "I always need something to do at parties, otherwise I just stand around and don't know what to say."

Wendi was excited that Claire was bringing the kids. She'd moved out of Erica's apartment after just a couple of days, once they confirmed Chad would be stuck in jail for a while. The kids were still at Claire's, though. Wendi had been allotted one supervised visit with the kids each week, and one additional video call.

Claire was grateful Wendi had accepted the foster situation, and was relieved to see her looking restored and energetic.

Seeing Wendi beginning to thrive made it easier for Claire to accept her own foster role as temporary.

Wendi had been working on her parenting plan with her social worker and was making good progress. She'd moved into her tiny house and she had started a certification program to become a peer counselor. Once she had that certification, she'd be able to get a job working with a local outreach agency to help women like her who were escaping from domestic violence and had found themselves homeless or nearly homeless.

Claire, Erica, and Wendi were all cautiously optimistic that Wendi would have her custody restored when they came to the ninety-day hearing. And, Claire assured all of them, she was fully prepared to unleash the fancy lawyers to make it happen, if needed.

⋆ ⋆ ⋆

When they were planning the party, the women had agreed they could all invite up to two people. And, as a group, they would also extend an invitation to the neighborhood association. At first, Sarah had argued they should only invite the neighbors who had been nice to them.

"Why would we invite the jerks who don't want us here to come and drink our fizzy water and eat our snacks?" Sarah had asked.

The rest of the women acknowledged she had a good point and were ready to protect their snacks—until Marta pointed out that inviting the naysayers was just as important as inviting the friendlies.

"I mean, the nice ones already like us," Marta said. "Inviting the ones who were shitty to us means we can take the high road and show them what a great place this is, not at all like they were saying it'd be."

Sarah grumbled something about the high road being suckier than the low road, but she was outvoted when the others recognized Marta was right.

"It'll be kind of nice to rub their noses in how wrong they were, too," Salina said.

"Not quite what I meant," Marta admonished.

Salina shrugged. "You do you, I'll do me."

★ ★ ★

Most of the people the women had invited were friends from camps or shelters. They'd had a long conversation as a group about who they wanted to have there.

Marta wanted to see if her daughter would come.

"Since I got stable here," Marta said, "she's finally started taking my calls. I don't know if she'll come, but I want her to see what we're doing here, let her see how much better this is."

"I hope she comes," Wendi said. "You think if she sees how good you're doing now, she'd ask you to move back in?"

"I don't know," Marta shrugged. "And I don't even know if I want to go that way. But I want her to know I'm doing well, and take that weight off both our shoulders."

They discussed possible guests a little longer, then Heather gazed over at the house that was supposed to be Cheryl's. It was still empty, but they had interviews for possible new members scheduled for the next day.

"If I can find her, I want to invite Cheryl to the party," Heather said.

Salina reached over for one of Heather's hands and squeezed it. "You sure about that?"

"I know we're filling the spot with someone else, but I want her to see what she could have. I want her to know it could be different for her."

"I don't think I'm going to invite anyone," Sarah said.

"Why not?" Karyn asked.

Sarah looked at her feet. "When I was in the camps, the only person who looked out for me besides me was Erica. And she's sitting right here. So ... I don't know, I guess I feel like I wouldn't trust anyone I knew before."

A few of the others nodded.

"I hear you," Jamilah said.

"What if someone tried to mess with us or mess up this place?" Sarah asked.

Erica had been listening but trying not to insert herself into their conversation. At this concern from Sarah, though, she pointed up at one of the cameras they had placed at the corner of the commons building. There were others in locations all around the site, tied to an app that ran through the commons computer and their phones.

"That's one of the reasons we have those cameras," Erica said. "They won't keep someone from trying, but they'll help us make sure they get caught."

"It's okay if you don't invite anyone," Karyn said. "You've got all of us!"

Sarah groaned like she was in pain but her smile gave her away. "Don't remind me!"

* * *

Erica had invited her mom and dad to come down from Olympia. They were so much more positive about this project than anything else she'd ever worked on, and she wanted them to see it for themselves. She was still nervous, though. What if they saw it and it—and she—didn't meet their expectations?

"You're proud of this place and these people, right?" Sam asked Erica.

"Of course."

"Then show it off," Sam said. "I heard Claire was inviting the mayor. Maybe that would impress them."

Erica laughed. "I don't know ... my mom says the longer you work in government, the less impressed you are when you meet an elected official."

* * *

For her part, Sam wanted to invite the work crew she'd hired, so they could see the fruits of their labor. The residents agreed she could go over her guest limit for that.

And Claire had, indeed, invited the mayor. She'd also gotten approval from the group to go over her guest limit, so she could invite the rest of the City Council and three women she described as her "fancy charity lunch friends from a past life." She was already starting to think about the next steps, and wanted to be sure the powers that be and the deep pockets that fund those powers saw what good could come from taking a chance, doing some hard work, and—yes—spending a lot of money. In the same vein, she and Erica had also discussed whether to invite Bruce, from Portland Promise. Erica still hated him, and Claire hadn't spoken with him since she pulled her funding after the luncheon. But as an organization, Portland Promise did provide services they wanted to link to—and both of the women realized that an uneasy truce is better than an active conflict.

"I kind of want to rub his nose in how good we did, too," Erica said when they talked about it. "Show him how much you can get done when you're in it for the right reasons."

Claire laughed a little. "Rubbing his nose in it isn't really the spirit we should go at this with ..." Then she lowered her voice. "Even though I totally agree."

They decided to add him to the invite list, and to do their best not to gloat.

"Yeah," Erica said. "Gloating is what he would do. So yeah, no. Not gonna go there."

★ ★ ★

Most of the guests had arrived, and Sam and Jamilah were inside the commons house talking to a couple of the women from the work crew. Jamilah looked outside and noticed Doug the Slug standing in the yard, talking with a couple of the neighbors.

"Look who showed up," she said, and nudged Sam in the ribs.

"Let's go say hi and make him nervous," Sam said.

They excused themselves from the conversation inside and went out to Doug and the neighbors.

"You made it," Sam said.

Sam recognized the two women neighbors as people who had testified in their favor at the City Council meeting. They smiled warmly. Doug looked at Sam, a little startled, then he smiled.

"Big step up without the porta-potties and the tarp," Doug said.

One of the neighbor women swatted his arm. "Seriously, Doug?" she asked.

He waved her hand away. "Sorry," he said. "But you know I'm right. I bet you're all happy not to be using those anymore."

Jamilah arched one eyebrow and nodded. "Sure. Who wouldn't be?"

He was holding a can of soda and used it to gesture. "Thanks for the soda," he said. "And—" He used the can to point out at the rest of the site. "This is impressive. It's not what I expected."

Sam and Jamilah just stood there quietly, waiting. It was a trick they'd learned from Erica. Just wait, and the other person will probably keep talking.

"I, uh, I owe you all an apology," he said.

Sam and Jamilah tilted their heads as if to ask, *Oh? You do?*

"I mean," Doug continued, "I'm not sorry for caring about my neighborhood. But ... you all said from day one that this would be something different from those other, filthy places. And it really is."

Sam and Jamilah looked at each other.

"Kind of a weird apology," Sam said to Jamilah, but clearly speaking so Doug would hear it.

"Truth," Jamilah said to Sam.

"It's so weird, though, that I think he means it."

"Yeah, me, too."

They both turned to look at Doug.

"Okay," Sam said.

"We will take your apology under consideration," Jamilah said.

Doug stuttered. "I—I— thanks?"

Sam winked at the neighbor women. "Pretty awkward, huh?"

One of the neighbors laughed. "Make him work for it," she said.

The other neighbor joined in. "It'll be good for him."

Doug, still confused, wandered off to find another group to talk with.

* * *

Wendi and Heather were sitting at one of the tables with the two kids. Heather was helping Ella work on a puzzle with oversized pieces, and Wendi watched Theo attack a coloring book with a green crayon.

"Not coloring inside the lines at all, huh?" Heather asked Wendi, who shook her head in response.

"Nope. We gave up on that a loooooong time ago."

Heather shrugged. "It's overrated anyway."

Wendi laughed a little then looked across the yard and nodded her head in that direction. Heather followed her eyes and saw Marta in front of her house, talking to a woman who looked like her younger twin. They spoke tentatively, taking turns. One would lean in to talk, then lean back just slightly, as if making room. Then the other leaned in to fill the space when she spoke, and leaned back. It was slight, but Wendi noticed it. She'd spent a lot of time with Marta over the last few weeks, especially right when her kids got taken. Marta was a physical person and Wendi knew she could gather you in a hug that felt like it could stop time. Watching this exchange, she saw that characteristic in the younger woman, too. And it seemed like both of them were fighting the urge to reach out and grab the other in a hug. Like they were afraid it might be rejected, but also afraid they might never get to feel that hug again. She reached her hand out for Theo and rumpled his hair with her hand. It was so easy to make mistakes. And so hard to fix them.

"Marta's daughter looks just like her," Wendi said.

"I'm glad she came. Marta was worried, wasn't she?" Heather asked.

"Yeah," Wendi said. "The way Marta tells it, she wasn't the best mom to her daughter. But she's been the closest thing to a mom I've had. I hope she gets another chance."

"That's what we're all about here, isn't it?" Heather asked.

Wendi nodded. "Yeah." Then a beat later she added, softly, "No Cheryl?"

Heather shook her head and kept her eyes on the puzzle piece she was holding. "No Cheryl."

"I'm sorry," Wendi said.

"It happens."

"Yeah, but it can still suck."

Heather nodded. "Yeah."

"She'll get another chance when she's ready."

"I hope so," Heather said, sounding not exactly hopeful. "But—" She took a breath and brightened slightly. "The rest of us are here. And that's big."

* * *

Claire looked over at the table where Wendi and Heather sat with the kids. She'd grown attached to those two little ones, and it was going to be hard to let go when the court restored Wendi's custody. But she had also grown fond of Wendi and was impressed by her determination to get her kids back. She loved seeing them all so happy and closer to thriving than they'd ever been.

You should be proud of all this, Chris said.

"I suppose so," Claire said. "But I'm not going to go around patting myself on the back like 'Look how wonderful I am for saving all these people.'"

Good, Chris said. *That'd be tone-deaf and arrogant.*

"Well, as long as that's clear ..."

I'm just saying ... good job. You were an important part of something good.

"Thank you, love."

Now, as much as I want you all to myself, you need to get off this porch and go talk to people.

Claire sighed. "I'm enjoying just watching them."

Claire Anderson, you are hosting a party, Chris said with a fake-stern voice. *You know better than to think this is the time to enjoy yourself.*

She laughed. "Wow, way to channel my mother."

She was right about some things. Go out there and talk to your guests.

She reluctantly stood up and brushed her hands down the front and back of her pants.

I think you should start with the mayor and your society friends, because they look very uncomfortable.

"I was kind of enjoying their discomfort."

That's my girl.

* * *

Claire made her way over to the space in front of Jamilah's tiny house, where the mayor and Bruce stood stiffly, trying not to look like they were standing stiffly. Bruce kept his hands folded tightly across his chest, and the mayor held a sweating can of sparkling water. They were chatting with three of Claire's socialite friends, and the mayor actually looked a little relieved when Claire walked up.

"Mayor," she said warmly, extending her hands toward him. "Thank you for coming." Since he was holding the can with one hand, she gripped his other hand with both of hers. She then turned to the others, who had expanded the circle slightly. She wedged herself in a little more.

"Bruce, nice to see you. And Carol, Dorie, Shirley—thank you for coming, too."

"This is really something," the mayor said and took a sip from his can.

Bruce sniffed and nodded slightly.

"It is," Claire said firmly as she raised an eyebrow at Bruce. "It's something important, and it's going to change lives for the better."

One of the rich women tittered with laughter and said condescendingly, "Now you just need to make, what, 1,000 more of these to solve homelessness in Portland?"

Claire bristled slightly but turned to her with a broad smile. "You know, Carol, I'm glad you said that. There's an important distinction. This site isn't trying to 'solve homelessness.' That's *their* job." She tilted her head slightly toward the mayor and Bruce. "At this site, we are trying to help these ten women. And, once they are on their feet, the next ten who come after them."

Carol pressed her lips into a tight smile, but her eyes glared at Claire. "I see."

"It's an easy mistake to make," Claire continued, throwing a little bit of Carol's condescension back to her. Then she remembered that she didn't need enemies here. She'd invited these people to get them on board, not to turn them further against her.

"What we found," she continued with a gentler tone, "was that the system we have all supported," she waved her hand around the circle to include everyone and landed with her gaze on Bruce, "helps a lot of people. And we need it. Bruce and Portland Promise do good work. But it doesn't help everyone. This site is a part of diversifying our support."

The mayor cleared his throat. "I was doubtful," he said.

"I know," Claire smiled.

"But I'm impressed," he said.

"Thank you."

Dorie spoke up. "It's much better than the trashy campsites you see on the side of the freeway."

"Someone very smart once told me," Claire said, "when you make people a part of designing their solution, then it is more likely to be something they care about, and take care of."

"Sounds like someone I know," Bruce said under his breath.

"And," Claire continued as though she hadn't heard him, "when we treat people who have less than we do with respect, it validates their existence as individuals. Which we all need, don't we?"

The others nodded, and the group was briefly, awkwardly, silent. Claire enjoyed just standing in it.

After a few seconds, she relieved them and clapped her hands once.

"Well," she said. "Mayor, I know you probably have several other events to get to, and we have a little presentation to make this place officially 'grand-opened.' If you'll excuse me, I'll get us started."

CHAPTER 30

Claire and Erica encouraged everyone to gather closer to the "stage" area they had set up outside the sliding doors to the commons house, making sure Sam and the residents were toward the front. They stood on the grass and faced out at the rest of the group.

"Can you all hear us okay?" Erica said loudly. People nodded yes.

"Since we have to yell because I forgot to get us a loudspeaker, we'll keep this kind of short."

"You're already kind of short," Sarah yelled from the group.

"Seriously?" Erica asked sharply.

Sarah and the other residents laughed.

Claire spoke up. "You know it's a real show when there's a heckler," she said, and put her arm around Erica's shoulders.

"Thanks for joining us today," Claire said. "We are grateful you could be here to celebrate the official opening for this project that so many people made possible." She stepped away from Erica and gestured for her to continue.

"We are the ones standing up here," Erica said, "but that's not because this project is ours. This project is owned and run by the women who live here. We're just the ones talking because they know we don't like public speaking, and they forced us to do it." She laughed and looked pointedly at the residents.

"It's true," Jamilah shouted.

The other women laughed and clapped.

"This project started," Claire said, "because I had some money and Erica had an idea. But it came to life because of Sam's hard work and vision," she gestured toward Sam, "because the City Council let us do something different," she extended her hand toward the mayor, "because the neighbors gave us a chance," she waved her hand toward neighbor Doug, "and—most important—because of the dedication and spirit of the women who live here."

She swept her hand broadly across the front of the group. She and Erica started clapping, and everyone else joined in.

As the applause died down, Erica started up. "The problem of homelessness, and all of the contributing factors that lead people into homelessness, isn't something any one person, government agency, or group can solve. We all need to do our part, because it affects all of us."

The group applauded.

"I am honored to know each and every one of you," Claire said, and made eye contact with every woman living at the site, and then with Sam, and then with Erica. "When I started this project with you, I wanted to help. As we finish it, I am so grateful to you for letting me into your lives. I have gained so much in this process. I'm honored to be here with you today."

"We love you, too, Rich Lady!" Sarah shouted.

Claire laughed.

Erica poked her. "How do you feel about the heckler now?"

"Pretty good, actually," Claire said.

"I want to remind you all," Erica said, "the only reason we are up here speaking is because the women who run this place are making us." She smirked and pointed at Sarah. "I guess you do want to speak, just from out there where you can make fun of us."

"Yup!" Sarah yelled and clapped. Heather was sitting next to her and reached over to lower Sarah's hands.

"Okay," Erica said. "Clearly you all are done listening to us. So we'll wrap this up. This project may be built and ready to go—but this isn't the end. It's just the beginning." She started to get a little choked up and caught herself.

"Now," Claire said taking over so Erica could pull it together, "we just have one last thing. This whole time we've been working on this site, we've just been calling it 'the site' or 'the project.' And that's a terrible name." She laughed, and the other women shouted agreement.

"We are very proud to announce that this site *does* have a real name," Claire said.

"And," Erica added, "even though our members made us come up here and do most of the talking, this part is something only they can do. Members have named this site, and we need members to tell you about it. So, Wendi and Marta, could you come up here please?"

Wendi moved Ella off her lap and handed her to Karyn. Marta squeezed her daughter's hand, then walked toward the front. Once they were there, Claire and Erica went inside the commons building. They came out carrying a large sign covered by a blanket, and propped it up on the ground between them, behind Wendi and Marta.

"We, um ..." Wendi started, and looked over to Marta.

"We knew we were going to speak here," Marta said, "but ... it's very different talking to all of you here than it was when we practiced in my cabin."

The crowd laughed supportively.

"You got this," Sarah shouted.

"You do," Erica said softly behind them. "Just tell us about the name."

"We talked about all different kinds of names for this place," Wendi said. "And there were a lot that were fine, but nothing seemed perfect."

"And then," Marta said, "right as we were coming up to the finish line ... or, maybe the starting line, depending how you want to think of this place," she said, and glanced back at Erica, "all kinds of things happened that set us back. Or could have."

"We lost one of our friends," Wendi said, "we had trouble with the neighbors, I temporarily lost my kids and had trouble with my ex-husband ... it was looking bad."

"But we made it through," Marta said. "Most of the things that were problems a few weeks ago are still problems today. It's not like some rosy happy ending. But—we're working through it, and we're getting there."

"We're figuring it out," Wendi said. "And the only reason we can is because of the support here, and because we all got more than one chance."

"When you screw up," Marta said, "you don't always get a chance to fix it." She looked at her daughter and her eyes welled up with tears. "But sometimes you do. Sometimes you get that second chance. Or third chance, or fourth."

"Or seventeenth," Wendi said, and laughed.

"And that's what this place means to us," Marta said.

Wendi and Marta stepped to either side and gestured for Erica and Claire to drop the blanket from the sign:

CAMP 17TH CHANCE

The crowd laughed and rose to their feet, applauding and cheering. The residents of the site hugged each other and cried. They'd reached the finish line ... or maybe the starting line.

EPILOGUE

In true government fashion, Wendi's ninety-day hearing ended up being late, at about 101 days. That extra time, however, allowed the women and the lawyers to get Wendi's case fully together and make a strong showing before the court. Wendi was just about to complete her peer-counselor certification, and she had already received two conditional job offers from agencies in town. One was with the YWCA, and one was with Portland Promise, Erica's old employer.

"Is it weird," Wendi asked Erica, "that I got a job offer from the same place that kind of brought us all together?"

"No," Erica said, "because you're a great candidate." She smiled. "You may hate working for Bruce, but that's your call, not mine."

The Portland Promise job paid a bit more, but Wendi was a little more drawn to the job with the Y because it would be working directly with women who had been abused and were trying to avoid or get out of homelessness. But she didn't want to turn away from a bigger paycheck. She couldn't believe that after coming from nothing and having to sell her plasma to buy food for the kids, she was in a position to be considering two different job offers. To decide what to do, she had worked through different income and expense worksheets with Erica and with her social worker from the courts. It looked like she could make ends meet with either job, and still have enough after expenses to begin saving for her own apartment. Once she found stability she'd eventually need to move away from the site, but for a while at least she could stay, and save, and have additional support to take care of the kids. She decided to take the job with the YWCA.

⋆ ⋆ ⋆

Claire was grateful for a little more time with Ella and Theo, but had been working on preparing herself for the reality they'd be moving out. And at the end of each day, when her muscles ached from chasing them around, that reality was a little easier to accept.

Following children around is a young person's job, Chris said in her head. She hadn't been hearing his voice as often lately, but every now and then he'd pop up.

"Soon, I'll be able to just visit them, and then leave when we all get tired," she said.

Sounds like a good deal.

"I think so, too."

She was also grateful for the chance to get to know Wendi a little bit better. Although they had both judged each other harshly at first, Claire had come to see how and why Wendi made the choices she did. This brave young woman was doing the best she could with the tools and resources she had. In her role as sort-of grandmother to Ella and Theo, Claire had also become a sort-of aunt to Wendi, and she enjoyed the opportunity to see the world through her eyes.

Wendi was now allowed two supervised visitations a week, and Claire's lawyer had arranged for Claire herself to be the supervisor. She either took the kids over to the site to spend time with their mom and the other residents, or occasionally picked Wendi up and brought her to the house. Claire left them alone during these times, and after Wendi's time was done with the kids she'd sometimes spend a little longer with Claire, chatting and catching up.

Claire had known almost nothing about homelessness before the entire project started, and she'd known even less about domestic violence and the women who tried to escape it. She started talking with her lawyers and an advocate from the YWCA, whom she'd met through Wendi, about how she might be able to help. Once every couple of weeks, she was attending a local advocates' meeting and learning more about the landscape. They were gearing up to work on legislation to better protect victims and survivors, and she was looking forward to heading to the state capital during the legislative session to lobby the state legislature for these much-needed changes.

★ ★ ★

After completing the site, Sam had a couple more short-term jobs she went off to do, and she was able to hire Salina for a few days' work a week on each one. She'd also introduced Salina to Women Build, an apprenticeship program for women who want to learn the building trades. Salina was doing great at it, and would be done with her apprenticeship and ready for work in a couple of months. One of the women in her apprentice program lived at a "cottage housing" community not too far from the project site. Like their site, this place had smaller houses and shared common areas. It wasn't specifically for people coming out of homelessness, but it was for people who wanted community as well as privacy, and didn't need a huge house. Salina had figured out that if she got steady carpenter work for six months, she'd have enough saved to buy into the cottage housing site and truly be out on her own.

* * *

Heather was doing well in her recovery, even while she still missed her friend, Cheryl. Cheryl hadn't come back, and Heather had gone looking for and found her a couple more times but hadn't seen her recently. Cheryl was falling further and deeper into the place Heather didn't want to go back to. It took a lot of strength and patience—mostly patience with herself—for Heather to move on and find her new path without her friend. She had found work in a warehouse. She didn't love it, but it gave her a routine and a paycheck. There were a lot of other folks in recovery working there, too, and management had allowed them to hold meetings before and after shifts. It was good community Heather needed.

Karyn, Jamilah, Linda, and Barb had all gotten jobs at the same warehouse as Heather, and they often had schedules that allowed them to go to and from work together. They were getting along well, and were talking about possibly trying to rent an apartment or house together when they were all ready to move to a more permanent housing situation. Erica had been working with them on basic skills and had each of them talking with a counselor to help work through the trauma they'd experienced living out on the street.

Jamilah, especially, was taking it slowly. Between medication and behavioral therapy, she was learning how to handle her stress and triggers, and what to do when they got out of her control. She was a little nervous about leaving the community at the site, but she also had a strong sense of independence that made her want to get things under control and manage her own issues.

This was true of so many of the women who came through the site. They loved the community and were grateful to have the opportunity to live there, but they wanted more. They knew it was supposed to be transitional, and were excited about the opportunity to go off and make their own way.

"You gave us boots," Jamilah said to Erica and Sam one time when they were sitting around together at the end of the day.

"What?" Sam asked.

"You gave us boots," Jamilah repeated. "There's this dumb thing people say, 'Pick yourself up by your bootstraps.' They usually say it when they are telling you why they aren't going to help you."

Erica nodded, seeing where she was going. "Yeah, like, 'Stop complaining—just pick yourself up by your bootstraps and don't look for a handout.'"

"Exactly," Jamilah said. "But the people who say that don't account for it being pretty hard to pick yourself up from your bootstraps when you don't have any damn boots."

Erica and Sam laughed. "Right," Sam said.

"So you gave us boots, you know?" Jamilah punctuated her sentence by kicking her leg into the air, showing off her work boots.

"As I recall," Sam said. "I literally gave you *those* boots."

"I *know*!" Jamilah said.

* * *

Marta and her daughter were talking regularly now, after a years-long silence. They were proceeding cautiously, but Marta was overjoyed at renewed contact with the daughter she thought she'd lost forever. She knew it would be too much—for both of them—for her to move back in with her daughter. It hadn't come up yet, but Marta was worried her daughter might ask, out of a sense of duty. So she worked diligently to find other options and show that she was not assuming her daughter would take her in.

Inspired by Wendi's pursuit of the peer counselor work, Erica recognized that Marta had been kind of a "den mother" for the group. While she'd focused a lot of her energy on Wendi, Marta had also been a calm and mothering presence for everyone else at the site. Not only did she help the other women, but the act of serving in this role also helped Marta. Erica talked with Claire, and they created a job for Marta as the on-site liaison. It gave her a little income that didn't interfere with her disability check, and it also formalized the role she played on-site. Although Erica managed the project, she lived off-site in her own apartment. They needed a point person on-site.

"You're making me, like, building manager?" Marta had asked.

"More like 'house mom,'" Erica said. "You don't need to fix the toilets or anything. Just help me take care of the place and the people here. Which," she pointed out, "you already do."

* * *

Once the site was up and running, Erica didn't have to spend nearly as much time on it, and knew she needed to find something else. She started looking at ads for other jobs, and went by Claire's house to talk about it. They sat at the island bar in Claire's kitchen, and Erica spread the different job postings out in front of them.

"Wait," Claire said. "You're leaving me?" She looked down at the job postings and started panic.

"No," Erica said. "What? Of course not."

"But you're looking for work." Claire pushed the pieces of paper away, and it took every ounce of her self-restraint to keep from crumpling them up and tossing them on the floor.

"I *am* looking for work," Erica said. "This isn't a full-time job anymore. You can't pay me for work I'm not doing."

Claire squinted at Erica. "Wow," she said. "You are *definitely* not a bureaucrat."

"You thought I was?"

"No! I just ... 'don't pay me for work I'm not doing' isn't something you hear very often. You really haven't figured out this capitalism thing, have you?"

"I thought we could work out something to keep me, like, on-call for the site, but then I'd go look for something else so you're not paying me for a job I'm not doing."

Claire leaned back in her chair and folded her arms across her chest.

"Nice thought," she said. "But I don't like it."

"You ... wait, what?"

"No," Claire shook her head. "I can't let you go off and work for someone else."

"But I just told you—"

"I know," Claire said. "But seriously. It's for your own good. Look how your last job ended. If I hadn't hired you, you would have been fired and possibly charged with assaulting that poor man, Bruce. Clearly, you need to stay with me because I'm the only one who can control you."

"You have *got* to be kidding me," Erica said.

Claire looked at her blankly, then broke into a smile. "Of course I am. Like I could control you."

Erica shook her head and started to tell Claire about the couple of jobs she was thinking of applying for.

"Oh—" Claire interrupted her. "I'm sorry—you misunderstood me. The controlling you part was a joke, but I'm dead serious about you not working for anyone else. I'm not going to let you go do that when we have so much more work to do."

Erica was confused. "What do you mean? We just opened, they have their governance system, everything is running well ..."

"Yes," Claire said. "That. One. Site. Is doing great." She leaned in. "So now we have to figure out what's next."

"Seriously?" Erica asked.

"More serious than I've ever been, Erica. You said it yourself when we were getting started—you had a placemat full of crayon with a whole list of things that needed to be done."

"I did," Erica said. "I do. I still have it."

"Great!" Claire clapped.

"It's a really long list."

"Then we'd better get started," Claire said. "What's next?"

Photo credit: Missy Fant

ABOUT THE AUTHOR

TEMPLE LENTZ is a nonprofit CEO and former local elected official. She has lived mostly in central Ohio, Chicago, and Vancouver, Washington. This is her first book.

ACKNOWLEDGMENTS

This book is set in a world of real problems that have been made worse by real people and real systems that get more and more broken every day. And it's inspired by real people doing incredible work to make things incrementally better, even when better seems impossible.

Some of the people who inspired this book know who you are, and some of you I've never even met. Thank you to Michael and Jamie for being the spark, to so many hardworking people struggling to put their own masks on first and then help others, and to the scrappy organizations scraping by and bringing hope.

Thanks to the wonderful team at Sibylline Press for believing in this story and helping bring it into the world. I'm proud to be among this fine group of writers.

Thank you to Kristen Tate and Nicole Ayers for your phenomenal developmental editing work, and thanks to Elizabeth, Kelly, Helena, Veronica, and Anita for being early readers and helping me test proof of concept and work out some of the kinks before taking it to a broader audience.

Ed and Andy Lentz, thank you for bringing me up to be a reader and a writer. It's the only way I know how to be in the world, and I learned it by watching you, OK?! And Wheeler, you may have gotten there first little bro, but now we both have books out in the world and I think that's pretty cool.

Jason, thank you for inspiration, idea-bouncing, and then for years of dinners, breakfasts, and patience … I guess after all that, now I can finally let you read it.

STUDY GUIDE QUESTIONS

1. How did the character of Claire develop and change throughout the story?

2. How did Erica's personal recovery affect her approach to her job and her work with her clients?

3. For the unhoused women, how did their past experiences affect their current situations?

4. How did the book affect your opinions or impressions of women struggling with homelessness?

5. The community the women are building serves only women and children. Why do you think they chose that path?

6. What is the significance of the name, "Camp 17th Chance"? What else could they have called it?

7. What issues did the book raise about how communities do or don't serve people in need?

8. Which characters resonated the most with you, and why?

Sibylline Press is proud to publish the brilliant work of women authors over 50. We are a woman-owned publishing company and, like our authors, represent women of a certain age.

www.ingramcontent.com/pod-product-compliance
Lightning Source LLC
Jackson TN
JSHW021942240425
83275JS00009B/49

* 9 7 8 1 9 6 0 5 7 3 8 9 6 *